Lauren Layne is the *Ne* ... re than two

Her books have sold over a million copies, in eight languages. Lauren's work has been featured in *Publishers Weekly*, *Glamour*, *The Wall Street Journal* and *Inside Edition*. She is based in New York City.

Lauren I

'Chic and clever! *Passion on Park Avenue* comes to life like a sexy, comedic movie on the page'
Tessa Bailey, *New York Times* bestselling author

'I couldn't put it down! Not only is the friendship between Naomi, Claire and Audrey refreshing and inspirational, the chemistry between Naomi and Oliver is off the charts! I love a sassy heroine and a funny hero and Layne delivers both. Witty banter and an electric connection between Naomi and Oliver kept me turning the pages late into the night. Lauren Layne knocks this one right out of Park Avenue!'
Samantha Young, *New York Times* bestselling author

'Strong characters and relatable situations elevate Layne's bighearted contemporary . . . This vivid enemi   digs into class differences, emotional baggage, an
parents' *Publishers*

'Featuring wine in coffee mugs, di
Naomi and Oliver being (almost) caught with their pa   t
for readers who love the dishy women's fiction of Candace Bushnell' *Booklist*

'Layne is one of the best authors writing today and I was reminded of that as I read this book . . . It was hot and sexy and sweet. I laughed and shrieked and cried, exactly what I want from a book' *Obsessed with Romance*

By Lauren Layne

Wedding Belles Series
From This Day Forward (e-novella)
To Have And To Hold
For Better Or Worse
To Love And To Cherish

Oxford Series
Irresistibly Yours
I Wish You Were Mine
Someone Like You
I Knew You Were Trouble
I Think I Love You

Love Unexpectedly Series
Blurred Lines
Good Girl
Love Story
Walk Of Shame
An Ex For Christmas

I Do, I Don't Series
Ready To Run
Runaway Groom

The Central Park Pact Series
Passion On Park Avenue
Love On Lexington Avenue

Standalone
The Prenup

LAUREN LAYNE
The Prenup

HEADLINE
ETERNAL

First published in Great Britain in 2019
by HEADLINE ETERNAL
An imprint of HEADLINE PUBLISHING GROUP

1

Cataloguing in Publication Data is available from the British Library

ISBN 978 1 4722 5877 9

Typeset in 11.55/16.25 pt Granjon LT Std by Jouve (UK), Milton Keynes

Printed and bound in Great Britain by Clays Ltd, Elcograf S.p.A.

Headline's policy is to use papers that are natural, renewable and recyclable
products and made from wood grown in well-managed forests and other
controlled sources. The logging and manufacturing processes are expected
to conform to the environmental regulations of the country of origin.

HEADLINE PUBLISHING GROUP
An Hachette UK Company
Carmelite House
50 Victoria Embankment
London EC4Y 0DZ

www.headlineeternal.com
www.headline.co.uk
www.hachette.co.uk

The Prenup

THURSDAY, AUGUST 13

⁓

*T*here are a few things I've missed about New York in the decade I've been away.

JFK Airport isn't one of them.

Current situation:

I'm fresh off a six-hour flight in coach, and thanks to my last-minute trip, and the resulting back-of-the-plane seat assignment, by the time the food/drink cart got to me, they were out of the cheese plate *and* white wine (horror).

I'd made do with Pringles and vodka, because there are some things a person shouldn't attempt while sober, and a middle seat between a fussy toddler and a man who brought his own onion-laden Tupperware was one of them.

As you can imagine, somewhere over Nebraska, I'd started fantasizing about the moment I'd get off the plane. Like, we're talking borderline erotic daydreams about stretching my cramped legs, breathing in non-recycled air, and listening to something other than the toddler's repeated demands for "banananananaanaa *NOW!*"

Now don't get me wrong, I could respect that the toddler hadn't yet learned just how many sugar calories were lurking in the humbly delicious banana, and he wanted it *now*. I could even get behind my onion-loving neighbor's mind-set that airplane food was rarely worth the risk.

Still, my fantasy of not being between the two of them was very, very real.

And yet.

My fantasy had most definitely not included the tense exchange with the airline after they'd made me gate-check my suitcase and then *lost* it. Nor had it included a mile-long taxi line once they'd finally located my suitcase on the carousel with a flight arriving from Denver.

Lastly, my fantasy hadn't incorporated a cab driver involved in a heated cell phone fight with his mother. Although, *that*, at least, I can sympathize with. I've had a few of those over the years myself.

I know what you're thinking:

Who is *this hot mess?*

Fair question. I'm Charlotte Spencer, age thirty-one. Sagittarius, in case that's the sort of thing you like to know about a person. Long blond hair, although not as naturally platinum as my skilled hair stylist would make you think. I've got blue eyes and a borderline unhealthy affection for mascara. I'm a New Yorker by birth, San Francisco resident by choice. Body type . . . eh, we'll go with *decent*, mostly thanks to a rather expensive personal trainer. And no, we're not telling her about the plane Pringles. Or the vodka.

My professional life is pretty badass, if I do say so myself. I'm founder and CEO of my own business, a social media management company called Coco (as in Chanel, *obviously*). I started it when I was twenty-one and had pretty great timing on the whole social media wave. When I started, some of the biggest retailers on the planet were desperate for someone to help figure out the whole social media thing and couldn't wait to hand over their money to a team of twenty-somethings who got it.

Fast-forward a decade, and if I were going to be completely crass, I'd be making *cha-ching!* noises right now, because I've always known I'd make a killer girl boss, and now, finally, my bank account agrees.

Let's see, what else . . .

Oh, relationship status? It's complicated. *Very* complicated.

But we're getting to that.

For now, all you need to know is that I'm back in New York after a decade away and I'm not entirely sure how I feel about it.

I rest my head back and turn to look out the window. Traffic is even slower than usual, thanks to an August thunderstorm, but Manhattan inches ever closer, its lights a blurry kaleidoscope through the raindrops on the window.

The taxi driver pulls his phone away from his face and glances at me in the rearview mirror. "Where to again?"

The words *Sixty-third and Lex* nearly roll off my tongue, and I bite them back. Apparently, ten years on the West Coast can't undo twenty-one years as an Upper East Side princess. But the last place I want to be tonight is my parents' house.

"Seventy-sixth and Madison. The Carlyle Hotel."

He goes back to his conversation without acknowledging my response, but he apparently heard me, because twenty minutes later, the taxi pulls up to the correct address.

I pay the fare, and a second later, the car door opens. I smile in gratitude at the hotel doorman who's already unloaded my suitcase from the trunk and is waiting with an oversized umbrella.

"Welcome to The Carlyle, ma'am."

Ma'am. Ouch. I make a mental note to stop putting off replacing my eye cream.

And while we're on the topic of appearances, I've forgotten how vicious the summer humidity can be on the East Coast. I feel my sleek blowout transforming into a poufy cloud with each passing moment. Thankfully, the hotel lobby is cool and dry, and I want nothing more than to check in to my room and make a hot date with a bottle of wine and a shower.

A glance at my cell phone tells me there's no time for that. The luggage debacle and traffic have already made me ten minutes late for my, shall we say, appointment.

I leave my suitcase and trench coat with the bellman to be taken to my room, and ask for directions to the restroom. I may not have time for a shower, but some occasions at least require a lipstick check, and this is definitely one of them.

A glance in the restroom mirror confirms that I'm a good deal beyond a simple lipstick check. At least half my mascara is under my eyes, and my lipstick is long gone, though my lip *liner* has managed to stick around in a very unbecoming manner. And as expected, the humidity-induced frizz is simply gorgeous.

A damp paper towel takes care of the mascara, a couple dabs of concealer hide the fact that I haven't had much sleep since getting The Call, and by the time I apply ChapStick and a swipe of light pink lip gloss, I feel mostly human.

Even better, the hotel is fancy enough to have complimentary mouthwash, and I pour some into the provided little cup, gargling as I pull my long hair into an intentionally messy bun. When you've survived three decades with naturally curly hair, you learn that sometimes the best method is to pretend that the frizz is deliberate and work with it, Carrie Bradshaw style.

I spit and rinse, then dig through my Prada purse—a thirtieth-birthday gift to myself from yours truly—until I find some much-needed eye drops and a lint roller, which go a long way to diffuse the *just got off a cross-country flight* look. A spritz of perfume to combat the onion-eating neighbor.

I'd purposely selected the blue dress I'm wearing because it's made out of some wrinkle-free material I like to call magic, so at least my wardrobe's on point. And now, for the final touch: I reach into the bottom of my purse, groping around until I find the stilettos carefully wrapped in their fancy Stuart Weitzman shoe bags. Yeah, I'm *that* girl, the one with fancy shoes in her purse. I love a good pair of sexy high heels, just not for walks over four blocks or the airport security line. Thus, I am a master of The Shoe Swap.

I slip my feet out of the gray flats, into the gray suede peep-toe stilettos, and voilà. I'm ready.

Or as ready as one can ever be for this.

I'm also late. Quite late. *Crap.*

I hurriedly put my makeup and the flats back in the purse, do one last smoothing of the flyaway hairs by my temples, and head toward the hotel bar. Like the rest of the hotel, the bar's fancy and dimly lit. It's not until I'm scanning and coming up empty that I realize . . .

I don't know what the guy I'm meeting looks like.

I mean, I know what the version of him ten years ago looked like. Long, curly black hair, pulled back into a man bun before man buns were even a thing. I scrunch up my nose, trying to remember other details. He'd been long and lean, almost coltish. Full, dark beard. Not my type at all, truth be told, but to give credit where it was due, I do remember that he had very nice eyes. They were light blue with thick, those-can't-be-real black eyelashes.

The trouble is, the bar is far too dark to see anyone's eye color, so I'm at a bit of a loss. I scan the room and come up empty. My palms get a little sweaty, and I hope he didn't leave because he thought I'd stood him up. I scan the room again, slower this time.

Get-a-room couple in the corner? Nope. Group of girls laughing shrilly next to them? No. Not the elderly couple either, nor the business meeting that looks to be two glasses of wine past productive. It's definitely not the single lady reading her book, nor the two dolled-up cougars on the prowl.

There's a man with his back to me who has the right hair—longish and black, although he seems a bit shorter than I remember . . . the man turns his head. Nope. Too old.

Next.

I look all the way to my left and see a hot guy in the far corner that I'd somehow missed the first time around. His clean-cut good looks, broad shoulders, and dark suit are pure fantasy material, and a reminder that buttoned-up businessmen are one thing that New York does *very* well. Guys in California tend to be a bit more casual. His attention is on his phone, so I can't get a good look at his face, but it doesn't matter, because as yummy as he is, now is definitely not the time and place to be ogling.

I drag my gaze away from Hot Guy and continue my search. Cute old lady reapplying her red lipstick. No. There's a couple giving off first date vibes. No.

Damn it! No man bun in the entire place. Maybe he *did* leave.

I pull out my phone to see if I have any missed messages, when I feel eyes on me. Not surprising, considering I've been standing in the middle of the crowded bar without taking a seat. What *is* surprising is who's doing the looking. The hot guy in the corner's attention is no longer on his phone. It's on *me*.

His blue eyes are so piercing, so direct, so . . . familiar.

My stomach drops out.

Oh.

My.

God.

The hot guy is *my* guy.

Somehow it had simply not occurred to me that my brother's lanky, awkward best friend from college would turn into . . . this.

My mouth is a little dry as his gaze holds mine. There's no trace of a smile on his face, though I could swear there's a hint of a smirk in his eyes . . . as though he's very aware what I'm thinking and is amused by it.

No, no. We can't have *that*.

I paste a confident grin on my face and make my way toward him. He stands when I approach, and I think we can say, without a doubt, he's not lanky. Not anymore. He's turned into male perfection: broad shoulders, lean waist, and long legs. If I had to bet, six-pack under the dress shirt. No, eight-pack.

Twelve-pack? Is that a thing?

I reach his table and he gives the slightest nod. "Charlotte."

The voice is the same. Gorgeous and lilting, and every bit as Irish as I remember.

"I almost didn't recognize you," I say breezily, lifting my cheek to receive his kiss.

Damn. He smells good too. Expensive and clean.

Why did nobody warn me about this?

"*Almost* didn't recognize me?" he says, lifting his eyebrows. "If I had to guess, I'd say you didn't have the faintest clue who I was," he says, pulling out my chair for me before settling back in his.

"Well, in my defense, you're not on social media. And your picture isn't on your firm's website." I know, because I've looked. "How was I supposed to know what you look like these days?"

"You could have asked your brother."

"Right, because that's something normal siblings do. Ask their brother for a picture of his best friend," I say, picking up the drink menu in an effort to hide my nervousness.

A tuxedo-clad server comes over for my drink order and I opt for a martini, because *strong* sounds like just the thing for this particular moment in my life.

The waiter disappears, and for a moment, my brother's best friend and I simply look at each other. He's clearly taking me in, assessing, but I don't mind because I'm doing the same, absorbing all the details I couldn't see from a distance.

The beard's gone, although there's a hint of a five o'clock shadow that draws attention to the Superman-worthy jaw that really never should have been covered up in the first place. His hair is as black as ever, though ruthlessly short now.

"What happened to your man bun?" I ask.

He blinks. "I'm sorry?"

I gesture to my own messy knot. "You know. Before, you wore your hair long."

I expect him to smile, but he doesn't; his blue eyes lock on mine. "I cut it."

I give in to the urge to roll my eyes. "Okay. Good talk."

"You look . . ." His gaze trails over me, more calculating than sexual, which, let's face it, is kind of insulting. "The same."

I wrinkle my nose. "I'm going to choose to interpret that as you saying I look like I did when I was twenty-one. I thank you for the compliment."

He shrugs as though he doesn't care one way or the other how I take it, then exhales a long breath, the first sign that he's as unnerved by all of this as I am. "Thank you for coming."

"You said it was urgent?" I ask, deliberately letting the question enter my tone.

I'm *dying* of curiosity here. I have been ever since his email came three days ago, saying he needed to discuss something urgent with me—in person.

After establishing that my brother wasn't dying of cancer or something awful, I'd agreed. Partially because I needed a break from work, partially because I was dreadfully curious, and partially because, well . . . a little sliver of me has known for a while that it's time—past time—to face this part of my life.

He waits until the server puts a wonderfully large martini in front of me, waits until I take a sip and somehow manage to withhold a moan at how good it tastes after the day I've had.

And then, as though he's been deliberately waiting until I had a little booze flowing through my veins, lets me know the reason I'm here.

"Charlotte."

"Yeah?" I give him an encouraging smile.

He looks nervous but determined.

Then he lays it on me: "I want a divorce."

THURSDAY, AUGUST 13

I can explain. Really, I can. Throughout my teens and early twenties, I was, um . . . how do I put this . . . ?

A bit of a handful.

I'm not sure when it started. Puberty, I suppose. Up until then, I was the perfect WASP daughter. I wore big bows in my hair that matched the adorable, little-girl dresses I wore to St. Thomas Church every Sunday. Eventually, I graduated to wearing headbands that matched the pastel cashmere twinsets, paired with flouncy skirts.

I played piano, I did ballet, I got straight A's at boarding school. Yes, *boarding school*.

I did everything exactly right.

Right up until the moment I quit being the good girl.

It wasn't some grand, overnight rebellion or anything, but somewhere around the age of fifteen, I found myself irritatingly and persistently *bored*. Bored with my parents, their friends, *my* friends. Bored with the Ivy League life laid out for me, the well-connected husband already picked out for me in pedigree, if not by name.

I made it until age twenty-one before I cracked—really truly, decided I couldn't do it anymore . . . *wouldn't* do it anymore.

My parents were . . . well, let's just say my failure to heel like my family's Cavalier King Charles spaniel did not go over well. See, there were a lot of things the Spencers of the Upper East Side didn't like. Jersey. Fried food. Catholics. Girls with short hair, boys with long hair.

And, as I learned during one particularly heated argument: college dropouts.

You'll get your degree, Charlotte Elizabeth Spencer, or you'll leave this house without a dime.

It was this *without a dime* part that was a bit of a problem. It shames me to have to admit it now, but back then, I really didn't have a clue where money came from other than Daddy's wallet.

Am I ashamed of this fact? Embarrassed? Absolutely. But it doesn't make it less true. I was born with a silver spoon, all my friends were born with silver spoons, and at twenty-one, I didn't fully comprehend where one could get *another* silver spoon, should that first one be taken away by stern parents.

I mean, I knew the basics. I knew I could get a job, obviously. I wanted a job. Craved it, even. But I also knew that the type of job I was qualified for wouldn't get me particularly close to the future I envisioned for myself. I had big dreams and no big cash flow to support said dreams if my parents cut me off. Which they made clear they would do.

And at twenty-one, the trust fund left to me by my grandmother was off-limits. Not because of my age, but because of my marital status; specifically, my *single* status.

Yep, that's right. That sort of thing still happens among the

richy-rich of New York. Grandparents leave grandkids money
that the parents can't touch until certain conditions are met. And
in the case of my marriage-minded Grandma Geraldine, that
condition was . . . drum roll, please:

Marriage.

Per Grandma Geraldine's stipulations: if I got married, I got a
six-figure chunk of change. Stay single; stay poor. Definitely a
dilemma for a twenty-one-year-old with no boyfriend in sight.
But I had a solution.

Enter Colin Walsh.

I didn't know much about my brother's law school bestie other
than the fact that he was Irish and a ridiculous overachiever, chas-
ing his JD and MBA concurrently.

Back then, I'd been quick to deem him *nerd*, and his shy intensity and man bun had done nothing to reverse my flippant
disregard. The guy was barely on my radar, save for the fact that
he hung around during holidays sometimes because it was too
expensive to fly back to Ireland.

It was my dumbass brother Justin who'd come up with the
idea.

See, with just months away from law school graduation,
Colin had plenty of job offers, some of them quite decent. But Colin
Walsh had some big dreams of his own.

The way my brother put it: "Colin's too smart to be anyone's
bitch."

I'll translate: Colin wanted to start his own company, to work
for himself. He wanted to build an empire. And he wanted to do
it in New York City.

It was this last part of his dream that caused a not-so-tiny hiccup for the Irish-born Colin. Taking a job with an existing US company would have gotten him a work visa. But to work for *himself* in the US, with no company to sponsor his visa? Colin needed a little something called a green card.

You get where I'm going with this, right?

I needed my inheritance; Colin needed to stay in the United States. The solution to both was the same:

Marriage.

To each other.

Now I wish I could give you a fairy tale here, I really do. But, the truth? I didn't even wear white. Well, that's not entirely true. I *did* wear white lacy underwear with a blue ribbon and "bride" scrawled across the ass, but we don't speak of that moment of frivolity, especially since it had been very much for my eyes only.

But really, my wedding day was like this:

Meet brother on steps of courthouse.

Have him reintroduce me to Colin because I'd met my groom only twice before then, and I didn't recognize him. (Guess I've come full circle on that, huh?)

Sign a prenup.

Repeat a bunch of mumbo jumbo in front of a judge, all while sweating profusely and trying to remember if I put on deodorant that morning.

Sign marriage certificate.

Shake hands with my husband, muttering something lame like, "Good times."

The next morning I'd been on a flight to San Francisco. Colin had stayed in New York.

I know. It's practically a Disney movie.

Now, okay, you're wondering why, after getting my hands on the money, I didn't get a divorce ASAP.

Simple. Grandma Geraldine—God rest her soul—was a wise old tramp. I had to stay married for five years, and I'd barely listened to my brother when he explained, but since green cards had stipulations too, the arrangement was just fine with Colin.

And then, five years came and went, and I was busy building my social media company, and then after that, I *stayed* married because . . . well, to be honest, it was *easy* to stay married. I mean, I didn't live like a nun. Colin and I got that figured out via a couple of awkward emails very early on that we'd both live our lives however we wanted . . . discreetly.

And separately.

I've had a few casual relationships in California, and they've all been aware of my tricky situation. Which leads me to the upside . . .

If any of those relationships got too intense, and it happened, a handful of times, there's nothing like a husband-of-convenience to gently let a guy you're seeing know *it's just not meant to be.*

It's not that I was callous—I let these men know the score upfront: that I was committed to building my company and not looking for anything serious on the relationship front.

It's been a good situation, honestly. For me, and I thought for Colin.

Until now, apparently.

I smile and refocus my attention to the present, and my husband's unsmiling face. *Damn, he's gorgeous.* "A divorce?"

I just want to make sure I've heard him correctly. He doesn't seem like the type to joke, but . . .

"Yes. A divorce, Charlotte."

Hmm. Okay then. The clipped use of my first name definitely lets me know he means business. Ah, well. I suppose I knew it was coming someday. All good things, and whatnot.

I smile to let him know there are no hard feelings. "I get it. Time to be free of the old ball and chain, huh?" I pick up my purse and pull a pen out of an inside pocket. "Where do I sign?"

He doesn't smile back. Nor does he look even slightly relieved or grateful that I'm being super cool about this.

"There's something you need to know," he says, holding my gaze.

I go still, because I suddenly realize that Colin Walsh isn't nearly as calm as he's trying to appear. He's holding back his anger, or at least frustration, by a very thin thread, and he doesn't seem like the type to lose his shit very often, which means whatever is under his skin is the real deal.

My smile falls. "What? What something?"

"Your brother," Colin says, leaning down and picking up a leather briefcase. He pulls a thick packet of paper out of the outside pocket, folds it back to a marked page, and sets the stack in front of me, his long finger indicating a highlighted paragraph.

I read it. And read it again.

And, one more time.

I look up. "Is this in English? I don't understand."

Except my heart is pounding because I'm afraid I *do* understand. And I can only hope I'm reading the formal legalese wrong.

Colin slowly lifts his eyes from his cocktail to meet my gaze. "This is our prenup. That highlighted section is your brother's idea of a joke, with very serious consequences for the two of us."

Oh God, I'm having déjà vu of my wedding day. No lacy white underwear, but I'm definitely sweating up a storm, trying to remember if I applied deodorant.

I glance back down at the prenup. "It says . . . it says neither one of us can file for divorce until . . ."

I can't say it. I can't even think it.

But Colin's apparently had more time with the concept, because he says it calmly, as though it's not about to turn my life upside down.

"We can't get divorced until we live under the same roof for three months. As husband and wife."

MONDAY, AUGUST 17

San Francisco

◡

"*I swear*, Charlotte, I swear to God, I literally don't know what's more upsetting to me. That you're leaving San Francisco, that you're *married*, or that those shoes are from four seasons ago."

I smile at my assistant's melodrama as I continue searching through my desk drawer, shoving aside stray paperclips and pink highlighters for stuff that I'll actually need for my three months in New York.

"You knew I was married," I point out.

"Sure, sure, technically. But I guess I always let myself think of the guy as imaginary. But Char, seriously. The shoes. They're hurting my eyes."

Poor Kurt. I'm not all that surprised that he put my outdated Blahniks in the same category as my relocation and my fake husband. I consider myself passionate about fashion. I know what's in, what's out; I know who's in and who's out. But Kurt Lovejoy (Kurt's his real name; Lovejoy was acquired because his given name of Kurt Ross didn't match his *brand*) takes the obsession to a whole new level.

"I'm jealous, you know."

"Of the shoes?" I ask, lifting my head and looking over at him.

"God, no. I mean, I get what you were going for. The red's a nice pop with the halter, but sweetie, round toes haven't been in for ages."

"Cut me some slack," I say, pulling a protein bar from my desk drawer and tossing it in the trash, since I'm pretty sure the health food company who made it went out of business a year ago. "I've already packed up most of the stuff in my condo and forgot to set out work clothes. I had to dig through the Goodwill pile for shoes to wear today."

Kurt makes a pouty motion with his lips and crosses his arms. "When do you leave? *Why* do you leave?"

Deciding my desk is full of nothing but coffee-stained notepads and cheap pens, I shut the drawers and stand to face my assistant. Kurt has a full seven inches on five-foot-five me, and I know for a fact our weights are roughly the same. He's got that sort of skinny, angular waif look that begs to be paired with long scarves and skinny ties, and Kurt delivers on both fronts frequently.

"You know you can come with me," I say, waggling my eyebrows enticingly. "You and New York's fashion scene could be soul mates."

"Don't I know it," he says with a dramatic sigh. "Unfortunately, my *other* soul mate just made partner at a law firm here. *Damn* our respective pesky lawyer husbands keeping us apart."

Kurt makes a face, but I know he's as proud of his husband

Lewis as he is in love. They've been together for nine years, two years longer than Kurt's been with me, so I don't begrudge his loyalty. Plus, while I'd love to have some moral support as I wade into unchartered Manhattan waters, I'm relieved to have Kurt here in my absence. Granted, most of my work is done via laptop, and I trust my carefully selected C-team to make the right decisions. But it'll be nice to have someone give me the unfiltered version of what's actually happening on the ground if I'm ever unavailable because of the pesky time difference.

Or like, say, because I'm *in jail* for getting in a brawl with my brother for landing me in this mess in the first place.

Oh, what, you thought I wasn't going to mention it? You thought maybe I was in denial about this whole debacle?

I only *wish* I were in denial. I only *wish* I could forget about the fact that I'm about to move to New York City in order to move in with a husband I haven't seen in ten years, all so I can divorce that same husband.

"Is he *delicious*?" Kurt asks, leaning forward, whispering unnecessarily since we're the only ones in the office. "Is that why you're leaving me?"

Wordlessly, I reach for my cell phone and pull up the proof. Some things are better shown than told, even if it's the grainy, too-dark photo I'd snuck as Colin had paid the bill on that fateful night.

Kurt makes a purring noise. "Oh, my. Oh, definitely delicious."

I shrug.

He lowers the phone and gives me a flabbergasted look. "He's hotter than anything I've seen in recent history, my own spouse excluded. Why are we divorcing him again?"

"Because I barely even know him," I say.

"What if you get . . ." He lowers his voice. "*Investigated?*"

I glance over my shoulder, then, to play it safe, I shut the office door. "You mean, how am I not in hot water for marriage fraud?"

He shrugs. "I've seen *The Proposal.*"

I smile. "It's like I've told you before, it really isn't like that. Or at least, it wasn't for us. Thanks to my brother doing his homework, we aced the interview."

Kurt's blue eyes go wide. "Interview? How am I just now getting the full story on this?"

"Not as scary as it sounds. We just had to prove that we'd known each other for a while. It helped that he'd spent holidays at my house in the past and we had a couple of photos to prove it. Wasn't hard to convince them that it was the age-old story of the pesky younger sister falling in love with her older brother's hunky best friend."

"And he convinced them that he was horny for his best friend's hot little sister."

"I guess," I say with a laugh. "Regardless, they didn't really seem to care. My brother says we didn't really have any of the red flags they tend to look for. There was no major age difference. We'd known each other a few years, at least loosely. Overall, the guy interviewing us seemed happy enough to believe Colin was just a nice Irish lad who came over here for school and got smitten with his best friend's sister."

"But he wasn't smitten."

I snort. "Hardly. Colin was—is—well, he's serious. Mostly he just ignored me, but if he ever did pay attention to me, I'm sure it was to roll his eyes at my penchant for purses and lip gloss. But he apparently managed to lie well enough, because nobody batted an eye. Thanks to you," I say, blowing him a kiss.

Because me buying real estate in a different state from Colin would have been a big red flag, Kurt and Lewis had done me a major favor. Actually, favor doesn't even begin to cover it. They'd bought me a house. I paid them back every penny, obviously, but technically, my home here in San Francisco is in their name, which means if anyone asks, I can technically be living in San Francisco part-time for work.

The arrangement was working just fine for everyone until my brother thought it would be hilarious to force us to live under the same roof and prove it in order to get divorced. Until Colin decided he wanted a divorce.

Men. Not on my happy list right now.

"So, in case I don't get to tell you before this all goes to hell, I've already told Lewis that if you go to jail, he needs to pull some strings so that you're incarcerated here in California. So I can bring you gift baskets."

"I'm not going to jail, Kurt." I hope.

"You might as well be. You're seriously going to live with someone you don't know? What if he's a serial killer?"

"He's not a serial killer. And I'm doing it because it's time to close this chapter of my life. *Past* time. I have a fake husband, Kurt. It's a little pathetic."

"Okay, fine, but why can't he come live here?" Kurt whines. "He's the one who wants the divorce. Make him move into your place. Well, technically, *my* place, but you know what I mean."

"Colin's job is less flexible than mine. I can work from anywhere. He can't. He doesn't have a Kurt," I say, trying to butter him up.

But Kurt's known me too long and knows me too well. He narrows his eyes. "You didn't even try to fight him, did you? You *want* to go back to New York."

Want to? No. Definitely not.

But . . . I think I need to.

That city and I have some unfinished business.

THURSDAY, AUGUST 20

New York, New York

*olin's apartment building is a surprise. Though, come to think of it, I've had so little time to actually envision what my life for the next three months will be like that *any* building probably would have been a surprise.

In the midst of moving across the country, handing over the reins of my company to my team, preparing to come face-to-face with my parents and a decade of baggage, and, oh yeah, play-acting at wife, a role I'm *quite* sure I'm ill-suited to, the details of the roof over my head have barely crossed my mind.

But they're crossing my mind now, as I take in my home for the next three months. And like I said, it's . . . a surprise. Colin had emailed me the address ahead of time; obviously, I haven't been gone from New York *so* long that I don't know my way around Manhattan street names to know that my husband and I would be shacking up in Tribeca.

But it's an odd choice for a guy like Colin. Tribeca is the *it* place for families. It has the best schools, a fancy Riverwalk Pier with putt-putt and fancy daycares. If you find yourself married and knocked up in Manhattan and can afford it, you move to Tribeca. Colin, for all intents and purposes, is single and childless, save for one wayward pesky wife.

If I had to guess, Colin's neighborhood of choice probably has more to do with the fact that Tribeca borders the Financial District, which is where Colin's law firm is located. Since he's a corporate attorney, I'm guessing he must find that the short commute is a fair trade for finding himself riding elevators with nannies, mannies, and golden retrievers.

Given all of that, I think in the back of my head, I've been expecting some place shiny and minimalist when the Uber drops me off at Broadway and Park Place (not to be confused with Park Avenue, darlings, that's Upper East Side territory).

I've come straight from the airport with only a suitcase and my laptop. Colin's assured me the guest bedroom is comfortably furnished, so other than a couple boxes of clothes and shoes arriving via UPS tomorrow, I don't have much stuff.

As you can imagine, the whole thing has left me feeling strangely in limbo. On one hand, I've left my San Francisco apartment more or less "as is," since I'll be returning to it. At the same time, this isn't a one-week getaway to Cancun or even a two-week escape to Europe. It's three months of not just visiting somewhere else but living there.

In the name of positive thinking, I've been trying to spin it in my brain as an extended vacation. After all, maybe if I call it a vacation, it'll start to feel like one. A girl can hope.

Anyway, where was I?

Oh right, Colin's apartment building. It's a high-rise, as

expected, but it's not sleek and shiny and modern. It's not a pre-war building either. Instead, it's somewhere in between, a newish building that's clearly been designed with a nod to old New York. The structure is sort of a cozy off-white instead of being comprised of shiny panels, and the ornate detailing around the windows gives one the sense that the building's been around a lot longer than I suspect it actually has.

I exhale a long breath, and before I can chicken out and go running back to San Francisco, I force my feet forward through the front door.

The lobby, too, is a surprise. It's white marble, but instead of feeling cold and unapproachable, it manages to feel warm and homey. The flower arrangements are lavish, but inviting, the doormen smiling and welcoming.

"Mrs. Walsh, I presume?"

It takes me a solid thirty seconds to realize the man behind the enormous desk is talking to me.

"Oh! No. I ... I'm Charlotte. Spencer. I kept my maiden name," I say, fumbling through the introduction like a newlywed who hasn't come to grips with her status as a married woman.

Which, of course, I haven't.

"Of course, I'm sorry. Mr. Walsh said his wife would be arriving today—I shouldn't have assumed."

"No worries." I give him a friendly smile, knowing I'm going to need allies if I'm to survive the next three months. "What's your name?"

"Matteo, ma'am."

I wince. "Does the job require you to call me ma'am? Or can we go with Charlotte?"

He smiles. "Well, *Charlotte*. I'll just need to see some ID, and I can hand over the keys to your new home."

Home. Ha.

Matteo and I make the exchange: me proving my identity, and him handing over a little fob that is the key to my prison.

Did I say prison?

I meant prison.

Matteo points me to the elevators, and I find myself on the fortieth floor, scanning the doors until I find Colin's apartment.

My apartment. Nope. It still doesn't feel right.

Though, I have to say, opening the door and seeing where I'll be serving my sentence for the next three months is a pleasant surprise. Yes, there are the expected whiffs of a bachelor pad. The TV is ginormous, the sofa clearly chosen with a mind to accommodate Colin's large frame. But as with the lobby downstairs, the rest of the apartment is surprisingly homey. The kitchen, while modern, is all white wood, the backsplash and counters bright white instead of the expected sleek, dark that I'd pictured in my head.

Everything is spotless, so I'm pretty sure the lone sheet of paper on the kitchen counter is for me. I'm right.

The smaller bedroom is yours. -C

I roll my eyes, tossing the note back on the counter. I wheel my bag down the hallway, sticking my head into a bathroom that is *super* tiny and I'm really hoping isn't what I'll be stuck with for the next three months. I have never been, nor am I currently, one of those girls who claims to be low-maintenance. I have a look, and my look needs a lot more counter space.

I flick off the bathroom light and continue to the end of the hallway. The doors to both bedrooms are open, and I can see at a glance which is the smaller—which is mine. I drop my bags just inside the door, but instead of entering and making myself at home, I instead turn and go into Colin's bedroom.

I've always thought you can learn a lot about someone from their bedroom. The theory isn't holding in this case. Colin's bedroom tells me almost *nothing*. The bed is large and the bedding white, reminding me of something you'd see in a generic, chain hotel. The furniture is large and a little more old-fashioned than I'm used to. Dark wood with sturdy black handles.

I wander into the walk-in closet, which is small by my closet standards, but I suppose when you have nothing but dark suits and white shirts, as seems to be the case with Colin's wardrobe, you don't need much space.

Still looking for more clues about what makes him tick, I reach out and spin the fancy, rotating tie rack. Not as neutral as I feared, but not exactly full of bright and fun tie options either. Mostly there are lots of conservative blues and dark reds. I pause when I get to a bright green tie, my eyebrows lifting when I see the pattern is little tiny Rudolph heads.

I smile. My husband has a Christmas tie! A dorky one. It's the most telling thing I've seen so far, though I don't know exactly what it's telling me. Was it a gift? A gag gift? Does he actually wear it?

I'll never know. I'll be out of his life for good before the holidays roll around. Back in San Francisco, celebrating Christmas the way I usually do. Christmas Eve at Kurt and Lewis's annual party, and Christmas Day . . . alone.

I punch out Colin's closet light and head back into the

bedroom. I yelp when I see someone standing in the door, putting a hand over my pounding heart.

"You scared the *crap* out of me."

Colin doesn't move from the doorway, his scowl never wavering. "You didn't see my note?"

"No, I did."

"And this seemed like the smaller room to you?"

"I wanted to learn a little more about my darling hubby."

His dark eyebrows go up fractionally. "And?"

"Do you ever wear the Rudolph tie?"

Instead of replying, he steps to the side, making space for me to exit his bedroom. "Out."

I pretend to write on my palm. "Note to self, spouse does not share his space well."

"While you're making notes, jot this down . . . stay out of my bedroom."

"Were you this much fun when we got married?" I ask.

"Were you this annoying?"

I give his chest an affectionate pat as I walk past him. "Oh, hubby. You haven't seen anything yet."

Thursday, August 20

*H*onestly? I thought my last retort was a pretty good zinger. A solid last word that would have him retreating into the kitchen to ponder what I meant. Instead, he follows me into the guest room—*my* room—managing to look disinterested by my presence and highly perturbed at the same time.

I give Colin a perturbed look of my own. "If we're going to survive the next few months, we're going to need to talk about boundaries."

"Says the woman who was just snooping through my bedroom."

I go to the closet and slide open the doors, inspecting the unimpressive space. "This is smaller than yours. Criminally so."

"It'll hold whatever's in that suitcase and then some."

"Yes. But not the stuff arriving tomorrow."

"What stuff arriving tomorrow?"

I turn. "You really thought I was going to move across the country with no more than what fits in an overhead compartment?"

He slowly lowers to the side of my bed, his hands clasped

loosely between his spread knees. "I guess I hadn't really thought about it. This whole situation is . . . atypical."

I sit beside him on the bed, not close enough to be weird, but it's still . . . weird.

I'm *married* to this guy. Objectively, I've known that for a decade now. But there's a distinct difference between having a husband in name only and seeing the flesh and blood man.

And Colin Walsh is a *man*. Those suits that seemed so boring in his closet aren't boring when they're on him. His shoulders are broad, his waist lean, his legs are long, and probably . . .

"Where do you work out?"

He glances at me. "Excuse me?"

"Exercise. Is there a gym in the building?"

"Oh. Yeah. I can show you where it is tomorrow. I go every morning at six."

"Which will feel like three to me, so . . . no, thanks."

"You'll have to get used to the time change at some point."

"Oh really? Will I?" My tone is more snide than before, my patience quickly evaporating at his lecturing tone and the fact that he's making me feel like a childish nuisance who's invaded his home.

"Just a quick reminder," I continue, flooded with all the frustration of the past week. "None of this is my fault. We both said our vows. We both signed that prenup agreement without reading it carefully. You're the one who initiated the divorce, necessitating this three-month stint as roommates, and yet *I'm* the one who's upended her entire life, moved across the country, and has a closet the size of a coffin. So how about a little patience?"

Instead of apologizing or acknowledging my very excellent

points, he lifts his eyebrows. "And here I thought I was supposed to have the Irish temper."

"Do you? Have a temper?"

"I have more important things to do with my life than lose my temper."

"As opposed to me, who just fritters away her days getting manicures and shopping?"

He doesn't bother to dignify that as he stands and goes to the door. "At least there's one upside to all of this," he says, turning and gesturing between the two of us.

"What *this*?" I ask. "The fact that we don't like a single thing about the other person?"

His smile is grim. "Exactly. With all this antagonism and bickering, if Immigration Services comes looking for us, there should be no doubt in their mind that we are, in fact, man and wife."

THURSDAY, AUGUST 20

I still can't believe you're back!"

I laugh as I'm pulled into what is probably the tenth hug of the evening, each one getting a little bit sloppier as our drink count ticks steadily up.

"I can't believe we're drinking legally now," I say, grinning at the petite honey-blond woman sitting next to me at the bar.

Meghan Barker was once one of my closest friends, and though our contact over the past few years has been mostly limited to birthday phone calls and Facebook messages, I'm delighted to find that the rapport of our teen years holds strong in our thirties.

"Oh, God," she says with a laugh, taking another sip of the Champagne she's switched to after declaring herself *over* the cocktails we'd started the evening with. "Do you remember the first time we tried Scotch?"

I wince at the memory. "I don't know who was more pissed, my dad that we'd helped ourselves to 'his best bottle,' or me that

I'd gotten grounded for trying something that tasted so god-awful. What a waste."

"It *was* god-awful," she agrees. "Though, to be fair, I seem to remember that usually when you got grounded, it was for things that were worth it."

"It certainly seemed that way at the time," I say with a smile into my own Champagne, remembering the rather numerous occasions my exasperated parents banished me to my bedroom for all sorts of classic teenage offenses. Helping myself to the liquor cabinet. My first cigarette. Letting Drew Callahan get to second base when I was supposed to be helping set up for the church fundraiser. Though, I would like to be very clear, I did help set up for the church fundraiser, we just wrapped up earlier than expected. And *then* I let Drew get to second base.

And all that was just during summer vacations. If my parents had known and grounded me for every bit of mischief I got into at boarding school, I'd have spent my entire teenage career under lock and key.

Still, I have a hard time mustering up much regret for those years of my life. I was a rule breaker but the harmless variety. Rebellious, yes, but the annoying kind of rebellious, not the dangerous variety.

"How *are* your parents?" Meghan asks. "I saw them a few months ago at . . . gosh, I don't remember. Someone's wedding, I think. They look exactly the same."

"They're fine!" I say, grateful that Meghan doesn't know me quite as well as she once did and doesn't realize that my voice is just a touch too high at the lie.

I don't really know how my parents are. I mean, I do. They're alive. Healthy, I think. I *hope*. But Meghan's words cause an unexpected pang at the realization that she's seen them more recently than I have. Her brief encounter with them at a wedding is about as much as I've had with them in the past decade.

If you walk out that door, Charlotte Spencer, don't expect to walk back in again, now or ever again.

I hadn't expected to. And I haven't walked back in again.

Years later, I can understand that my mother said those words in anger and probably no small amount of hurt. She'd just found out that her only daughter had not only gotten married without telling her but had booked a flight to San Francisco for the very next day. Looking back, it's easy to see that I'd been young and more than a little careless with my parents' feelings.

Just like I also know that there were two sides of the war that was my youth, and not *all* the mistakes had been mine. I can't even remember how many nights I'd sit on my bed, pep talking myself to gather the courage to go downstairs to talk to them. Just to *talk*. To tell them about my dreams, about things that excited me in hopes that they could be happy *for* me, if not necessarily *with* me.

I'd wanted—needed—someone to listen. To at least try and understand, even if they couldn't support. Instead, I'd gotten dismissive eye rolls and comments that it was my youth talking. I'd gotten sent back to my bedroom with instructions not to speak again until I'd come to my senses. But worst of all were the icy silences, as though they hoped if they didn't move, or blink, or speak, that I'd suddenly become the perfect cookie-cutter daughter they so clearly wanted.

Strictly speaking, my parents hadn't thrown me out of the

house. The twenty-one-year-old Charlotte and thirty-one-year-old Charlotte know that I was the one who bought that plane ticket; I'm the one who got married for the sole purpose of financial freedom from them. *I'm* the one who left.

But let me tell you, when your own mother tells you not to come home—ever—it takes a little while to get over.

About ten years, in my case. And I'm *still* working on it.

"So, okay, we covered work stuff," Meghan says, propping her chin on her hand and looking at me with the fuzzy smile of someone a few drinks in. "You're doing amazing, like I always knew you would. Your parents are healthy. Now, onto the good stuff . . ."

Her face contorts, and I laugh. "Are you trying to waggle your eyebrows seductively at me?"

Meghan laughs along with me. "Blame it on the booze, and give me a break. It's been forever since I've had a night out!"

"But mommyhood suits you," I say, affectionately waving a finger around her face. "Raphael is nearly three and you've still got your new mom glow."

"I do," she says with a little smile. "Though to be fair to Camden, some of the glow is the newlywed glow. I didn't think we needed to be married to be good parents, and I'm sure that's true, but there's definitely something extra special about making it official." She bats my arm. "Well, why am I bothering telling you! You've been married longer than any of us."

I give her a wry look. "Colin's and my situation is hardly anything like yours and Camden's."

Like me, Meghan settled down from her wildest teen years, but she still knew how to break a few of the Upper East Side rules. For starters, she'd nearly given her conservative mother a heart attack by doing the whole family thing out of order: *baby*, then husband. And like me, when Meghan and Camden finally got married last year, it was in a small civil ceremony at the same courthouse—by the same judge, no less, that had married Colin and me.

Unlike Colin and me, however, Meghan and Camden are very much a love match, and together with Raphael, they've made the world's most adorable family.

"So, what's going on with you two?" Meghan asks, reaching for the menu to peruse our next wine option that I don't need, but I'll probably drink anyway, because it's been a long time since I've done irresponsible, and it feels delightful.

"I still don't understand how you did the whole long distance thing for so long," she continues. "Weirdest marriage *ever*."

You have no idea.

Although, she probably has *some* idea. For obvious reasons, Colin and I have always maintained we'd reveal the true circumstances of our marriage only when absolutely necessary, which means we've only told a handful of people the truth.

Even still, I'm pretty sure most of the people closest to us, Meghan included, have a fairly good idea why we got married. They're just too polite to say so.

"*So?*" she presses, a touch impatiently and a lot curious. "Are you guys like . . . together now? For real?"

"We're trying to make it work," I say slowly, testing out the line Colin and I agreed upon. It's a hell of a lot easier than trying to explain that for the first time in our marriage we have to actually spend time in the same state, all so we can get divorced.

It's a *bit* much to explain to a friend I've barely seen in ten years.

"I'm so glad," she says, sounding genuinely excited. "I don't know Colin all that well, but he knows one of Camden's coworkers, so we've ended up at some of the same holiday parties. He's so . . . hot."

I let out a nervous laugh, knowing she means it as a compliment, but since I'm new to this wife thing, I'm not entirely sure how to act. Smug? Possessive? Proud? Humble?

Why yes, I did *bag the hottest Irish import since Guinness made it to the States!*

I decide to infuse a bit of honesty into the situation as much as I can, without putting Meghan in a weird place on the very off-chance she were to get interviewed by Immigration Services about the nature of our marriage.

"He is hot," I say. "He's also impossible to read."

"Well, *yeah*," she says, unsurprised. "He's a man."

"No, this isn't your run-of-the-mill, closed-off alpha stuff. I mean he's like a whole other level of unreadable," I insist. "I have no idea what he's thinking, and the only time I get a glimpse of what might be going through his head when he looks at me, I'm pretty sure he's thinking about how much he dislikes me."

"Could be," Meghan surprises me by saying. "But I guarantee there's at least one other thing he's thinking about when he looks at you."

"What's that?" I ask warily.

She leans forward and gives me a grin I recognize well from our teenage years. "Sex, darling. Obviously."

She looks so tipsily scandalized by her own assessment that I don't have the heart to tell her that's *so* not a factor in Colin's case.

FRIDAY, AUGUST 21

~

*T*he next morning starts with a crisis and a decision: *coffee or pills?*

My nose makes the decision for me. I wouldn't say no to an Excedrin, but I'm also painfully—pun intended—aware that my trusty bottle of headache fighter is currently a six-hour flight away in my San Francisco medicine cabinet.

I could go snooping around Colin's stuff looking for pills, but in my current state, I'm not equipped to deal with him hounding me. Not to mention, I'm not entirely sure the man even owns painkillers. He doesn't strike me as the type to make bad decisions.

Well, other than marrying me, of course.

I roll out of bed, pausing for a second when I stand to make sure the world doesn't spin. It's a hangover all right, but not the worst I've ever had.

I open the bedroom door, turn left as I'm used to doing at my bedroom at home, and stop just in time to not collide with the wall. I pivot and shuffle toward the smell of coffee and the sound of kitchen noises.

Colin is standing at the kitchen stove dressed in slacks and an undershirt, his hair still damp from a shower. He does a double take when he sees me.

"What are you wearing?" His accent is thicker than usual when he says it, lilting and a little bit husky.

Since answering stupid questions is a no-go before coffee, I ignore him, instead opening and closing cupboards until I find the mugs. I feel a little pang of homesickness when I see they're all matching black, and a far cry from my Kate Spade mugs with the bright polka dots, but as long as it can act as a vessel for caffeine, all is forgiven.

I pull the heavy metal carafe off the fancy coffee maker, grateful for its heft because it means Colin's made a very big pot.

"What are you wearing?" he asks again, and because I've taken the first sip of sweet, sweet salvation, I humor him.

"Pajamas."

"Where's your robe?"

"Well, Grandpa. I live alone, so I don't need a robe."

"Well, you don't live alone anymore, so yes, you do need a robe."

I look down at my pajamas, trying to figure out what's got him acting all constipated. I tend to sleep hot, so even in winter, my pajamas consist of shorts and a tank top. The tank top is low-cut, but my boobs aren't spilling out, and the shorts, while tiny, aren't showing pubes, so why he's all aflutter is beyond me.

"Quick refresher from yesterday. I'm your roommate, not a guest. You don't get to tell me what to wear," I mutter, going around to the barstool and settling.

He shakes his head and turns back to the stove. He holds up a metal bowl. "I was about to scramble some eggs. Want me to make any for you?"

My stomach rolls and I can't stifle the groan.

He smirks over his shoulder. "Late night?"

I press my fingers to the center of my forehead where the headache seems to be focused. "I caught up with Meghan and somehow forgot about the fact that I'm not twenty-one anymore."

"Meghan . . . short? Pink hair?"

I smile even through my pain. "Still short. Hasn't had pink hair since we were seventeen and she was going through her rebellious stage."

As opposed to my own rebellious stage, which hadn't come until a couple of years after that. A rebellious stage that got me into the mess I'm in currently. Well, not the hangover mess. That was one too many glasses of a nice Spanish Tempranillo that followed the cocktails and Champagne. And needless to say, we had not consumed nearly enough tapas to absorb the wine.

I glance at Colin's broad back, noting the slight flex of muscles as he moves around the kitchen.

"You already went to the gym?" I ask. "I thought you were going to show me where it was."

"It's six forty-five."

"You say that like I slept until noon," I say.

"I like to be at the office no later than seven thirty."

I roll my eyes. "What a thrilling life you live."

He shoots me a look over his shoulder. "Don't act like you're in any shape to go to the gym. How's the headache?"

I wince. "*Touché.*"

I devote myself to my coffee and am a little surprised when he sets a plate of steaming scrambled eggs in front of me.

"What is this?"

"Breakfast," he says unceremoniously, sitting on a barstool, though he keeps a seat between us.

"I don't eat breakfast."

"Maybe you should. Especially if you're in the habit of late nights."

"I'm not, actually," I admit, staring at the eggs and trying to figure out if they sound like just the thing to help my headache or if they'll merely tip the scales toward queasy.

"Not in the habit of drinking?" he asks.

"Not like I did last night," I say, picking up the fork and gingerly taking a bite. "Not when I have to work the next day."

The eggs are pretty good, and my next bite is more enthusiastic.

Out of the corner of my eye, I note that Colin eats methodically. Not inhaling his food, but not savoring it either. He's got a pile of something green on his plate—spinach, maybe, and I'm grateful he spared me that, since I'm new to this breakfast thing. Vegetables are pushing my luck. Normally, I'm more of a coffee kind of gal, and occasionally, a raspberry smoothie that Kurt brings me when he tells me I'm acting hangry.

The exception is Sunday brunch, but brunch isn't breakfast. There is no spinach at brunch, not the way I do it. It's all about mimosas and French toast piled high with whipped cream.

"Do you like brunch?" I ask Colin.

"What?" He doesn't look at me.

"Brunch. You know, a boozy weekend breakfast? Where you eat just a little too much, preferably something with Hollandaise or syrup, and want to take a nap after?"

He wipes his mouth and takes the plate to the sink, rinsing it and putting it in the dishwasher using the same robotic efficiency with which he eats.

"Are you done?" he asks.

I look pointedly down at my plate, which is almost entirely full since I've taken all of two bites.

"Right. Well, put it in the dishwasher when you're done."

I give him a mocking salute as he pours himself another cup of coffee and heads back toward the bedroom.

"So that's a no on liking brunch then?" I call after him, mostly to be annoying.

Colin doesn't reply, and I don't expect him to.

I sigh. One morning down. Only about ninety more to go.

Kill me.

FRIDAY, AUGUST 28

⌒

"*H*oney, your *hair*. Do they not have hairdressers in New York?"

"Hey! I'm not going to do Skype calls anymore if you're going to criticize my appearance."

Kurt blows me a kiss through his on-screen camera. "I missed your face."

"I missed yours too."

And it's true. I have missed him. But . . . this whole working remotely thing has been more successful than I expected. Granted, it's only been a week, but I've been a little surprised to realize how much more I get done when I don't feel obligated to sit in on every possible meeting. Not to mention, the three-hour time difference means that I feel like I get a jump-start on every day.

I make a mental note to use that three-hour advantage to make a hair appointment. I left San Francisco in such a hurry that I missed my standing appointment to keep my mushroom brown roots from showing, and the grow out's not pretty. But neither is the process of finding a new stylist who knows his or her way around light blond hair, so I've been putting it off.

The way Kurt's eyes keep widening in horror tells me I've put it off too long.

"Seriously, I'm going to go put on a hat if you keep doing that."

"Oh, God, *no*. That's worse. Hats and your face shape are no good."

"Remind me again why we're doing this?"

He smiles. "Because you love me. And I love you. Speaking of *lovvvvvve*, how's the hubby?"

I slouch down at Colin's kitchen table, which I've taken over as my makeshift office until I can get around to renting proper office space, and tell him the same thing I told Meghan. "I don't think he likes me."

Kurt shakes his head. "Nonsense. Everyone loves you. You've got that *joie de vivre* that men find positively irresistible and women want for themselves."

"Yeah, well, Colin doesn't seem to appreciate my joy for life. I think he thinks I'm annoying."

"Are you?"

I purse my lips. "I *may* find it a little intriguing to push his buttons. But in my defense, he has a lot of them. The guy's so tightly wound."

Kurt fans himself. "Oh, God. My Kryptonite. The first night I stayed over at Lewis's house, I put my fork in the dishwasher tine-side down, and I thought he was going to lose it. It was some of the best sex we've ever had."

"Yeah, well. Colin and I are most definitely not having sex."

"You're married!"

"Not *really*. I barely know the guy."

"So? Get to know him."

"I've been trying," I say, fiddling with my necklace. "Not because I want to sleep with him, but because I don't see any reason why the next three months have to be completely unbearable. But he seems perfectly content to just pretend I don't exist, even when we share the same fridge, breathe the same air . . ."

"You could seduce him," Kurt says, as though I haven't spoken.

"Okay, one-track mind. You're not listening. I'm not interested in him like that. He's grumpy, structured, and he lives on the other side of the country. I just don't see why we can't be friends."

Kurt shakes his head indulgently. "You never could stand it when people don't like you."

"Well, why doesn't he like me?" I demand, sitting up straight. "I'm easy to like. I get along with everyone."

"Mmmm. And how are your parents?"

I lift a warning finger. "Off-limits, and you know it."

"So you haven't seen them yet."

"No," I grumble, trying to dodge the pervasive stab of guilt and failing.

"Do they know you're living in the same city as them these days?"

"I'm working up to it. You don't know them, Kurt. They're not regular parents. They're not even regular *people*."

"Okay, fine. One battle at a time. We'll start with your spouse. How have you tried to win him over?"

"I made him coffee this morning. He didn't even say thank you."

"Who usually makes coffee?"

"Him."

"Do *you* say thank you?"

I open my mouth then shut it. "Fair point. Okay, so what do I do?"

"Remind me of your ideal endgame?"

"My not *dying* over the course of the next three months?"

He rolls his finger. "Non-hyperbolic version."

I sigh. "I'd settle for not feeling so inferior whenever he's around. I can deal with the fact that we're not going to be BFFs, but it's been a long time since someone's made me feel so . . . inadequate."

"Have you asked him what he thinks of you?"

"Um, no. How exactly does one have that conversation?"

Kurt places his hand over his chest. "Okay, pretend I'm you . . ."

Kurt flutters his eyelashes and twirls an imaginary lock of hair. "Hi, Colin? I know my hair looks kind of skanky right now, but that aside, I'm just wondering why you think I'm scum?"

Kurt shifts positions slightly to the other side of his chair then scowls before speaking in a low, lilting voice. "I don't disdain ye, lass. I'm just a wee bit shy is all."

"That is the worst Irish accent I've ever heard."

"But he does have an Irish accent, right?"

"Yeah. But—"

I break off when I hear the front door open.

"Gotta run," I tell Kurt.

I slam my laptop shut before my friend can say goodbye, not wanting Colin to know we were talking about him and his sexy accent.

Did I say sexy?

Yes. Yes, I did. Because even though his accent's not quite as thick as it was ten years ago, there's still something distinctly hot about a man with an accent, especially when he looks like this one.

He's wearing a blue shirt today with his standard dark gray suit, and it brings out the bright blue of his eyes even more than usual. Blue eyes that blink once too fast when he sees me, as though he's still not used to seeing me in his home.

Colin gives a quick incline of his chin, his version of a greeting, as he closes the front door.

We've been at this for a week, so I know what happens next. He puts his briefcase in the hall closet, goes to the kitchen for a glass of water and sometimes an apple, and then retreats to the bedroom. Sometimes he stays in there most of the night, except to eat, reading or watching TV. Some nights he'll head back out, to do I don't even know what with his evenings.

He's never outright rude. He's considerate of noise. Cleans up after himself—and me, if I do something crazy like leave a baguette out on the counter. He speaks to me if I ask him something. He continues to put eggs in front of me every morning if I'm up at the same time as him. But like I told Kurt, I can't shake the sense that he doesn't like me. Or at the very least, wishes I wasn't here.

Which I can understand. I don't particularly want to be here either. I still have pretty regular fantasies about strangling my brother for getting us into this mess, especially since Justin's been continuing to ghost me. I can't even blame him. My brother's an exceptionally intelligent man. Avoiding the sister whose prenup you manipulated is a very smart strategy for preserving personal safety.

Still, Justin *did* get me into this mess. He got both of us into this mess, and we're stuck with it. And simply wishing the situation away isn't going to work. Something's got to give, and I guess it has to be me.

"Hey, do you want a drink?" I blurt out, as he opens the coat closet to set his bag inside.

Colin slowly straightens and gives me an unreadable look. "What?"

"A drink," I repeat patiently. "Alcohol optional. Consumed while in my company. That part is *not* optional."

"A drink here?"

I shrug. "Why not? You've got that fancy bar cart with all the fixings. And I make a really good martini."

"Vodka or gin?"

"Either. Both. Bond drank vodka."

"Churchill drank gin."

"Bond was hotter," I counter.

Colin's hands slip under his open suit jacket, finding his hips as he studies me. "You're a 007 fan."

"I'm a Daniel Craig fan. And Pierce Brosnan. And Connery. Okay, yes, fine. I'm a 007 fan."

He nods. "All right then. Ever had a Vesper?"

I shake my head. "It sounds vaguely familiar though."

"It's vodka and gin. Plus, Bond drank one in *Casino Royale*."

"Ah *ha*! So you're a Bond fan too. What do you know, we *do* have something in common!"

He doesn't smile, but his gaze seems slightly friendlier than usual.

"All right," he says finally. "Let me make one quick phone call, and then I'll make us one."

I wait until he's out of sight, listening for the click of his bedroom door before I hop out of my chair and do a victory dance. What it lacks in coordination, it makes up for in enthusiasm.

I've just figured out what my project will be while my real life in San Francisco is on hiatus: I *will* figure out what makes this guy tick, and I *will* make him like me.

Kurt wasn't entirely wrong about me. I do like people to like me. They don't have to love me. Just . . . adore me, a little bit. Not because I'm vain, but, well . . .

I suspect it probably has something to do with the deep-seated guilt of just how awful I was in my early twenties. Self-centered, reckless, and a little ungrateful.

I've been making up for it ever since.

I have no idea how long Colin's phone call will take, and quite honestly, I don't really need him to make the cocktails. I love to entertain, and added at-home bartending to my cocktail party and dinner party skills a long time ago. And though this particular cocktail is new to me, it's nothing a little Google can't help with.

A quick search later, and I see that this mysterious Vesper is pretty close to a martini. I pull the vodka and gin off the sleek bar cart Colin keeps in the corner of the living room and find a bottle of the third ingredient, something called Lillet Blanc, in the refrigerator.

I contemplate shaking it. It's very Bond after all. But the picture of the drink I found on the Internet is perfectly clear, and shaking the cocktail will make it cloudy.

I put two cocktail glasses in the freezer to chill and then snoop around Colin's kitchen until I come up with a crystal mixing glass and a bar spoon.

The mixing glass is small, so I have to make the drinks one at a time, measuring carefully, pouring over ice, and stirring for a good minute or so to get the liquor ice cold before straining into the glasses.

I'm digging around in the refrigerator for a lemon to garnish the drinks when Colin emerges from the bedroom.

He pauses, looking at the two finished cocktails in surprise. "I said I'd make them."

"I heard you." I hold up the lemon. "Do you have a little—?"

I mime the motion of making a lemon twist to garnish the drinks.

Colin shrugs out of his suit jacket and drapes it over the back of the barstool, rolling up the sleeves of his dress shirt as he walks toward me.

He opens a drawer and pulls out a channel knife, but instead of handing it over, he reaches out for the lemon. My fingers close around the fruit reflexively, so accustomed to living alone, to doing things my way, that I immediately resist giving up control.

Colin's apparently used to being in control too, because he continues to reach for the lemon. Only, I'm holding it so tightly he can't grab the lemon without also grabbing my hand.

Things that are not sexy: lemons.

Things that *are* sexy: Colin Walsh holding my hand holding a lemon.

It shouldn't be. I know that. But the second his fingers make contact with mine, I feel it in places I have no business feeling anything as it relates to this man.

Still, my hand doesn't pull back, and, I realize belatedly . . . neither does his.

I lift my gaze to his and see something that looks like a flash of heat—if a bit angry heat—before he tugs the lemon out of my hand.

Clearing his throat, he adds a lemon twist to the cocktails with an adeptness that tells me I'm not the only one who knows his way around the home bar.

He hands me one of the glasses before lifting his own in a silent toast and taking a drink. "Not bad."

"You sound surprised."

He studies his drink for a moment. "No. Well. A little. I've never had a woman besides female bartenders make me a beverage."

"And you thought we were incapable?"

"Don't put words in my mouth."

"Well, what else am I supposed to—"

Colin reaches out and sets a single finger along the base of my cocktail glass, managing to tip it toward my face without spilling a single drop. "Shut up and drink your damn drink."

I take a sip, not quite sure what to expect. "Oh! It's good."

"You sound surprised," he says, mimicking my earlier statement.

I make a *ha ha* face then take another sip of the drink. "I didn't know quite what to expect with the vodka and gin together, but it's . . . pleasant, isn't it?"

He shrugs. "Bond thought so."

"So, is this your drink of choice?" I ask, settling on a barstool, determined to lure him into conversation, and maybe, just maybe—something resembling civility.

"I've been known to order it."

"But is it your *favorite*?"

"What am I, twelve?"

"I didn't ask you to please rate your favorite Power Rangers in reverse order," I say, striving for patience. "I was just asking if this is your go-to drink order."

"No."

God give me strength.

"So what is your go-to drink order?"

"Are you always this talkative?"

"Yes. Most people find it extremely charming."

"Most people aren't married to you."

"Only because I've been taken since I was twenty-one." I flutter my eyelashes.

He rewards me with a very slight upward tilt of the corner of his mouth. "I don't think that guy knew what he was getting into."

"Oh, please. You've been dealing with me for all of one week. Don't tell me that the twice annual emails or text messages over the past decade were too much for you to handle."

"I survived."

I spin my drink in a slow circle. "Why did we last so long, do you think?"

He gives a casual shrug. "I never really had reason to end it."

"Until now."

"Until now," he agrees.

"What changed? I mean, I'm not complaining, I'm just curious."

"I guess I realized I'm an adult. No longer a kid in need of a green card."

"And I'm no longer a rebellious girl in need of her trust fund to escape her parents."

"No. You're not."

I narrow my eyes because there's a little something extra in his tone.

"What's that I'm hearing?" I say. "Judgment? It sounds like judgment."

"I just find it interesting that you've been in the city for a week and haven't seen or spoken with your mother. Or father."

"How do you know I haven't called them? Or seen them?"

"Your mother told me."

I nearly spit out my drink. "You talk to my mom? When?"

"She texted me yesterday when she hadn't heard from you."

"She *texts*?"

"Yes, Charlotte. Both of your parents are savvy enough to have mastered text messages. Something you might know had you taken the time to stay in touch this past decade."

"Hey. My relationship with my parents is *not* your business. I don't go around asking the last time you've seen your parents."

His jaw tightens.

I give him a vaguely smug look. "So. Then you're not really one to talk now, are you?"

He stares me down, and I stare right back, and damn it. He wins, because I cave.

"What did she want?" I ask.

"Your mother?"

I nod.

Colin shrugs. "She knows you're back. Knows about our situation. Wanted to see how you were."

"She could have called me," I grumble.

"Would you have picked up?"

"Yes." Maybe. Probably. Possibly not.

It's not like I've had no contact with my parents. We've thawed slowly over the years, mostly due to my brother's persistence. I call on birthdays. We talk on Christmas. I saw them at my grandmother's funeral and at my brother's wedding in the past couple of years.

It's just . . . chilly. We don't understand each other. They're two of the most opinionated people on the planet, and yet they somehow manage to be both baffled and outraged that they got an opinionated daughter who refuses to subscribe to the life they'd laid out for her.

"So, did you know my mom once grounded me for getting my hair cut?"

"Yes, of course. I keep track of all your past haircuts and have a list of all the times you were grounded as a child."

I let out a little laugh, delighted by the dry sarcasm, but I forge ahead to make my point. "I was seventeen. I read an article on pixie cuts in *Cosmopolitan*, thought it would look cute on me, so I went to the salon, showed them the picture, and came home with a pixie cut."

"Fascinating stuff."

"My mom was so horrified, she grounded me for a week. I missed the spring formal. Because of a *haircut*, Colin."

He sips his drink. "How old are you?"

"You know exactly how old I am."

"Yes. I do. Which is how I know that this episode with the pixie whatever happened a *long* time ago. Perhaps it's time to let that one go. Perhaps it's time to let it all go."

"You're not wrong."

His hand freezes midway toward setting his glass on the counter, and it's oddly gratifying to know I can surprise this man. "I'm not?"

I shrug. "Like you said, it's been long enough."

With that, I stand and pick up my own glass, and head back toward my bedroom.

"Where are you going?"

"To call my mom," I call over my shoulder. "If you hear screaming, be a good husband and make me another drink, would you?"

SUNDAY, AUGUST 30

Is it still too hot to be wearing leather pants? Absolutely.

But it's a small price to pay for showing my parents that, while we might be meeting on their turf, I'm still me. The version of me that pairs leather pants with red patent leather shoes and a black silk camisole. No cardigan. It's the no cardigan that will get my mother, mark my words.

What? I said it was time to let it all go, not become a doormat.

The cabbie gives me an impatient look in the rearview mirror, and I realize my stalling time is over. With a grimace, I shove open the cab door and step onto a street I haven't set foot on in a long, long time.

I look around, somehow completely unsurprised to see that the street I grew up on looks exactly the same. You often hear people say how New York City is always changing, and it's true. Just not on the Upper East Side. Or at least not on Sixty-third Street.

I glance at the row of town houses as the cabbie drives away, and on a closer look, a few things *have* changed. The Steins' door is dark blue instead of red. Mrs. Krause's home has gotten a facelift, no doubt by its new owners, considering Mrs. Krause had been in her late eighties when I was a girl. Trees are taller, flowerpots refreshed, but the essence of the street is still exactly as I remember it.

Finally, I fix my gaze straight ahead, at the home I grew up in. My parents' town house has changed . . .

Not at all.

There's still the dark gray door. The perfectly kept steps. No flowerpots at this house. My mother finds them messy. The welcome mat is strictly practical. No cheeky puns or friendly sayings, just a place to wipe your feet before entering the pristine foyer.

Sounds fun, right?

And now you're wondering what I'm doing here. I was told, after all, that if I walked out the door, I was not to come back.

Yeah, well, I'm sort of wondering what I'm doing here myself. One minute I was making strained small talk with my mother, and the next she was informing me she'd see me at five for Sunday dinner.

Note that I said *informing*. Not *asking* if I was available, or if I'd like to come over. It was simply there. A command. I haven't had Sunday dinner with my family for the better part of two decades, but you'd have never guessed it from my mom's casual insistence.

And, so . . . here I am. Preparing to enter the lion's den.

I manage the steps just fine, but the front door gives me pause, and I realize just what sort of mind games ten years can play.

Do I knock? Or merely . . . enter?

The thought of knocking feels unthinkable. I've burst through this door hundreds of times. Thousands. But I'm not an eighth grader bounding home from school any longer. I'm a thirty-one-year-old woman.

And this is no longer my home.

If you walk out that door, Charlotte Spencer, don't expect to walk back in again, now or ever again.

The prideful part of me wants to reverse court and prove to my mother that you reap what you sow. You tell your only daughter never to come back, maybe she won't.

And yet the other part of me, the one that's grown up, the one that's determined to be a kinder, better person, suspects that my mom's demand that I be here for dinner tonight wasn't uttered out of bossiness or control-freak tendencies, but out of fear. If I had to guess, I'd say that my mom was terrified that if she didn't *make* me come for dinner, I wouldn't.

Of course, it still irks that she hasn't learned me well enough to know that the tighter she tugs the reins, the more I pull back, and that had she merely invited me to dinner, I'd be inside playing nice instead of lurking stubbornly on the porch.

Grow up, Charlotte.

Strangely, it's Colin's voice I hear in my head. Not that I've heard him utter those precise words, but close enough.

And it's him I'm determined to prove wrong when I open the door.

I'm a little surprised to find it unlocked. And the second I step inside, I'm surprised by the slap of emotion. I'd thought it would be like stepping into a stranger's home, or at best, a little sliver of my past.

My reaction is much more visceral than that, and much warmer. This is my *home*. Or at least it feels like it. Everything, from the click of my heel against the dark wood floor, to the elaborate flower arrangement on the entryway table, to the smell, is familiar.

A *nice* familiar, I'm a little surprised to realize. The first door to the right was my dad's office, and poking my head into the dark room, I see that has remained the same. Same dark wood desk, same faintly woodsy smell. The computer's been upgraded—a newer model Mac, which surprises me. I'd have pegged my dad as a PC guy for life.

I back out of the room and head toward the parlor, and yes, they call it that. My parents are, oh, how do I put this . . .

Stuffy as heck.

No casual meals are eaten around a friendly kitchen table, no snacks to be nibbled at the kitchen counter. Meals, even breakfast, were formal, seated affairs in the dining room.

Even the before dinner ritual had been stuffy, with mandatory "cocktails, conversation, and nibbles" in the parlor, and don't even think about showing up in bare feet, shorts, or with messy hair.

Growing up, "cocktails" had meant lemonade or Shirley Temples for me, but I'm most definitely planning on a more adult beverage option tonight. For obvious reasons. Sure enough, I find my mom exactly where I expect to—in the parlor, and again the sheer familiarity of the moment washes over me.

Mom turns to face me, and the butterflies dislodge from my stomach and seem to lodge in my throat when I meet her familiar blue eyes.

She looks the same. Same pearl necklace, same muted red lipstick, same shoulder-length bob, and perfect posture.

But not exactly the same. Like the street outside and the home itself, there are subtle changes. Soft changes. Crepe paper lines around her eyes and silver mixed in with the straight blond hair.

My mom's gaze, too, is softer than I remember it being, though just for a moment before she lifts her chin slightly. "Charlotte. Good, you're here. You're still on that lax California schedule, I suppose."

My mother, ladies and gentleman. Let the record state that I'm exactly three minutes past her five o'clock summons.

"Where's Dad?" I ask, glancing around the room, then doing a double take. There's a man standing at the wet bar, but it's most definitely *not* my father.

"What are you doing here?" I blurt out.

"Charlotte, be polite," Mom says, not liking my West Coast manners any more than she likes my willy-nilly time table, apparently.

Colin idly lifts a cocktail glass in greeting. "Wife."

"You said you had plans," I accuse. I haven't seen him since he left our place around noon.

"I do, and they involve Sunday dinner with Eileen and Paul."

"Since when has your weekend plans involved dinner at my parents'?"

"Since always," my mother answers for him. "Colin, would you be a doll and fix Charlotte something to drink? I'm going to go find your father. He's out in the garden again, doting on his herbs. And then I'd like a nice glass of white wine when I return."

Herbs? The father I remember tolerated the outdoors to golf, and only then when it was to advance a business deal. He most certainly didn't go outside willingly. And he'd never dote.

I stare after my mom's back as she leaves the room then shake my head. "I can't figure out what's more surprising: that you do regular dinners with my family or that my dad has a herb garden."

Colin shrugs. "It's been part of his quest to figure out what he wants to do with his life after retirement. Model airplanes, photography, and writing the next great American novel have all been ruled out," Colin says, not turning around as he fixes a drink at the bar.

"You know him better than I do," I murmur, walking toward him.

He glances down at me as I approach, his gaze skimming over my outfit. His expression is detached, as usual, but I don't miss the way his eyes linger on the V-cut of my camisole before dropping to my leather pants.

"Nice outfit. Where'd you park your motorcycle?"

I let out a little laugh and accept the drink he holds out.

"What is this?" I take a sip and smile. "A Vesper."

He shrugs, reaching up to pull down a wine glass, filling it from a bottle of white wine chilling in an ice bucket. He sets it aside, presumably for my mom, then picks up his own glass once more.

"You really come here every Sunday?"

"Most."

"*Why?*" I ask, trying to wrap my head around why a grown man would willingly put himself in this situation on the regular.

"I enjoy your parents."

"Really."

He looks away. "It's nice. To have people in the city to . . ." He clears his throat. "I don't have family in the city. And neither do they."

There's no accusation in his tone, but I feel the guilt all the same. I left. Justin left. Colin stayed.

I suppose a son-in-law who stayed beats a daughter who left.

"She's glad you're here," Colin says softly.

I'm startled by the comment, but before I can respond, my mother sails back into the room, surprisingly graceful for a woman on the north side of her sixtieth birthday.

My father's right behind her, and my heart squeezes at the sight of him. I don't know what I was expecting, given this whole herb garden hobby. Overalls. Dirt under the fingernails. A beard.

But he looks the same. There's no sign of stoop in his broad shoulders. His hair is more salt than pepper now but still thick and perfectly combed into the same side part he's worn my entire life.

"Dad."

My dad's not a particularly smiley guy, but he smiles when he sees me. "Charlotte."

I hand my glass to Colin, who takes it without comment, and acting on instinct, I throw my arms around my dad, who stiffens a little in surprise.

We are not a hugging family.

But he chuckles and pats the back of my head a little awkwardly. "Good to have you back."

Back.

There's a comfort to the word I didn't expect. I'm not back— not for good. It's just a three-month reprieve from my real life until I can ditch my pesky husband, but in this moment, I let myself pretend that I'm home.

"Whiskey, Paul?" Colin asks, as I pull back from the awkward hug.

My dad nods, accepting the glass that Colin's already poured.

There's an easy casualness to their exchange that makes me feel . . . weird.

The fact that they're *my* parents, that this was *my* home, even the sense of familiarity when I stepped into the house—it's an old familiarity. The kind that you inherit, not the kind you've earned.

Colin has *earned* the familiarity. He's been here. For the life of me, I can't figure out if I'm annoyed or grateful.

"Charlotte, come. Sit," Mom says, as she gracefully lowers to the love seat, crossing her legs and gesturing to the opposite love seat.

My mom's navy slacks, navy pumps, and yellow sweater set are perfectly suited to the conservatively decorated room. My leather pants, not so much. Still, I do as instructed, nodding in thanks as Colin retrieves my cocktail and places it back in my hand.

Then he surprises me by sitting next to me, my father taking his place beside my mother. It's a weirdly domestic scene, one that suits the three of them, and leaves me feeling very much the newcomer who hasn't read this part of the script.

"We were so glad to hear that you and Colin decided to try to make your marriage work."

I choke into my cocktail and glance at Colin in bemusement.

But his expression betrays nothing, and I look back at my parents. *Surely* they don't think—?

There is no sense of irony on their faces, no knowing smirks. Which I guess I should have figured. I don't remember either parent having much of a sense of humor, but they're also not stupid. There's no *way* they think that Colin and I got married for real.

Right?

Ten years ago, Justin had very specific instructions about my arrangement with Colin:

Don't tell a single goddamn person the truth.

We'd all known that those close to us would make their own assumptions, obviously, but on the off chance we were suspected of marriage fraud, we hadn't wanted to put anyone in the position of having to lie for us.

That had included my parents, but I always thought they'd figured out the truth about why we got married. They were well aware of the stipulations of the trust fund from my grandmother, and it couldn't have been much of a leap to put together the fact that Irish-born Colin would benefit as well.

Then again, I wouldn't be surprised in the least if they believed what they wanted to believe for stubbornness' sake.

Or wishful thinking.

I get another one of those pangs at the thought that my parents have been clinging to hope that their rebellious daughter would return home to patch things up with the dutiful husband.

But. It's been a decade. Surely they don't think that Colin and I have been *actually* married for that long.

Surely he hasn't let them think that.

"Naturally, it's something to celebrate, so I thought I'd throw a small get-together."

"Wait, what?" My attention snaps away from the unreadable man beside me and back to my mom.

"People want to see you, Charlotte," she says, as though this explains everything. "Just yesterday Irene Hicks asked how you were."

"Irene Hicks. As in Mrs. Hicks? My seventh-grade teacher?"

"Since she was one of your favorites, I invited her over on Friday—"

"Wait." I hold up a hand, feeling panicked now. "Friday—"

"For your party," she says, sounding exasperated with me, as though I'm the one talking crazy. "Colin, I already called your office and talked to Stephanie about your schedule. She said you're wide open."

Out of the corner of my eye, I see Colin hesitate for just a second before nodding. "Sure. Friday night sounds good."

"Oh, *does* it?" I ask sarcastically, giving him a quick dark look before turning back to my parents.

"Mom, I really appreciate the sentiment, but I think a party would be weird."

My mother looks affronted. "My parties are never weird."

"No, I know, I just mean . . ." I take a breath. "I mean it would be weird to have a welcome back party when I'm not back for good."

I stumble over the announcement slightly, feeling fifteen again. I'm fully braced for disappointment and/or a guilt trip and am a little puzzled when I get neither.

Instead, my mom waves her hand in a dismissive gesture she's picked up in the past ten years, because I definitely don't remember it from my childhood.

"Oh, who knows what will happen?" she says.

I do! I know what will happen! In three months, I'll have gotten out of this ridiculous marriage trap my brother got me into, and I will go back to my real life.

I wait for Colin to chime in, but instead he stands. "More wine?" he asks my mom.

"You're a doll. You picked a good one, Charlotte."

My head drops forward in defeat.

SUNDAY, AUGUST 30

*S*omehow, I make it all the way through cocktail hour, dinner, and dessert.

And then? Then I give in to the urge to *lose it*. The second the cab door closes behind Colin, I whirl on him, punching his shoulder.

"Ouch," he snaps. "What the hell?"

"Don't *what the hell* me. I'm the one who gets to *what the hell*. Are you seriously telling me you've been going over there every single Sunday night for ten years, and you haven't once told them you married me to get your green card?"

"No," he says, unperturbed.

"So you *did* tell them."

He hesitates. "No, I mean I don't go over there every Sunday night. I've missed a few."

I punch him again, and this time he grabs my wrist. "Stop doing that."

I try to wiggle my arm away, but he holds firm, so I settle for glaring. "What was your plan? To just wait for me to come back to New York and deliver the bad news? Let them think you're the patient, abandoned husband while I'm the selfish, disloyal airhead?"

He doesn't reply, and my mouth drops open.

"Oh my God. That *was* your nefarious plan."

"*Nefarious?* I didn't have a *plan*, Charlotte. I'm not a cartoon villain. I didn't set out to let them think anything. I saw an aging, lonely couple who missed their grown children. You flitted off to San Francisco without a backward glance. Justin's wife's work took them to Frankfurt. It didn't hurt me any to join them for a home-cooked meal, so I did."

"And in all those dinners, you couldn't find the time to tell them why we got married?"

"I'm sure they know."

"*Really?*" I let the word drip with sarcasm. "Because I didn't hear you once correct my mother's assumption that you're wildly in love with me and have been patiently waiting for me to return home."

His head snaps back as though the concept is abhorrent. "She does not think that."

"Well, she definitely wants to believe it. And I'm betting when I head back to San Francisco, you won't be telling them that *you're* the one who asked for a divorce."

His fingers tighten on my wrist. "Now who's the one acting like the put-upon spouse? Don't pretend that you want to stay married to me. Not when it's just the two of us. And don't pretend you ever wanted to get married in the first place. It was a business transaction, pure and simple. For both of us."

He's right, but in this moment, nothing between us feels businesslike. He's still got my wrist in a viselike grip. His expression is murderous, and I expect mine is too. We're both breathing hard, with just a few inches separating us in the back of the cab, and I don't think it's my imagination that the tension between us is just slightly tinged with sexual awareness.

Ten years ago, I married a quiet Irish boy who did absolutely nothing to get my blood pumping.

Now, however, I can't deny that grown-up Colin isn't *just* objectively good-looking—he's fiercely attractive. *To me*.

His gaze drops to my lips, and I wonder if he feels the pull too. I wonder if he wants to kiss me as badly as I want him to. He releases my wrist abruptly, turning his head away, and making a noise that sounds an awful lot like disgust.

Well. That answers that question.

I struggle to contain my disappointment, even as I register the sudden coolness on my arm where his fingertips had been.

"It's just one party," he grumbles. "We'll get through it. Then we can tell your parents the whole truth."

"The truth. Meaning that you want a divorce," I say, just to be very clear that I won't be the lone bad guy in this situation.

"Yes," Colin says in a clipped tone, as the cab pulls up outside our apartment. "That I want a divorce."

He climbs out of the cab without another word, and I pause just for a moment before following suit, frowning in irritation and more than a little confusion, at how much his announcement bothers me.

Friday, September 4

Whatever easy tolerance Colin and I had developed during that first week evaporates following the disastrous dinner with my parents.

All week, we've been acting like the strangers we are, barely speaking except for absolute essentials.

Where'd you put the can opener?

Did you move my phone charger?

Can you please turn off that god-awful music?

The last one is me because Colin apparently likes jazz, which has always sounded like chaos to my ears.

Mostly, we've avoided each other. I found a co-working space where I've rented a small office. I spend all day there, and then I've made it a point to catch up on the Manhattan social scene in the evenings. I've caught up with friends I haven't seen in years, flirted with hot Wall Street guys over martinis, and just generally let myself remember how much I love this city.

I love it with as much enthusiasm as I hate my husband.

I've been half hoping for a hurricane. Not the really destructive kind, just . . . you know, rough enough that my mom will have to cancel this damn party.

But Friday rolls around, and though the day is oppressively humid, there's zero chance of extreme weather canceling the party. Even if there was, there are stronger forces in this world than hurricanes.

My mother is one of them.

To her credit, she hasn't nagged me about the party. Not about showing up, what to wear, how to behave. There are no lectures about not embarrassing her or unsubtle reminders to change absolutely everything about my personality.

Instead, it's as though she merely expects me to be there, expects me to behave.

She's treating me like an adult.

Which means . . . I have to act like one.

Given Colin's and my deliberately misaligned schedules these days, I'm fully expecting to merely meet him there rather than coordinating our arrival. We'll have to play nice for the evening, but we're not on the clock until the party officially starts at six. Until then, I imagine we'll be doing what we've been doing: pretending the other doesn't exist.

Which is why I freeze in the process of putting my earrings in when I see Colin in the kitchen, drinking a glass of water.

"I didn't hear you come in."

His only response is a shrug. He's wearing a navy suit with a white shirt and bright blue tie. The tie matches the color of my cocktail dress almost exactly, and perversely, I want to go change so we don't match.

I don't, mainly because the scrappy blue dress is the coolest item in my wardrobe that can satisfy my mom's "cocktail attire" dress code. And considering it's an atypically hot September, the fact that the dress has very little fabric, while still looking some-what formal, means that I'm sticking with it.

Colin's gaze rakes over me. "Nice nightgown."

I ignore him, pulling a glass out of the cupboard and pouring myself a glass of water, because even with the AC blasting and the dress being blissfully shy of fabric, it still feels hot in here.

I jump when I feel the brush of fingers against my back and whirl around.

"Easy," he says, holding up a hand in surrender. "Your zipper's undone just a bit. I was going to fix it."

"No. I've got it." The back of the dress is mostly open at the top, with a crisscross pattern running across my shoulder blades. The zipper is near the bottom of the dress, running halfway up my back, and I realize after a moment of flailing that the zipper tab is just out of reach.

Colin's dark eyebrows lift. "Need a hand?"

"Fine," I mutter, turning around. "Don't get frisky."

"I'll try to contain myself."

And contain himself he does. He makes absolutely no effort to linger as his fingers brush against my back, fixing the tag with as little contact as possible before pulling away.

The brevity of the touch does nothing to lessen the impact on my pulse, and I grit my teeth in irritation at my misplaced attrac-tion to a man I don't like.

I take a gulp of water and turn around to glare at him. He's glaring right back.

"So. Tonight should be fun."

He rolls his shoulders. "At least you don't have to wear a suit in a goddamn heat wave."

"I didn't realize robots registered body temperature. That's some pretty advanced AI."

"A robot? That's what you're going with?"

"It's the best scenario I can come up with for why you are the way you are."

"Which is what?"

"Impassive. Unreadable. Incapable of human emotion."

He carefully sets his glass on the counter. "How do you figure that?"

"You never smile. Or laugh. Even when you get mad, you tamp it back down immediately."

"I see. So because I don't *show* every emotion, I must not have any."

"Do you?" I ask curiously.

He picks up his glass and puts it in the dishwasher. "Are you ready to go?"

"See, this is exactly what I mean! Whenever I try to talk about anything personal, you shut down."

"Not all of us are wired to open up to perfect strangers, Charlotte."

"A stranger," I repeat. "Seriously. I'm your—"

He steps closer. "You're what . . . my wife? No, you're not. Not in a way that warrants you access into my innermost thoughts. I didn't know you when I signed the marriage license, and I don't know you now. And you don't know me either, so perhaps you'll want to consider withholding judgment."

I think this over, because . . . he's not wrong.

"Fine," I say slowly. "I'll make every attempt to withhold judgment if you do the same."

"What?" He looks confused and annoyed as hell.

"Ah, look! There's some emotion. I believe they call that one irritation. But I'm serious. You can't call me out for judging you without knowing you when you're doing the exact same thing."

"I'm not."

"You are," I say, stepping forward. "You've made it plain since our very first meeting that you don't like me. You didn't like me back then either."

"You were twenty-one and a brat."

"I absolutely was," I say because it's true. "I was selfish, but let's not forget that we both got something out of this arrangement, so spare me the sanctimonious lecture. And—" I press on before he can object, "I would like to point out that people are allowed to grow and change. And I have."

"Have you?" Colin murmurs.

"Yes. Something you might have noticed if you weren't so busy brooding and avoiding me."

"All right," he says affably. "Prove it."

I frown. "Prove what?"

"That you've changed. Prove that you're not still obsessed with getting your own way and doing the exact opposite of what your parents want just to spite them."

"That was never—" I break off. "Okay. That was a big part of who I was at that stage in my life. But it's not anymore."

"Like I said. Prove it."

My eyes narrow in suspicion. "How?"

"Give your parents tonight."

"Um, did you not hear me agree to the party? Am I not dressed to impress?" I say, gesturing down my body.

"Your mom wants more than for you to simply show up in a tiny dress, and you know it. You had a vision for your life, and that's fine, but your mom had a vision for your life too."

"And let me guess. That vision's come to involve you," I say drolly.

"Look at that, folks. Smart *and* pretty."

I grin. "You think I'm pretty?"

"I think *you* think you're pretty." But his voice isn't as irritated as usual, and his eyes are almost smiling. I think.

"So what is it you want from me tonight?" I ask. It comes out a little breathy, and I clear my throat. "I mean. How can I prove I'm not the . . . what was it, twenty-one-year-old brat?"

"I already know you're not a twenty-one-year-old brat. I'd like to see that you're not a *thirty*-one-year-old brat. Do something unselfish."

He doesn't say "for once," but I'm pretty sure he's thinking it, and it stings. And irritatingly, I want to prove him wrong.

I don't just want him to like me. I want him to respect me.

"Fine." I lift my chin. "What do you have in mind?"

"Just for tonight, let your parents think we're trying to work it out. For real. For one night, let them have their fantasy. That you and I are . . . you know . . ."

"Doing it?"

Colin goes still at my words. "I just meant . . ."

I give him a brotherly pat on the arm and turn to head toward the door. "I know what you meant. For tonight, let them think that I'm trying to be a wife for real. There's just one problem," I say, looking over my shoulder as I pick my purse up off the end table.

"What?" he asks warily.

"In order for that to work, you'll have to prove that you're trying to be my husband. For real."

"Which means, what, I follow along behind you and carry your purse?"

"How about a smoldering look across the room?" I suggest. "That way we won't have to talk to each other, but people will think you can't wait to drag me home and have your way with me."

Colin gives me a dark look, and I sigh. "No, no, dear, I said *smolder*, not glare. Don't worry, I'm sure you'll have *plenty* of opportunity to practice at the party."

Friday, September 4

"Charlotte, dear, you look exactly the same as I remember."

"Well played, Mrs. Hicks. I was literally just talking to my mom about how you were my favorite teacher."

"Oh stop that. Irene, please. We're both adults now, though one of us is on the uncomfortable side of middle-aged."

I hadn't been lying about Mrs. Hicks being my favorite teacher. She'd been young and pretty and fun, and unlike Mrs. Bunting, Mrs. Hicks hadn't busted my chops for painting my nails during morning announcements.

She's not so young anymore—neither am I, for that matter. But she's still fun and pretty, her blond hair neatly styled into an elegant chignon, her makeup perfectly applied to flatter her fifty-something skin. For all her talk about middle age, Mrs. Hicks—Irene—strikes me as the epitome of aging with grace. Her lips don't have that telltale injection pout, her forehead doesn't have the perfectly smooth Botox kiss. She looks natural and soft, and I make a mental note that *this* is how it's done.

"I was so touched when your mother included me in your welcome home party," Irene says, taking a sip of her wine. "I still love teaching, but it's nice to be surrounded by adults. Especially when that adult conversation doesn't center around the supposed college aspirations of twelve-year-olds who I know for a fact are more concerned with their first kiss than they are their eventual SAT scores."

"Please tell me my mom wasn't one of those types of parents," I say in a loud whisper.

Irene laughs because we both know my mom was *exactly* one of those.

"You'll understand when you have one of your own," Irene tells me.

I give an indelicate snort. "Let's just say on my road of emotional maturity, I'm still a lot closer to my first kiss than I am to my first kid."

"An event that I still like to tell myself I played a part in."

I turn toward the masculine voice that's just joined the conversation and do a double take before letting out a delighted laugh. "Drew Callahan! What are you doing here?"

I give my high school boyfriend a one-armed hug, careful not to spill the drink that Colin pressed into my hand shortly after we'd gotten to the party.

"You look so good!" I say, drawing back and giving his arm a fond pat.

I mean it. Drew's a bit thicker now, the body of a man instead of the lithe form of a boy. And while his hairline isn't quite what I remember, the twinkling, friendly blue eyes definitely are. We dated for nearly three years in high school, a practical lifetime in the teenage timeline. Though, the fact that we went to the same boarding school probably made it a little easier, without parents to loom over us.

Our relationship was an easy one, as I remember it, but then, so was our parting of ways when we went off to college, which was all the confirmation I needed at the time to know that he wasn't *the one*. Still, I remember him fondly, and his face amidst a guest list primarily made up of my parents' friends is *very* welcome.

"You're not looking so bad yourself," he says, giving me a familiar grin. "Do you not age?"

"Exactly what I was telling her," Mrs. Hicks says emphatically, before drifting subtly away to join another conversation. I can practically *hear* her devising to give us young things some privacy.

"You know, I never did get a straight answer on if I was your first kiss," Drew muses, as I turn to face him fully.

"Gosh, if only I can remember. It was so long ago, and all . . ." I say teasingly, since we both know he wasn't my first kiss any more than I was his.

My first kiss was with the grandson of the elderly couple who lived across the street. His name had been John; his grandma had called him Johnny, much to his chagrin. He'd been visiting his grandparents for the summer from Texas, and I thought his accent was just about the best thing my thirteen-year-old self had ever heard, even if the kiss had been a sweet, awkward peck of a thing.

"I'm just going to go ahead and keep lying to myself," Drew says.

I smile. "Solid plan. How the heck are you? Where's—?" I

look around the room for Drew's wife. I'm blanking on her name, but I remember seeing their wedding photos on Facebook a couple of years ago.

"Andrea," he supplies, holding up his left hand, which I belatedly realize is bereft of a ring. "We ended up on the wrong side of the divorce statistic."

"Oh, I'm sorry. I hadn't heard."

He shrugs. "It was relatively painless, at least as much as those things can be. We just sort of . . . drove each other crazy, and not in the good way." He leans forward and lowers his voice. "Of course, maybe if we did marriage *your* way, we'd have had a shot."

I laugh, hoping he doesn't notice the nervous tinge to it. "My way?"

His smile is friendly. "Don't think that theories over your marriage haven't dominated every dinner party of our mutual friends for years now."

"Hmm." I sip my wine. "What's the prevailing theory?"

"That you're Charlotte Spencer, and you make your own rules. And speaking from personal experience, I imagine that living on different coasts is a pretty brilliant way to stay married. How'd you make it work? Weekdays doing your own thing, sexy weekend escapades?"

"Something like that," I say noncommittally.

There's no accusation in Drew's tone, but the conversation makes me uncomfortable anyway. I know I promised Colin not to embarrass my mom, but I didn't account for how wrong it would feel to be asked to lie outright, especially to someone I used to care about.

I scan the room, subconsciously seeking the one person who

might possibly understand. Colin's in the far corner of the room talking to my dad's business partner and his wife. My husband's not looking at me, but he apparently senses my gaze, because he meets my eyes across the room and lifts his eyebrows in silent question before resuming his usual default state when it comes to me. *Glowering*. And I must be starting to know the guy because I've got a pretty good sense of what he's thinking: *Here's what I think of your goddamn smolder.*

I hide a smile and turn back to Drew, who's thankfully, changed the subject away from my thorny marriage, and is filling me in on our mutual friends from high school. I continue to smile and nod through the rundown on who's divorced, who's had twins, and who's feuding with whom before I give in to the urge to excuse myself.

Not because I don't enjoy Drew, not even because the conversation's boring me, but I just need a minute to catch my breath and gather my thoughts. Being back here among people from my old life is stranger than I thought it would be. Which is saying something, because I'd been expecting it to be strange. It's like being in a time machine where you're surrounded by people who don't know you now, but even worse, you realize maybe never knew you then—not really.

With a quick glance to make sure my mom isn't watching, I slip out of the room, and before I realize where I'm headed, I take the stairs two at a time until I'm standing outside my old bedroom.

I push open the door.

I'm not expecting it to look the same, and it doesn't. The bed's in the same place, but the bedding is navy and taupe instead of the teal duvet cover I'd begged my mom for during my all-things-Tiffany-Blue phase. The nightstand is a dark cherry wood instead of white, and there's a bookshelf where my dresser used to be.

I know I'm not the first adult woman to have her childhood room turned into a more all-purpose guest room, but I'm still caught off guard by the wave of forlornness that rolls through me. I hadn't realized how much I was hoping to see something familiar in this room until it wasn't there.

I sit on the side of the bed and give a quick jump of surprise when I see someone standing in the open doorway. Though I'd come up here for a moment of silence, the forlorn feeling eases slightly when I see my father.

"Hey, Dad."

He looks hesitant. "May I come in?"

I shrug. "Your house. For that matter, this stopped being my room a long time ago."

"Not so long ago. If I remember correctly, your mother held off changing things in here until just a couple of years ago."

"Really?" I ask, genuinely surprised. "I'd have thought she'd have rid the house of all things Charlotte before my plane even touched down in San Francisco all those years ago."

He gives me a chiding look I remember with perfect clarity. "Perhaps you don't know your mother as well as you thought you did."

"Perhaps not," I say, smoothing a hand over the unfamiliar bedspread. "Perhaps she didn't know me either."

He surprises me by laughing. "No, definitely not. But then, I don't think she would have ever claimed to know you well. It was part of what frustrated her—and me—so much. You just never seemed to be thinking what we thought you were thinking."

"Or what you wanted me to think," I point out.

"True," he admits. "Justin was fairly easygoing, and it didn't really occur to us until you came along that not all children adhered to the plan you'd laid out for them."

"Well, props for trying to enforce your plan for as long as you did." I don't *mean* to say the words, which come out with a slight edge. But apparently time doesn't heal all wounds, because mine are still there. Not as raw as they once were but not entirely healed over either.

My dad looks away, and I expect him to give one of his weary *Charlotte's so exasperating* sighs and leave, the way I'd watched him do so many times in the past. Instead, he surprises me.

We've already established that my father isn't exactly a fuzzy, heart-to-heart kind of guy, so it's both nice and a little strange when he comes and sits beside me on the bed. He exhales, but it's a thoughtful sound, not an annoyed one. For a few moments, neither of us says anything.

He breaks the silence. "We thought you'd come home, you know."

Wow, so we're doing this. The conversation has been a long time coming, but I confess I didn't think it would happen in the midst of a party, and I sort of always imagined the showdown would happen first with my mother.

I look over. "She told me not to."

This time he does give in to the weary sigh, but it doesn't annoy me as much as it used to. "Charlotte, when you—if you—have children, you'll learn that there's nothing quite so difficult in the world as watching them try to pull away from you. And you pulled hard, and you pulled often."

"I know," I whisper.

"It's probably not entirely your fault," he shocks me by saying. "You are your mother's daughter after all."

I blink in surprise. "Mom's the very opposite of me. She's always done *everything* she's supposed to."

"I don't mean you get your rebellious streak from her; I mean you inherited her stubborn streak. As well as, perhaps, your tendency to speak and act first, think later. Especially when things don't go your way."

"I'll have you know I've gotten much better at that over the years," I say.

"I'm sure you have, but your mother still gives in to the urge to say things she doesn't mean when she's frustrated."

I don't pretend to misunderstand. "You mean like when she told me to leave and never come back."

"She didn't tell you *to* leave," he says, with impressive gentleness. "That was your decision."

"True," I admit. "But she hardly gave me a hug, well-wishes, and told me she couldn't wait to hear all about my California adventure at Thanksgiving." I risk another glance his way. "Neither did you."

In that moment he looks older than his years, and he bows his head. "No. No, I didn't, and I have some regrets about that."

It's not *quite* an apology, but I'm still shocked by how much it means to me to hear it. To know that they haven't been leaving all the blame on my shoulders all these years, that the shoddy state of our relationship isn't *entirely* my fault.

Plenty my fault, definitely. But not entirely.

I reach over and hold his hand, giving it a squeeze. He squeezes back; there's a lifetime of communication in the silent gesture.

"Is now a good time to ask if you're ever going to take Coco public?" he asks, a playful note of hope in his voice.

"Wait, what?" I laugh in surprise. "You follow my business?"

He gives an embarrassed shrug, and I'm surprisingly touched. "It's not Apple, but it seems to be doing well."

"High praise," I say, amused. "And I would love to talk business with you. But maybe not when there are thirty people downstairs in your living room?"

He winces. "Sorry about the party."

"I don't mind the party."

"And yet here you are, hiding in your bedroom. I seem to remember that was always more Justin's move during your mother's parties."

"Ha, that's definitely true." I smile at the memory.

Justin and I had been a pretty cut-and-dried introvert versus extrovert case study. He'd been personable enough when required, but if given the choice, he would choose books over people every time.

I'd never met a party or person I hadn't liked. Even during my rebellious years, if we want to call them that, I still knew how to sparkle and shine, even if it was in a too-much-black-eyeliner kind of way, and not the pearls and discreet blush my mom would have preferred.

Hiding away from the crowd has never been my style, but my dad's right. I *am* hiding out right now. I look down at my hands, trying to identify why I feel so atypically *uncomfortable*. It's nothing that anyone's said or done. Everyone's been welcoming and seems genuinely glad to have me back.

And maybe that right there is *exactly* what's making me

uncomfortable. The fact that nobody's even questioned my right to be here, in this house. The fact that everyone, from old teachers to old boyfriends, to my own parents, seems to think I belong here.

Even though I turned my back on all of them and have *barely* looked back over the course of ten years. I can tell myself whatever I want about my growth and change and maturity, but it doesn't take away the fact that I could have done *a lot* of things better.

I look up at the ceiling. "How do you not hate me?"

"Biology," my dad says without hesitation. "I'm physically required to love you."

I laugh. "Fair enough. What about *like*? Do you like me?"

"I do," he says, again without hesitation. "I'm not going to pretend to understand you any more now than I did back then. But I've had a few years to watch you from afar, and I get what you're doing. I respect it."

"What *am* I doing?"

"You've started your own business. Built something for yourself that's all your own, nothing to do with your connection or the power of the Spencer name in this city."

"Such modesty."

"Pride," he corrects. "Now, I could have gone with a few more visits over the years. But it doesn't change the fact that I'm proud of you."

I blow out a long breath. "I have a lot to make up for, huh?"

"Showing up to your mother's party is a good start. It meant a lot to her."

"And hiding out in my bedroom? Was that on her wish list for the evening?" I ask dryly.

"Well, you escaped up here so that you had an opportunity to talk to your dear old dad, did you not?"

"Oh, absolutely," I say, starting to take the easy out he's offering, but then realizing I don't want to start this tentative peace treaty between us with a pretense.

"Dad, about me and Colin . . ."

He gives a slight smile, and there's a definite note of sadness. "You're not going to live happily ever after?"

"Okay, I have to ask," I say slowly. "Did you and Mom really think we would?"

"Does she think it's a real marriage? No, not really. I'd like to think we're both too smart for that. *Hope*, though. That's different. I'll confess that she's let herself hope that it could be real. So have I, for that matter."

Ugh. That's both extremely sweet and a little bit sad, thinking that they've been secretly longing for Colin to become their son-in-law *for real*.

"But it's been ten years," I say slowly. "Surely you sort of figured that—"

"That Colin really likes living in the US?" my dad says slyly.

"Yeah," I say, relieved that it's out there without having to be spelled out.

"I know. Your mother does too. But I guess I'll have to admit to having some of the same old-fashioned sensibilities as your grandmother when she put a marriage stipulation on your trust fund. And that old-fashioned part of me wants my only daughter to find a nice man."

"And you think that's Colin?" I say, not bothering to keep the skepticism out of my voice.

"What's not to like? He's polite. Successful. Respectful. Considerate."

"Uptight? Boring? Absolutely impossible to get along with?"

"He's a tough nut to crack," my father says. "I remember those early years when Justin brought him around, I wasn't sure the boy had more than ten words inside of him. Came to realize he just chooses his words with care, as well as choosing who he uses those words with."

"I don't seem to be on the very exclusive list."

"May I ask . . . given that the marriage was of the, ah, convenient variety, what compelled you to not only move back to New York but to move in with Colin?"

"That," I say, "is a great question for your stupid son. And sort of a long story."

One of which I am all too happy to tell.

FRIDAY, SEPTEMBER 4

❧

"Greenwich and Christopher, please."

My head snaps up in surprise, and I look across the cab at Colin, who's just given the taxi driver an intersection that is most definitely not our apartment.

"What's in Greenwich?" I ask.

"Dinner." He leans his head on the headrest and closes his eyes.

"You didn't eat at the party?"

He opens his eyes and meets my gaze. "Did you?"

"I had . . ." I think back to the cucumbers topped with crab and cream cheese, the nibble of carrot and hummus, a single bite of some sort of sesame beef in a lettuce cup.

Three hundred calories, *maybe*.

"No, not really," I admit. Then I frown. "Wait, is that an invitation?"

"An invitation to what?" Colin's eyes are closed again. "To dinner? I'm going to get something to eat. You're welcome to join, or you're welcome to have the cab make a second stop."

"Wow. Romantic," I mutter, looking out the window.

"Why would I be romantic?"

Apparently I *really* didn't get enough food, because I'm feeling unusually irritable at his dismissive attitude, and I'd like to blame it on a good old-fashioned *hanger*.

"*Hey*," I say, not bothering to soften the edge of my voice. "You're the one who suggested we play husband and wife for the entire evening. Which, by the way, would have gone better had you bothered to talk to me even once. Or even stand beside me."

"I didn't exactly see you clamoring to stand by my side."

"Yeah, well, I forgot my sweater," I snap. "I wasn't properly dressed to withstand the chill you emit anytime I'm near."

"Well, next time bring your parka," he snaps back. "If Immigration Services comes sniffing, we can't afford to have an entire roomful of people notice we're barely civil."

"Look on the bright side, at least we're doing a *fantastic* job of selling our impending divorce. And for what it's worth, we don't need to worry about convincing my parents. I talked to my dad. He already knows why we're married. The real reasons."

His eyes snap open and he turns toward me. "You told him?"

"No. He already knew."

Colin frowns. "I've seen your father nearly every week for the past ten years, and he's never indicated he knew of our arrangement."

"Of course he knew," I scoff. "Anyone who spent any amount of time with us back then knew it was hardly a love match. And I'm pretty sure he noticed that we literally spent zero time together."

"For all they knew, I could have been sneaking into your bedroom when I came and stayed with your family on holidays. Or that we met every weekend to have conjugal visits."

I wrinkle my nose. "Gross."

"*Gross?*"

I laugh because he sounds genuinely affronted. "Oh, come on. *You're* the one who just referred to any physical relationship between us as conjugal visits. What is this, prison? And you know full well we weren't exactly setting off sparks back then. I could literally see your lip curl in disgust whenever I opened my mouth, and I never really dug the whole man bun, bearded homeless vibe you had going on."

"Homeless," he mutters, looking out the window. "Jesus."

"Water under the bridge," I say, patting his leg in a sisterly gesture to prove my point about the lack of zip between us, even as my palm registers his leg is appealingly firm.

"And I accept your gentlemanly dinner invitation," I add, because I'm more aware by the minute how hungry I am. "Where are we going? What's at Greenwich and Christopher where they only serve Guinness and soda bread?"

"Yes, because that's all we Irish bumpkins eat."

"And potatoes. Don't forget potatoes."

He turns his head back toward me, the city lights casting shadows across his face. "Back then?"

"What?" I ask, not following.

"You said we weren't exactly setting off sparks *back then*. Interesting distinction."

My stomach drops at the intensity of his gaze, but I try to play it off. "You know what I meant. Just that back then, we couldn't stand each other, and my parents knew it. Just like they know we can't stand each other now, no matter how much my mom might dream of her baby girl marrying her surrogate son. I didn't mean that we were setting off sparks *now* . . ."

I'm babbling, and true to form, he says nothing in response. And because I'm realizing this man won't come out of his shell on his own, I decide to nudge him. "Are we?"

It's his turn to look confused, and I'm pleased to have thrown him off-balance for once. "What?"

"Are we setting off sparks? Do I set you all aflame?" I say, giving him my best Jessica Rabbit look, which, honestly, isn't all that good.

"No," he says curtly.

And though I can't say for sure given the darkness inside the back of the cab, I could have sworn his gaze lingered on the hem of my dress as he says it.

FRIDAY, SEPTEMBER 4

⁓

"*O*h my God," I say, pushing my plate aside and exhaling with the sheer pleasure of a perfect meal. "I think that was the best thing I've ever eaten."

"Better than the boiled potatoes you were expecting?" Colin asks over the top of his red wine glass.

"Don't get me wrong, I love a good shot of Jameson and shepherd's pie on St. Paddy's day," I tell him. "But no cuisine can compete with pasta."

"I wouldn't know. You ate most of mine."

"We agreed to split them."

"No, you 'suggested,' we split them, didn't take no for an answer, and then ate the lion's share of each."

"An exaggeration," I retort.

Well, sort *of* an exaggeration. My pesto was one of the better things I'd ever put in my mouth, but his short rib ravioli gave it a definite run for its money.

"So," he says, topping off both of our glasses from the bottle of

Barolo he ordered for us to split. "How was your reunion with your first love?"

"The pasta?"

He surprises me with a grunt of a laugh. "No. Drew."

"Oh, right," I say, sipping the wine. "It was good to see him. Did you know he's divorced now? That always makes me sad when people our age are divorced already. How does that happen?"

I wince when my brain catches up to my words. "I guess I'll be joining the ranks in a couple of months, won't I?"

Colin studies me. "Silver lining. Our divorce will free you up to rekindle things with Drew."

Huh. The idea excites me not at all. Not that there's anything wrong with Drew, but the truth is I haven't put that much thought into what happens after this thing with Colin and I wraps up. I've avoided thinking about it, if I'm honest. Lately I've been feeling sort of itchy about my life in general, and for now, it's been easier just to leave my future as one big question mark.

"I don't think so," I say aloud.

"Why not?"

I give an irritated huff that he's pushing this. "I don't know. No spark, I guess."

Yes, Drew looked great. Yeah, he'd been funny and nice, and charming, and I have nothing but good memories of our time together. But whatever physical chemistry we'd once had is long gone, at least on my side.

"Plus," I admit, "I guess in my head, I'm not really available."

He shifts, looking uncomfortable with the train of conversation. "You mean because of our arrangement?"

"I guess. I mean, I know our situation is anything but typical, but it was easier to forget that I was technically married when I was in California. Here, everyone *knows* I'm married. Everyone knows *you*. And what's really throwing me off is that some of these people seem to think we're really, truly married."

He gives me a sharp look. "What do you mean?"

"I spent nearly three hours today making small talk with some of the city's biggest gossips. Were you aware that people think we've actually been married for real, and that we just have some really weird modern relationship where we only see each other on weekends?"

Colin flinches. "I may have let that rumor percolate. Deliberately."

"Really?" I ask, fascinated. "Why?"

"To avoid suspicion over the motives of our marriage. My accent's faded over the years, but there's still no mistaking that I'm not from around here. The possibility that we'd marry for the sake of my green card isn't a huge leap to make."

"True. Though, I disagree on the accent. It's faded a little, but it's still very much there. And, for what it's worth, it's the one thing you had going on back then."

"Excuse me?"

"Well, the beard and bun thing didn't work for me when we got married, and I thought you were super nerdy, but even I could admit that the accent caused a few flutters." I glare down at my glass, realizing it's making me admit things I probably shouldn't. "Damn you, wine."

"Very deep thoughts, Charlotte," Colin says dryly.

I shrug. "I never pretended to be deep."

"No, you don't pretend, do you?" he says thoughtfully.

"Um, I've pretended to be married for a decade. I'd say I'm pretty good at it."

"Yes, but like you said, that was easier when you were in California. It wasn't a daily charade you had to keep up. Tonight you were jumpy. You don't like lying, and you don't like pretense."

"No argument there," I say. "I hate having to lie about our domestic bliss. About the reasons I'm back here."

"Two more months," he says quietly. "Then we can file for divorce and end this chapter of our lives."

"Yeah. And then what?" I ask, more to myself than him.

"You go back to California," he says, though there's a slight question in his voice.

"Right," I say automatically, because that is the plan. Or at least it's been the plan.

But for some reason, the thought doesn't click quite as well as it should.

SATURDAY, SEPTEMBER 5

*S*ince I've been in New York, I haven't been putting my phone on Do Not Disturb when I go to bed, wanting to be available for my team while I'm in a different time zone.

A fact I regret when my cell rings *way* too early the next morning. I blindly grope for it on the nightstand, eyes still closed as I swipe to access the call.

"Yeah. Hello?"

"You ratted me out to Dad?"

My eyes fly open at the sound of my brother's voice, and I sit upright. "Justin?"

"Hey, Charlie."

"What time is it?" I pull the phone away from my ear. "Oh my God, *six*? On a Saturday? What is wrong with you?"

"It's noon here."

"And what, you couldn't do the math?" I gripe, shoving my hair out of my face.

"You've called me about a hundred times in the past couple of weeks. I thought you'd be happy I called."

"Ah *ha*! So you have been seeing my calls," I accuse.

"And may I just say, God bless Caller ID."

"You've been screening me! Your only sister!"

"It's *because* you're my only sister that I know you well enough to know that you needed some time to cool off. But obviously, you're still peeved if you told Dad about the prenup."

"*Peeved*?" I say in disbelief. "Just, you do realize that your pre-nup shenanigans required me to leave my company, fly across the country, move in with a stranger, live with him for three months, all so that I can become a divorcée?"

"In my defense—"

"Really? *Is* there a defense?"

"In my defense," he continued, "I never imagined you two idiots would stay married for ten years without ever seeing each other in the meantime."

"What *did* you envision?" I ask skeptically.

"That maybe some forced proximity would make you realize you two were good together."

My mouth drops open. "You were *matchmaking*? I thought you were just being a stupid jerk. I can't decide which is worse."

"I was being stupid, yes," he admits. "Can we please remember that I was twenty-four, had passed the bar exactly four days prior, and I wasn't *exactly* at the height of professional maturity? But a jerk? Honestly, Charlie, in my head I swear I thought I was doing a good thing."

"By forcing me to live with a mute who hates my guts?"

"It's like I said, in my big-brother-knows-best brain, I thought you and Col would be good for each other if you'd just give each other a chance."

"And what have we learned from all these good intentions? Oh yeah, it's that *big brother knows nothing at all.* How could you possibly think we'd be good together? We're opposites."

"Exactly. He was so serious all the time—"

"Still is," I interrupt.

My brother is used to my interruptions and ignores it. "He's serious and a little uptight. You were all over the place. I thought you could lift him up, and he could ground you."

"And we'd live happily ever after?" I say sarcastically.

"*Again.* I was in my early twenties. What were *you* doing in your early twenties? Oh yeah, getting a nose ring, learning to sky-dive, pushing our parents' every button, and marrying a guy you barely knew."

"I got rid of the nose ring," I say, picking at a loose thread on the comforter.

"Exactly, because you grew up and realized it looked ridiculous on you. Just like I grew up and realized that my little prenup surprise was a little ridiculous too."

"Can't you undo it?"

"Not really," he admits. "I may have been dumb at twenty-four, but I was good. The prenup's already on file. Any court worth their salt will see the stipulation, as well as the fact that you and Colin clearly signed it. Without reading it, by the way."

"Oh, well excuse us for not suspecting our brother and best friend would set out to ruin our lives."

"Ruin? Really?" he says sarcastically. "It's three months out of your life, and I've seen Colin's place. It's hardly a rat-infested shack."

"Did you know that he goes to Mom and Dad's every Sunday? I think he does it to make us look bad," I grumble, flopping back against the pillows.

"He does it because you live in California, and I married a woman who works for the World Bank in Germany. As far as daily routines go, our parents don't have kids, and he doesn't have parents. I think it's good they've filled a gap for each other."

"I'm just saying, how would *he* like it?" I'm still irritated with the entire situation. "How'd he like it if we flew to Dublin and got all buddy-buddy with his parents, if we weaseled our way into favorite child status with *his* mom and dad?"

My brother is silent for a long moment. "Col's parents are dead, Charlie."

I sit up once more, this time nausea mixing in with the shock. "What?"

"They were in a car accident a couple of years ago. Why do you think he didn't come to my wedding?"

"I don't know," I say, running a hand through my hair. "I thought you were just like, trying to save me the awkwardness . . ."

"Yes, because everything's about you. He was at their funeral. He asked me not to say anything because he didn't want to intrude upon anyone's happiness."

"Oh God," I groan.

"I'm sure he didn't expect that you'd know," my brother says kindly.

"No, you don't get it. It's *bad*." I'm out of bed now, rummaging through drawers. "When I first got here and found out he was having dinner with Mom and Dad every week, I said some things . . ."

He groans. "What sort of things?"

"Just ... you know, snide little comments about how if he didn't spend so much time kissing up to our parents, maybe he'd have more time to visit his own ..."

"Oh God. Charlotte!"

"I know," I shriek. "You have to help me. What is the national flower of Ireland?"

"The Dudladilly," he replies.

I pull out a black sports bra and begin wiggling into it. "Really?"

"No. I have no idea. Why?"

Isn't it obvious? I have to fix this.

"I have to go," I tell my brother, sitting on the bed, and shoving my feet into sneakers.

"Why? Where are you going? What are you doing?"

He knows me well enough to sound panicked, but for once, my plan is pretty safe.

"Don't worry, nothing weird. I just have to go buy Colin flowers. Sympathy flowers. And apology flowers. It's going to be a really big bouquet."

I hang up on my brother's weary sigh.

SATURDAY, SEPTEMBER 5

$\mathcal{C}$olin's a perpetually early riser, but not, apparently, when he has a pasta dinner and a half bottle of wine at eleven the night before, because when I get back from my frantic flower mission, his bedroom door's still closed, and the coffee's not on.

Breathing a sigh of relief that I have a moment to gather my thoughts, I set the flowers on the counter and put on a pot of coffee. At this point, anything I can do to endear him to me after a seriously awful gaffe seems like a good plan, and coffee is always a good start.

It also gives me a chance to arrange the flowers. None of the local florists in the neighborhood were open this early, but Whole Foods was.

Unfortunately, Whole Foods' flower selection, while pretty and varied, had only modest-sized arrangements. After my blunder, the man deserves a bouquet the size of a small pony.

I settled for buying lots of *little* arrangements—six, to be exact—and now I set about unwrapping them, snipping the rubber bands, and combining them into one giant mess of flowers.

"Hmm," I puzzle aloud, as I realize that I have no idea where Colin keeps his vases—or if he even owns any. And even if he *does* have a vase, I'm reasonably sure it won't be one large enough to fit my self-assembled arrangement.

I purse my lips and study my handiwork. My flower "bouquet" is a lot more akin to a bush. One that takes both my arms to pick up, and even then, I drop a handful of blooms on the way to Colin's door.

I hesitate briefly, realizing I forgot the coffee, but since the flowers are a two-armed affair, I'll have to make two trips: one to deliver flowers and grovel, and a second to deliver coffee and grovel again.

In true Charlotte fashion, I didn't think my plan all the way through, because even though it takes me about five times of rattling the doorknob, and about twenty more dropped stems before I can get his bedroom door open, he's apparently not a light sleeper and doesn't budge from beneath the covers.

Fantastic plan.

Here I am, sneaking into a sleeping man's bedroom with enough flowers to fill the back seat of an SUV, standing at the foot of his bed and . . . watching him sleep.

I don't mean to, I'm just trying to figure out my next move, but even as my brain races through *what now* options, I take in the fact that even at his most vulnerable, he's still got that slightly haunted, closed-off vibe. There's no softening of his brow while he sleeps, no slight smile indicating pleasant dreams.

I clear my throat. No movement.

"Colin," I whisper. Nothing.

I say his name louder, but he still doesn't move, and the thorns from some pokey flower are making my situation kind of desperate.

His bed frame doesn't have a footboard, so I lift my knee to the foot of his bed and awkwardly manage to nudge his foot. "Colin!"

That does the trick.

He bolts upright, and . . . *oopsie*.

The bed covers drop all the way to his waist. It stops short of telling me whether he sleeps naked, but he definitely sleeps shirtless, and, well, all I can think is, *very, very nice*, said in an Irish accent in my head.

That first day in the bar before he'd told me he wanted a divorce, I'd guessed he had at least a six-pack, and I give myself a mental pat on the back for being proven right this morning. Colin's chest is broad, sculpted, and covered in just the right amount of hair. And interestingly enough, I may have hated that beard back in the day, but the dark shadow on his jaw at the moment is extremely appealing, especially when paired with the mussed dark curls.

"Charlotte, what the hell?"

"What the hell am I doing in your bedroom, or what the hell is with the flowers?" I ask.

He drags his hands over his face, rubbing his eyes slightly, then shakes his head and repeats. "What the hell?"

"Okay, so that's *what the hell* to both, then. Well, okay. I'm in your room to deliver the flowers. And I'm delivering flowers because I'm really, really sorry."

"For?"

I take a deep breath. "Your parents. For their passing. And for not knowing and saying some really insensitive things about how you didn't make time to visit them, and . . . oh God. It's so awful, and I'm so sorry. Really sorry. And I want you to forgive me. You have to say that you do."

Colin doesn't say he forgives me. He doesn't say anything at all. He just sits there with the sheet pooled at his waist, his eyes still looking slightly fuzzy from sleep, his hair rumpled and adorable.

"Okay," he says.

"Okay, you forgive me?" I ask.

"Okay, you can get out of my room now."

"Fair enough. I made coffee. I'll go get it." I heave the flowers upwards slightly, as I lose a couple of tulips to the floor. "Can I set these down first?"

"Please don't."

I pretend I don't hear this, mainly because if I don't put the flowers down soon, I may die of blood loss.

Colin sleeps on the right side of the bed, so I scoot around to the left side and leaning over, I awkwardly deposit the flowers on the bed. They take up *a lot* of room, and he makes a grumbling noise.

I make a quick sprint for the kitchen, hoping coffee will make up for the fact that he'll probably have to wash his bedding to get rid of all the flower pollen and dirt that are now all over his bed.

I'll wash the sheets, I amend. Right after I cook him breakfast.

I pour us each a cup of coffee, and when I go back into his bedroom, he hasn't moved except to turn his head to stare at the flowers as though he doesn't quite know what to make of them.

"Coffee?" I ask rhetorically, going around to his side of the bed. I hand it to him, but he doesn't reach out to take it, so I set it on the nightstand.

Without warning, Colin reaches out and jerks the hem of my cami upwards.

"What the—"

"You're bleeding," he announces unceremoniously, as he looks at my exposed stomach.

"Oh." I glance down at the red scratches on the left side of my torso. "Yeah. Roses weren't a great choice for my plan."

"So, you actually had a plan?" he asks.

"As much as I ever do."

His lips twitch a little at that, and I suck in a breath as he sets his thumb near the largest of the cuts along one of my ribs. "The cuts look pretty shallow. Do they hurt?"

"Paper cut pain," I say, taking a sip of my coffee.

His gaze flicks up. "So, the worst kind of pain on the planet?"

I smile. "Pretty much."

He lets my shirt drop, though I notice it takes him just a second too long to remove the finger that had been resting against my stomach. I also notice that my body is throbbing in ways that have nothing to do with any cuts from the flowers.

He reaches for his coffee mug, and I nudge his calf beneath the blankets, a silent command to scoot. I count it as a victory when he moves toward the center of the bed instead of ordering me out.

"I really am sorry," I say softly, meeting his eyes. "About your parents. Mine drive me crazy, but to lose them . . . especially to lose them both at once. I can't even imagine what that must have been like."

He looks down at his mug. "How'd you find out?"

"Justin called this morning. Finally," I mutter.

Colin gives a grim smile. "Yeah. He's been avoiding me too."

Sensing he doesn't want to talk about his parents—and who could blame him—I shift topics. "So you haven't talked to my brother? About the terms of the prenup?"

"No, we talked," he says, taking a sip of coffee. "Right after I dug out the paperwork and saw what he'd done."

"I thought he was just being a dick, but he claims that his dumb-ass twenty-four-year-old self had good intentions."

"Oh yeah? I didn't really give him much of a chance to explain himself through the cursing."

"At least one of us gave him a solid verbal reaming. I was too groggy to do much but sputter at him, but I feel pretty good about the fact that I tattled on him to my dad last night, which means it's only a matter of time until Mom finds out and calls Justin, and *that* conversation will be far more savage than any damage you or I can do."

Colin nods in agreement. "I'm not *entirely* sure I want to know, but what did he claim were his good intentions?"

"Matchmaking." I waggle my eyebrows. "Apparently, by forc-ing us to live under the same roof, we were meant to fall *madly* in love."

Colin grunts, which I'm learning is his default morning method of communication.

"So naturally," I continue airily, "I told Justin that we couldn't be *too* mad at him for his plan, seeing as it's worked marvelously, and you haven't been able to keep your heart locked up, nor your hands off me."

I'm sort of hoping to get a rise out of him, but he's either made of sterner stuff or is just really used to me, because he merely rolls his eyes and points to the flowers.

"So, after you robbed a garden, what was your plan? Start a nursery? Build a greenhouse?"

"Oh, that reminds me, where do you keep your vases?"

"My what?"

"You know. Flower vase. The bouquet won't all fit in one, but I can break them up into smaller bouquets and fill lots of vases."

I don't tell him that they actually *started* as smaller bouquets. Somehow, I doubt he'll appreciate my panicked need to make an impact. Especially since said *impact* is starting to make his room smell decidedly feminine.

He shakes his head. "I don't have any vases."

I tsk. "How can you not have a single vase?"

"Because until right now, I've never had a single flower in my home."

"Well, that's just silly."

"Feel free to survey the heterosexual men in your acquaintance who live alone, and ask them how many of them have vases."

"I would, but that would take far too long," I say with a sigh. "I fear my little black book filled with available men is close to bursting."

"Is it now?" he says, and I pause in the process of taking a sip of my coffee because there's a slightly dangerous element in his tone, something almost . . . predatory.

I meet his eyes, and for a single moment, they seem to darken before he looks away. What do you know? He *does* know how to smolder.

"Out," he orders, kicking slightly at my hip. "I need to get up."

I try and fail to rid my brain of dirty thoughts at the image his phrasing conjures.

"Because I may need to know at some point," I say, standing up by the side of the bed and gesturing over him with the mug. "Do you sleep half naked, or all the way naked?"

He glowers up at me. "When would you *ever* need to know that?"

"You know, in case the marriage fraud investigators come knocking. As your bedfellow, I would know."

"*Bedfellow?*" He points to the open door. "Out. Now. And close it behind you."

"Well, that answers that question," I say with a pleasant smile. "You sleep all the way naked. You wouldn't need me to close the door if you had boxers on under there."

"Charlotte."

"Okay, okay, I'm going," I say. "There's just one more thing . . ."

I move quickly, not giving him any time to reject me as I set my coffee mug on the nightstand and, careful not to bump his coffee hand, I wrap my arms around his neck. He freezes, but I hold tight, forcing him into the hug.

"I really am sorry," I whisper softly, near his ear. "I'm sorry you lost your parents. And I'm sorry I was insensitive about it."

I mean it to be a quick hug, assuming he won't be tolerant of anything longer than that, but just as I intend to pull back, Colin's free hand comes up, his palm resting against the back of my head.

"Thanks," he mutters gruffly.

For a moment, neither of us moves, and I'm suddenly all too aware of the fact that I'm leaning over him, the low-cut neckline of my tank leaving the tops of my boobs pressed against his chest, which is very bare and very warm.

His head moves ever so slightly toward me, his cheek pressing against mine. The scratch of it against my skin makes me tingle as I wonder what that slight rasp would feel like on other parts of my skin, wondering what he'd do if I pulled back just enough to press my lips to his, to challenge his insistence that there are no sparks between us.

I don't get the chance to find out, because I kid you not, in the sort of crappy timing that you think only happens in movies . . . the doorbell rings.

Literally. The *freaking* doorbell. Rings.

I jump in surprise, straightening as he pulls away from me. We stare at each other in a moment of surprise, both at what just happened, as well as the fact that someone's at the front door at seven on a Saturday morning.

"Groceries?" I ask, since he gets all of the groceries delivered.

He shakes his head. "Nothing scheduled."

The doorbell rings again, and I spring into action, exiting his bedroom and pulling the door shut behind me—partially because he asked, and partially because I need a minute. I stay still just for a moment, eyes closed, ordering my heart to stop pounding.

The doorbell rings again.

"God, okay, *coming*," I mutter, half jogging to the front door.

I open it to see a woman I don't recognize, and though I try really hard not to make snap judgments about people I haven't met, who I haven't even spoken with, I'm just going to come right out and paint a mental picture for you . . .

She's got a mean face. Pretty. Definitely pretty, in a patrician, no-carbs kind of way. Her hair is long, thick and very, *very* red, her eyes bright blue. Great mouth. Very Angelina Jolie. All good features, *in theory*, except the pretty blue eyes are cold, the full mouth a little hard, the perfectly shaped nose turned up, not due to genetics, but because she's actually looking down her nose at me. She's also tall. Did I mention tall?

"Hi," I say, smiling, because she may be mean, but I am not. "Can I help you?"

She looks irritated by the question. "I'm here to see Colin."

Colin, first name. Not Mr. Walsh. A social call, then. *Interesting.*

"He'll be right out. We weren't expecting anyone so early."

My use of *we* is a polite but pointed opportunity for her to explain who she is and what she's doing here, but she doesn't take the bait.

I try again, extending my hand. "I don't think we've met. I'm Charlotte. Colin's wife."

It's the first time I've used that phrase, and I'm not at all sure how I feel about the fact that it doesn't feel nearly as strange as it should to be saying it aloud.

But I don't have time to dwell on it.

If the woman's face is mean, her smile has a downright malicious note to it. Slowly, she reaches out to shake my hand. "Nice to finally meet you. I'm Rebecca. Colin's fiancée."

SATURDAY, SEPTEMBER 5

~

"*C*harlotte. Charlotte, damn it. Open the door."

I don't move from where I sit cross-legged on my bed. Colin rattles the doorknob, but I've locked it.

I hear him sigh. "I'd like to speak with you about this."

I scowl at the closed door. *Oh, you'd like to speak with me about this, would you? You'd like to speak with me about the fact that it's been nearly a month since you've told me you wanted a divorce, and not once have you bothered to mention the very pressing reason* why.

"Charlotte. Please."

I tilt my head a little at that, both at the unexpected use of *please* when he usually just barks orders, as well as the faint note of desperation in the way he says it.

The moment doesn't last long. He rattles the doorknob again. "You're acting like a child," he snaps, the quiet, desperate note of his voice replaced with irritation in its purest form.

Strangely though, it's this irritated Colin that has me climbing off the bed and crossing to the door to unlock it. He's quite right, sitting in a locked room is a bit immature, and I refuse to participate in any activity that would allow him to transfer blame for this situation onto me.

He's in the wrong, 100 percent, and I want to make sure he knows it.

The moment I open the door and see his face, I realize he does know it. I wouldn't go so far as to say he looks *miserable*, but he's definitely not a happy camper. He's pulled on his robe, a heavy, dark blue thing that he wears whenever I'm around in the early mornings or late nights, as though to protect his virtue.

And now I understand why. Probably for Rebecca's sake.

Speaking of her . . .

I glance down the hallway. "Is she still here?" I keep my voice low.

"In the kitchen," he answers curtly, his voice equally low. "May I come in?"

The fact that he doesn't just push his way past me the way he usually does when he wants something confirms my suspicion that he knows exactly how badly he's messed up.

I step aside so he can enter, surprised at first when he shuts the bedroom door, until I realize he's probably just trying to keep his two women separate.

Two women. I'm trying very hard not to think of him as a pig, and failing.

"So, a fiancée and a wife," I say casually. "Tricky, tricky. No *wonder* you're in such a bad mood all the time."

He meets my gaze. "I was going to tell you."

"Oh, I'm sure," I say, letting my voice take on a breezy tone. "You were probably just struggling to find the time and opportunity, right? It must have been difficult, what with us *living across the hall from each other*."

He closes his eyes.

"Sorry, sorry," I say, holding up my hands. "You talk. I eagerly await all the excellent reasons why you couldn't have bothered to mention that you were engaged to another woman."

He opens his eyes again, and they seem more silver than blue in this light, and I wonder if that's what happens to them when he feels guilty.

"I don't have one." His voice is quiet.

"Don't have what?'

"A good reason. I don't have *any* reason. I kept meaning to tell you, but the time never seemed right, the words never came out, and . . . I don't know why. I realize that's not an excuse."

"No, it's really not," I agree. "Honestly, dude, I have to ask, where has she even been? Have you kept her locked in a cellar somewhere? Did she just escape? Is that why she showed up this morning looking ready to throw down?"

He rubs a hand over his face. "It's a bit complicated."

"You don't say."

His hands drop, and he looks a little lost. "Shit. *Shit.*"

I smile, because it's about as close to Colin losing control as I've seen. And God help me, even though I'm mad, which I have every right to be, and a little hurt, which I probably don't have a right to be, I feel myself caving.

"You're really engaged to her?" I ask softly.

He hesitates, his blue silver eyes flicking away from me and then back. "Yes."

I get a weird sinking sensation in my stomach, but his answer tells me everything I need to know: that this isn't about me.

"Colin," I say gently. "You're married to me for fake. If you're going to marry her for real, I'm *really* not the one you should be groveling to right now."

I'm giving him full permission to exit this conversation to go make things right with Rebecca, and I expect to see relief on his face, and honestly, wouldn't mind a little gratitude. A kissing of feet at my benevolence wouldn't be out of place.

He doesn't move.

Instead he stands there, looking at me with a conflicted expression. Then he frowns, as though irritated with himself for feeling conflicted. Actually, scratch that. Knowing him, he's probably irritated with me, even though I spelled out his next move for him.

Maybe I wasn't clear enough. I lift my arm and point to the door. "Go. Rebecca just endured watching another woman open her fiancée's front door wearing pajamas, and don't think she didn't notice that you were only wearing briefs when you came dashing to the front door. If you still want to have a fiancée at the end of this day, *get out there*."

This time he nods slowly in agreement and steps backward toward the door, his eyes on me the whole time. He hesitates, and his next words are almost shy. "I never meant to . . . hurt you."

I give him a bright smile. "You didn't." *Lie.* "Now *go*, man, for the love of God."

He nods again and turns away.

"Oh, Colin?" I call, unable to resist.

He gives me a look over his shoulder, and I smile even wider. "Briefs, huh? That's *adorable*."

He slams the guest room door.

SATURDAY, SEPTEMBER 5

⟶

A minute later, I'm almost regretting my decision to send Colin after his woman.

It's not that I'm eavesdropping. It's just with the way Rebecca is yelling, it's *literally* impossible not to hear her entire side of the conversation, even with my door shut.

"Well, what the hell am I supposed to think?" she shouts. "I come over here to see if you want to grab breakfast, and both of you are in your underwear? And then instead of reassuring me, you chase after *her*."

My mouth drops open. *Underwear!* These are pajamas, thank you very much. Little ones, admittedly, but trust me, had I opened the door in my *actual* underwear, she probably wouldn't have stuck around long enough to yell at him.

I hope she wraps up her tantrum soon though. My coffee's out there.

I pace the tiny confines of my bedroom and try to force myself to process everything without the benefit of my usual caffeine amounts.

Colin's engaged.

He's *been* engaged.

This.

Entire.

Time.

I'm not holding the actual engagement against him. We're not actually married in the way that counts.

But it, um, would have been nice to know. Preferably *before* I started having sexy thoughts about him. Before I let myself have the crazy thought that maybe, just maybe my brother might have been right about his theory of Colin and me being good for each other . . .

"What'd you do, fuck her in a bed of flower petals?" Rebecca shrieks, her voice closer now, clearly having seen the flowers on Colin's bed.

I wince. *Yeeeeah.* That whole situation probably doesn't look good for Colin. *Good luck explaining that one,* husband.

I stand still for a moment hoping to overhear Colin's response, but his voice is merely a low murmur through the closed door, and I can't make out any actual words.

I pick up my cell phone and tap the corner against my bottom lip, debating my next move. I could—probably *should*—simply wait for Colin to give me the full story, but at the rate Rebecca's going at him, that could take a while, and I want answers now.

I *deserve* answers, damn it. I don't expect the man to tell me *every* detail of his life, but we're in this whole married mess together. Something as massive as his second wife waiting in the wings is sort of a crucial detail.

I decide to send a quick text message to Meghan, because of all my friends, she's the most plugged into the downtown social scene, and, thanks to our wine-fueled reunion, she knows that things between Colin and me are tricky. Plus, she has a toddler. The chances of her being awake early on a Saturday are better than my still-single friends.

My message is brief and to the point. **Do you know anything about Colin hanging out with a Rebecca?**

Meghan replies immediately, bless her. **Tall? Red hair? Pretty in a scary, vaguely plastic way?**

That's her.

Rebecca Hale. Lawyer at the same firm as Colin. Officially, they're colleagues.

My stomach feels icky as I reply. **And unofficially?**

Rumors. Nothing substantiated, but they do seem to show up at a lot of the same events and leave at the same time.

The nausea increases. I know I can't judge him. I have no grounds to be mad. I don't get to play the betrayed wife card, because I'm not his wife. Not in the way that matters. And as I've said, I've had plenty of flirtations of my own over the years.

But this isn't a flirtation. The woman introduced herself as his fiancée. He proposed to her. To *her*. She's not even nice. To be fair, I don't really know her—maybe she's a doll deep down, but I can at least attest that she makes a horrendous first impression.

How is it that he can't stand me, but he *loves* her?

Does he love her? He must, if he proposed, but . . . God does that ever make me feel queasy.

I take a deep breath and try to think about it the way he would—all rationally and robot-like. I suppose, if my emotional chip was damaged like his, he and Rebecca make sense. It's probably nice for Colin to find someone who shares his affliction for having something stuck up his ass.

My phone buzzes again with a message from Meghan. **Why do you ask?**

Oh, no reason. She's just in his bedroom.

Long story, I text back. **Drinks this week?**

She texts back. **Definitely. I'm here if you need to talk.**

I send a *thank you* text back, knowing that Meghan's probably got it in her head that Colin's cheating and I suppose technically he is. *Non*-technically, I have no reason to be upset, no reason to be jealous, and yet, well, here I am stomping around my room like an *actual* wife.

I hear Colin's bedroom door click closed, the angry murmur of voices telling me they're still having it out and that the kitchen is finally fair game.

Coffee. Maybe some coffee will help rid me of the weird feeling in my stomach.

I open the door softly and creep down the hallway. I look around the kitchen for my mug then realize that I left it on Colin's nightstand following our strange hug. I wince, realizing what that will look like to Rebecca.

I feel sorry for him. Almost.

I get a fresh mug, and half a cup later, I'm starting to feel mostly normal.

I hear Colin's bedroom door open and freeze, debating for a crazy instant to dive under the table and make myself scarce, until

I remember that I live here too, and that I'm just as much a victim in this whole mess as they are.

Rebecca doesn't glance my way as she strides into the room and toward the front door, every rigid line of her body and pinched mouth indicating that their fight is far from over. Colin follows, dressed now in sweats and a white T-shirt, his posture just as tense as Rebecca's.

Only after she jerks open the front door does she glare at me over his shoulder. She doesn't say anything, but the expression conveys plenty: *die*.

"It was nice meeting you," I call. "We should grab coffee sometime. Compare notes."

Her eyes narrow, and Colin gives me an *I'm going to kill you* look over his shoulder.

I give him a wide smile.

He murmurs something that sounds like a promise to call her later and steps forward to kiss Rebecca's cheek. She doesn't say a word to him or to me before she disappears.

Colin slowly closes the front door, his shoulders sagging forward slightly. Prior to Rebecca knocking on our front door this morning, I'd have acted on instinct and gone to him. Touched a hand to his back to comfort, even a hug.

Now, I don't move. He is not mine to hug. Or touch. Not that he ever was, but everything is entirely different now. Without a word, he goes to his bedroom, and I frown in confusion. *What?* Oh, hell no. There is no way we aren't going to talk about this. I let him off the hook so he could talk to Rebecca first, not so he could avoid me completely.

But before I can charge after him and demand answers, he

reappears, coffee mug in one hand and his blue bathrobe in the other.

Colin sets his coffee mug on the counter and comes toward me, robe in hand, and drops the heavy fabric onto my shoulders, shoving my hands through the armholes as though I'm a child. He knots it at my waist with impatient efficiency and then steps back. "From now on, wear that damn robe around the apartment."

Oh. Right. Because that'll fix *everything*.

But when he retreats to his room and closes the door, I don't go after him after all. A big part of me still wants answers, obviously.

But a smaller, less logical part of me isn't ready to hear them.

Sunday, September 6

At ten o'clock the following morning, I do the unthinkable.

"Charlotte?" My mother's surprise is palpable as she opens the front door and sees me standing on her front porch. "Dinner's not until five . . . *p.m.*," she adds, as though thinking I got confused and am in fact five hours late for a really early breakfast meeting. Though, if I *had* shown up at five a.m., I wouldn't be surprised if my mom had opened the door looking exactly as she does now, dressed in a summery yellow blouse, navy skirt, and navy pumps, armed and ready to face the day.

"I know," I say, adjusting my purse strap on my shoulder and trying not to feel self-conscious for standing on the front porch of my own home. Well, *former* home. "Can I come in?"

"I—" She looks nonplussed. "I was just about to go to church."

Right. I'd forgotten that it's Sunday. One of the side effects of working remotely and setting my own hours without a physical office or in-person meetings to attend is that I've tended to lose track of which day is which since moving to New York. The fact that my personal life is, shall we say, complicated, hasn't helped matters.

To my knowledge, my mother hasn't missed Sunday service aside from one nasty bout of stomach flu when I was eleven, and I don't expect her to miss it now.

"Sorry," I say automatically. "I'd forgotten. I can just come back for dinner, and—"

"Would you like to come with me?"

The question catches me off guard, and I think, based on her slightly stunned expression, it catches her off guard as well. But there's something else beneath her surprise. A little flicker of hope mingled with steel, as though she's fully braced for me to reject her.

"Sure," I say slowly. "I'd like that."

Her smile is quick, but it's so happy and genuine that my eyes feel suspiciously prickly all of a sudden.

"I'll just grab my wrap. Would you like to borrow one or—" Her gaze lingers pointedly on my bare shoulders.

The old me would have pointed out that it's already eighty degrees and humid, and that my sundress, while sleeveless, is hardly inappropriate, and *no*, I don't want a *wrap*.

New me merely smiles. "Sure, thank you."

I step inside and wait for her to return from upstairs with two wraps in hand. I'm relieved to see that the one she hands me, while not exactly my style, is a light cashmere and the lavender color works well with the green of my dress.

"Where's Dad today?" I ask.

"One of his fishing trips with your Uncle Steve," she says, picking up her purse from the table in the foyer.

"Does he still bring home that enormous cooler of fish that leaked all over the floor?" I ask as we step out into the sunshine.

"*Not*," she says in a crisp tone, with a knowing smile, "anymore."

I smile back, remembering the rare occasions when I heard my parents argue, remembering how often it had to do with, as my mother had phrased it, "those infernal fish."

As we've established, my dad is not the outdoorsy type, or at least he wasn't prior to his herb garden stage, but my Uncle Steve is sort of the black sheep of his family and moved to North Carolina to embrace all things remote and nature. He flat out refuses to come into the goddamn city, which means that when my dad wants to see his brother, he flies to North Carolina and comes home with the aforementioned cooler.

Or at least he did. I'm not the least bit surprised that my mom put the kibosh on that routine, nor am I surprised my dad let her. He doesn't even really like fish.

"You know," I muse as we walk down the quiet sidewalk, "it just occurred to me that Uncle Steve's sort of my spirit animal."

Mom makes a huffing noise. "How do you suppose that?"

"He flew the coop," I point out. "Just like I did."

"There's a difference between the swampy bayous of North Carolina and San Francisco."

I open my mouth to point out that geographically speaking, swampy bayous isn't the right way to describe North Carolina, but since I'm pretty sure she just came the closest she ever has to complimenting my adopted hometown, I let it slide.

Also . . .

I frown a little, as I realize that the mention of San Francisco doesn't cause the usual knee-jerk reaction to remind her—and myself—that it's home.

Nor does thinking about California cause even a flicker of homesickness. That can't be right. San Francisco is my life. It's where my work is, my friends, my home . . .

And yet, even though I've only been in New York for three weeks, I have the most unnerving feeling that I never left. And the ten years I spent in San Francisco are strangely fuzzy somehow. I try to shake off the feeling, making a mental note to call some of my girlfriends when I get home. I just need a reminder of my life there, that's all.

As we walk up the steps of St. Thomas and step inside the church, I'm relieved, if not exactly surprised, to see that of all the things in my life, *this* changed the least in my time away from New York. Everything is exactly as I remember, even the smells.

Though I wouldn't exactly volunteer this fact to Mom, once I moved to California and weekly Mass was no longer mandatory as decreed by my mother, I sort of let myself lapse into a Christmas and Easter kind of gal . . . if that.

Sitting in the familiar church though, instead of the old restless feeling I remember from past Sundays, I find the quiet and the rituals soothing, and by the time we step back out into the sunshine a little over an hour later, I confess I seem to breathe just a little easier than I have since Rebecca knocked on my door yesterday morning.

As a teenager, I was always anxious to get on with my day, impatient with my mother's ritual of lingering outside the church steps following the service to mingle with her friends. Today though, I follow her lead, greeting familiar faces, and even enduring a couple of honest-to-goodness cheek pinches from a few of the older ladies.

"Well," Mom says in a satisfied tone, as the group slowly begins to dissipate. "Shall we?"

"Shall we . . ."

"Talk, dear. We may have been apart for some time, but you're still my daughter, and I still know when there's something on your mind."

"What gave me away? Maybe the fact that I showed up on your doorstep unannounced for the first time *ever*?"

She ignores my gentle sarcasm and begins walking in the opposite direction of home.

"Where are we going?" I ask, falling into step beside her.

"Brunch. There's a place just around the corner that serves the most perfect mimosas. They fresh squeeze the orange juice by hand. And they're bottomless. That means you can have as many as you want."

"*Mom!*" I give her a teasing, scandalized look. "Where was *this* part of the Sunday routine when I was growing up?"

She gives me a look I can only describe as saucy. "Maybe had you stuck around past your twenty-first birthday, you'd have been introduced to this part."

"Touché," I mutter, holding open the restaurant door for her.

The hostess asks if we want to sit inside or out. I say *out*, just as she says *in*. Rough start.

We sit inside.

The second the server arrives with a water pitcher, my mom orders bottomless mimosas for both of us, and in any other circumstance I may have been annoyed at the old, familiar habit of her deciding what I want without asking, but in this case, I'm all too happy to follow her lead. The second I turn down bottomless mimosas is the second you should just put me out to pasture.

The mimosa, as promised, is pretty darn perfect, but as delicious as that first sip is, it unfortunately doesn't do much to diffuse the slight awkwardness we've managed to avoid up until now.

And by slight awkwardness, what I actually mean is the elephant in the room. I've mentioned that despite the strain of the past ten years, Mom and I haven't had *anything* to do with each other. While we didn't exactly break the ice at my brother's wedding, we at least cracked it, and there have been birthday and Christmas phone calls that were cordial, if not exactly warm.

But in all of those tense exchanges, we've never once mentioned *that* day. The day I'd defiantly shown her the plain wedding band on my left hand and proclaimed that I had the funds I needed to get out from under her thumb and "build my empire."

Yeah, I do believe those were the *exact* words I used, and no, I am not proud of them. In hindsight, I don't even know that I can really blame her for responding the way she did, which was with ice-cold rage and that whole *don't bother coming back* business.

So, while on some level, we both seem to have tactically agreed to chalk that day up to temper and pride (her) and temper, pride, and a side of immaturity (me), the scars are still there. Scars that I know won't fade until we air out the wound, but . . .

I can already feel today is not that day. I'll need my full armor for that conversation, and right now I so do not have my full armor.

"Mom, did you know Colin was seeing someone?" I say, deciding to get right to it.

My mom's Champagne flute had been halfway to her mouth, but she sets it carefully down without taking a sip, the slight *clink* of the base of the glass brushing her bread plate the only signal that she's rattled.

"A woman came by yesterday," I babble on. "Her name's Rebecca, and they work together, and—"

"Yes, I know Rebecca."

My mom's tone doesn't give me much information, and I try to play it cool as I fiddle with my spoon. "You've met her?"

"Many times. As you said, they work together, and she's been his companion on several occasions at various functions."

Companion. Such a polite word.

"Has she ever been to dinner? Family dinner, I mean, on Sundays?"

"Goodness, no." My mom seems genuinely affronted by the suggestion. "Why would she?"

I'm surprised by the depth of my relief. I don't know why, but I don't think I could bear the mental image of Rebecca and Colin laughing across my family dinner table from my parents.

Though, who are we kidding? There'd be no laughing with that foursome, just long dreary talks about the electoral college, Plato, and the stock exchange.

"Do you think—" She sips her drink, and I notice it's a big sip. "Do you suspect she and Colin . . ."

"Yes," I say quietly, saving her from having to come up with a phrase polite enough to meet her standards. "Yes, I think they *definitely*."

She huffs. "Well, that hussy."

I choke on my drink. So much for polite phrasing. "Mother."

"Well, honestly, Charlotte, he's a married man."

"Yes," I say slowly. "But you know—you have to know that he and I—" I flounder for words. "Didn't you and Dad talk about this? After the party?"

"We did, but I see no reason why the initial circumstances of your marriage and the distance of the past few years have to dictate what happens between you and Colin now."

I pretend to clean out my ears. "I'm sorry. Are you suggesting that the fact that our marriage was fake and we literally haven't spent a single moment together in a decade, shouldn't affect us?"

"Hush," she says with a frown, as she picks up her menu. "That isn't the sort of thing you want someone overhearing."

I roll my eyes and pick up my own menu, mostly because I'm starving. Colin and I did a hell of a job avoiding each other after Rebecca's appearance yesterday, and since he was hogging the kitchen last night, I skipped dinner and am thus starving.

I order the French toast, and Mom gets some healthy-sounding quiche before she surprises me by asking a blunt question.

"Why me?"

"What do you mean, why you?" I ask, smiling in thanks as the server tops off my mimosa from a crystal carafe.

"You're upset about this Rebecca situation, and you came to me. Why?"

"Honestly? That's a good question," I admit. "I didn't really think about it. I was just up all night thinking about it, I needed to talk to someone, and next thing I knew, I was on your front porch."

It's a lame answer, but the one I try to tell her with my eyes is the real one. The better one. *Because you're my mom.*

I hope she understands. And I think she does because her eyes seem just a little misty before she turns and gives the server a chiding look for dropping a minuscule amount of mimosa onto the white tablecloth.

"So, about this Rebecca woman," she says.

I make a grunting noise and slump down a little in my chair. But instead of telling me to sit up straight the way she used to, she simply studies me for a moment.

"It matters," she says softly.

I look up. "What?"

"His relationship with her bothers you. It shouldn't, but it does. Do I have that right?"

"Unfortunately," I say, my voice quiet as I sit up straighter once more. "I know I shouldn't be upset. That I have no right to be upset. Our marriage isn't a real one; I don't even know the man, not really. And yet I've gotten to know him a little in these few weeks, and when she showed up, I felt . . ."

I take a breath, not quite sure how to explain. "I don't know what I felt, or what I'm feeling, but whatever it is, I feel it *here*," I say, placing my fist just below my boobs. "It's just like . . . a knot."

My mother says nothing as she takes a sip of her mimosa.

"She's all wrong for him," I babble on. "I think that's my problem with the situation."

She gives a slight knowing smile. We both know that's not my problem with the situation—not my only problem, anyway.

"Well," she says finally. "What are you going to do about it?"

"Well, if I knew that, I wouldn't be here," I say in exasperation. Then I backpedal. "No, that's not what I mean, I just . . . I could *really* use some advice here."

She nods in understanding. "What did Colin say about the situation when you discussed Rebecca?"

"We didn't discuss it. I mean he started to, but then I tried to be the bigger person by suggesting he resolve things with her first. I figured after that was over, we would talk, but instead, he refuses to even look at me."

"Hmm. That *does* sound like a man, doesn't it? They like to pace around like caged animals when they have something on their mind that they don't want to deal with."

"Okay, so . . . what do I do?" I ask, leaning forward, a little desperate. "You've been married for nearly forty years. Any advice?"

"Space," she says immediately. "Give the man a bit of space. Especially *that* man. He's more complicated than most."

"Space," I repeat. "Okay, that sounds simple enough. I can do that."

My mom nods. "Of course you can. Though, if I might suggest . . ."

"By all means . . ."

"Put a time limit on how much space you give him. You never know when a little space can turn into a decade. The damage is harder to undo then."

"But not impossible to undo the damage," I say softly, knowing we're no longer talking about Colin and me. "Right?"

She gives me a little smile. "No, dear. Not impossible."

SATURDAY, SEPTEMBER 12

I take Mom's advice and give Colin some space.

I also take her advice and put a time limit on it. One week. One week is how long I give Colin to come out of his sulk on his own.

For the past seven days, he's done an impressive job of pretending I don't exist. He skipped Sunday dinner after my mom and I went to church under the guise of having to work—I think we both know who he was "working" with. And since then, every time I've been in the apartment, he finds a reason not to be.

I've been understanding; in fact, I've even tried to help him out. I've made a point of longer days at my rented office, happy hours with girlfriends I've wanted to reconnect with, and I've done more shopping in the past week than in the past year.

But a full week after Rebecca rang our doorbell, he's still pretending I don't exist, and . . . time's up. I take control of the situation.

The Saturday morning following church with my mom, I find Colin on the couch in the living room reading a William McKinley biography all casual-like, as though he's not a man with a wife *and* a fiancée.

"Can we talk?" I ask.

He looks up, his gaze going slightly wary as he carefully places a bookmark between the pages and sets the book on the coffee table before gesturing for me to sit in the chair across from him.

"So," I say, sitting and crossing my legs. "Do you want to go through the whole song and dance of me explaining what I want to talk about, or do you want to just skip that part and dive in?"

"She's my partner at the firm," he says, apparently going with option number two. "Her name is Rebecca Hale, and we've been working together for four years."

"And sleeping together for how much of that time?" *Whoops.* That didn't come out quite how I meant it to, but I don't backtrack. I really want to know the answer.

"We became, ah, involved, about a year and a half ago."

Nope, I lied. I didn't want to know.

"*Involved*," I repeat. "That's a nice euphemism."

"Don't," Colin says a little sharply. "Don't pretend that you and I have a real marriage and that we haven't had an agreement since the very beginning."

"I wasn't!" I say. "I know we never promised fidelity in this whole arrangement. But I don't understand why you wouldn't have just *told* me that you're engaged. Isn't that sort of a crucial detail in your life? In our life, since—like it or not—you're stuck with me in a big way for two more months."

He sighs and drops his head forward, and in spite of myself, I feel *almost* bad for him, especially when he lifts his head and looks a little . . . lost.

"Honestly? I didn't know for certain that I *was* engaged."

"That's . . ." *Huh?* I search for words. "That's definitely not what I expected you to say."

"I know. None of this is expected." He crisscrosses his fingers and looks at the floor.

When he lifts his head, he looks calmer. Slightly.

"Rebecca's known about the arrangement between you and me from the beginning. After we became . . . close, I told her the full story. About my green card, about your inheritance, everything. I wanted—needed—her to understand why she and I needed to be discreet. She was fine with it. Things were fine. Until a couple of months ago."

"What changed?" My reigning theory is possession by a dark spirit, though evil twin body swap is also a contender.

"Her birthday. She turned thirty."

Ah. I hate to have anything in common with her, but I have to admit I sort of understand. I'd be lying if I didn't have some pretty intense *my eggs are rotting and my life has been a total waste* moments when I came up on my thirtieth.

Many of those thoughts, interestingly enough, had to do with this man here, and the worry that I'd given the prime of my life to a man I didn't even *know* at the expense of finding The One.

But at least Colin and I, on some level, can take some accountability for our situation. We got ourselves into this mess when we said our vows and again when we signed that damn prenup without reading it carefully.

Poor Rebecca—yeah, I hear it, and I can't believe I'm saying it either. She simply made the mistake of falling in love with an

Irish guy, and not at the time in his life when he'd been hard up for a green card.

"Let me guess," I say with a small smile. "Rebecca's biological clock started ticking louder, and with it her marriage timetable?"

"That about sums it up. She told me I could marry her, or she'd find someone who could."

"Whoa," I say, my sympathy for Rebecca evaporating. "She gave you an ultimatum."

"Come on," he says, giving me a look. "You can't blame her. In a year and a half, I couldn't even take her on a proper date. Any time we went to a restaurant, we had to pretend we were colleagues."

"Yes, I'm sure *everyone* bought that." I don't even try to hide my sarcasm.

"Look," he snaps. "I tried. I've been trying to do right by her, *and* by you—"

"By me! You've treated me like a pesky fly since I walked into the apartment, and you didn't even tell me the entire situation!"

"You're right," he says, digging his hands through his hair. "But it's like I said, I haven't known where she and I stand. She barely speaks to me at work unless she has to."

"What changed? How'd she go from 'put your babies in me' to not speaking?"

He looks right at me. "You."

"But you said she knew about me. Our arrangement."

"She did. But then, when I realized I had to marry her or lose her, I started looking into the divorce process. Read through the prenup, learned about your brother's little game . . ."

"Ah," I say, everything clicking into place. "Rebecca was okay with you having a wife you never saw. Not so much a wife you *live* with."

"Well, actually, she was okay with it. At first. And then she looked you up, and it all sort of went to hell."

"Looked me up?"

"I hadn't told her anything about you prior to the prenup situation, and she made it a point to know as little about you as possible. I suppose I thought it would be easier for her if you weren't a real person in her mind. No offense."

"None taken." *I wish she weren't a real person in my mind either.*

"Then," he continues, "when we realized what the next three months would hold, you suddenly became real. She Googled you." He glances up. "You were apparently not what she was expecting."

"What was she expecting?"

"I don't know. We got into it a little after she saw your photos online. Even more so after she saw some picture on Facebook of the two of us at your mom's party. I just wish . . . I wish . . . I wish you didn't look like that," he says, dropping his hands and giving me an exasperated look.

My lips twitch. "Like what?"

"Shut up," he says irritably. He flops back on the couch, looking so boyish and out of sorts that I feel myself softening.

I stand and move around the coffee table to sit beside him on the couch, pulling one leg beneath me so I can face him.

"Colin." My voice is gentle. "Are you engaged to Rebecca, or not engaged?"

He lightly runs his palm over his jaw, and I notice that he still hasn't shaved today, which is all the proof I need of how far off his game he is.

"Engaged," he says slowly. "It's why she was so upset, I think. It hurts. It hurts knowing I'm with someone else, even platonically."

I let out my breath on a huff, hating this situation. For me. For him. Even for Rebecca.

"So where do things stand now?" I ask.

"She'll cool off. You and I will get through the next two months. Somehow."

"Two months in which I'll be stuck wearing your bathrobe," I grumble.

"You could get your own robe," he points out. "Or get something to sleep in that doesn't show so much . . . skin."

I bite my tongue to keep from pointing out that the morning before Rebecca had rung our doorbell, he hadn't seemed to mind all my skin. At all.

"All right," I say, giving him a sisterly pat on the knee. "What do you need from me other than to keep my skin to myself?"

"Well, you can start by getting rid of all the dead flowers all over the apartment. When I said I didn't have any vases, I did not mean to fill every single cup in the house with flowers that are now dead."

I wave my hand. "What else?"

"Well, actually," he says slowly, "Rebecca brought up a good point last week—"

"In between the screaming?"

"Yes, in between the screaming," he says, refusing to rise to my bait. "And quite frankly, it's something I should have thought of before now."

"Okay . . ."

"Well, we're following the prenup's stipulation that we live together—"

"Oh, trust me. I'm *well* aware of all those joys."

He continues. "The problem is, when these months are up, it's not going to be enough for us to say we lived together for the required amount of time. We'll have to prove it."

"I don't know how we can. Your place is already paid for, so we can't cosign a lease. I guess we could put my name on the utility bills."

"What's the address on your driver's license?"

I wince. "My old address in San Francisco. I tried to keep it as my parents' address for as long as possible, but eventually I needed a California driver's license."

"I thought as much." He sighs. "How do you feel about a trip to the DMV?"

SATURDAY, SEPTEMBER 12

⌐

"*S*o. The DMV on a Saturday. Not one of your better ideas, hubby."

"No," Colin says grimly as he shifts in the uncomfortable folding chair where we've been sitting for the better part of an hour. "No, it was not. But it's either this or take time off work."

"Cutting into your precious Rebecca time?" I say to needle him.

But he doesn't look up from his iPhone, much less respond.

"Not that you aren't fabulous company," I ramble on, "but you realize you didn't have to come with me, right? I'm the one with the California driver's license that needs to get updated."

"Actually, we both need new IDs," he says, putting his phone away. "Mine still has my old address. I need it to match yours."

"Didn't you move into your current place like two years ago?"

"Yes."

"Aren't you supposed to get a new ID with your new address within like, ten days of moving?"

"Also yes."

I gasp in mock dismay. "Colin Walsh. You are not the rule follower I thought you were!"

He rolls his head slightly to give me a baleful look. "You, of all people, who were there on my wedding day, know that an out-of-date ID is the least of my worries when it comes to following legal technicalities."

True. Very true. I hold out my hand. "Let me see your ID."

"Why?"

"I'm bored. I want to make fun of your picture."

He rolls his eyes but complies and pulls his ID out of his wallet.

I study it. "This is so weird."

"Why?"

"You're not smiling in your photo. I barely recognized you without your usual cheerful grin!"

He attempts to snatch it back, but I pull it out of reach and study it closer. "Let's see, hair, black. True. Eyes, blue. Yup. Height and weight seem about right. And ooh, you used to live in Midtown. How was that?"

He doesn't bother to respond.

I tilt my head at the ID, trying to figure out why it seems a little off to me, even though the info is all correct, save the outdated address, and the picture is about as decent as a DMV photo can ever be.

Then it hits me.

"This isn't a driver's license," I say, turning toward him. "It's just a photo ID."

"I know."

"Where's your driver's license?"

"I don't have one."

I sit up straighter. "What do you mean, you don't have one? Everyone has one."

"Not in New York, where almost nobody has cars."

Fair point. In California, it's almost unheard of not to have a car, even in a city with good public transportation like San Francisco. In Manhattan, almost nobody has a car.

"Still," I say. "There's a difference between not having a car and not being able to drive a car because you don't have a license. Did you let yours expire or something?"

"Never had one," he mumbles, starting to pull his phone out again.

I grip his wrist. "Wait, you've *never* had a driver's license?"

"I've never had an *American* driver's license," he clarifies. "I had an Irish one. In my teens."

"Wait. *Wait, wait, wait.* Are you telling me you haven't had a valid driver's license in over ten years?"

He shrugs, but I don't let it go. "You seriously haven't *driven* in over ten years?"

"That is correct."

"But—" An awful thought occurs to me. "Oh. Colin. Is it because of your parents, because of how they—"

"No," he interrupts. "Their accident was just a couple of years ago. My aversion to driving in the States started long before then."

"How. *Why?* This makes no sense to me."

He lifts a shoulder. "It's just ... when I first got here, I was fully aware of just how daunting driving in New York was for people new to the city."

"True. I grew up here, and it still terrifies me," I admit.

"Precisely. Now imagine if you grew up driving on the other side of the road. Let's just say Manhattan was not exactly the type of place I wanted to practice driving backward."

I tap his ID against my palm for a moment then hand it back to him.

"That's it?" he asks sarcastically. "No more snide jokes?"

"No more jokes," I say pleasantly. "Do you have any plans this afternoon? And tomorrow?"

"I don't think so. Why?"

"Because, hubby. You and I are going Upstate for a little week-end getaway."

"No."

"Non-negotiable," I say pleasantly.

"Why would I agree to that?"

"Because you owe me," I say, not above playing the Rebecca card. "For failing to mention you were engaged. *For three weeks*."

He hesitates, as I knew he would. His starchy moral code won't let his conscience off scot-free on that one.

"What's Upstate?" he asks warily.

"Wide open roads."

"For what purpose?"

"Oh, I think you already know," I say, standing up as my number is finally called. But just in case he *doesn't* already know, I turn back and give him a wide smile. "I'm going to be the best driving teacher you've ever had."

Colin's groan follows me all the way to the counter of the DMV.

SATURDAY, SEPTEMBER 12

⌐

"*I* cannot believe I let you talk me into this," Colin says from the passenger side of our rental car.

"Don't you want to learn how to drive?"

He hesitates. "I suppose. I just don't understand why it has to be an extended nightmare."

"By extended nightmare, you mean weekend getaway?"

"Same damn thing," he grumbles.

I smile because I'm beginning to think he enjoys our banter every bit as much as I do.

"Okay, so since we left in such a hurry—"

"Whose fault was that?"

"I didn't have time to put a road trip playlist together—"

"Thank God."

"But, lucky for us, I do have all my workout playlists downloaded onto my phone, so we'll have something to listen to. How do you feel about Madonna?"

"I prefer quiet."

"Don't be grumpy just because I don't have any Irish jig music ready to go."

"Irish *jig* music?" he says, giving me an incredulous look.

"Fine, what *do* you like to listen to?"

"Well, according to you, 'Danny Boy' on repeat."

"We can download 'Danny Boy.' Here," I say, fishing my phone out of the center console and handing it to him. "Have at it."

"Madonna's fine," he grumbles. "What's your passcode?"

"My birthday."

To my surprise, Madonna's "Holiday" begins playing mere seconds later.

"You know my birthday?" I ask, changing lanes to get around a semi.

"Apparently."

"How?" I press.

"Oh, you know," he says, dropping my phone back into the console and stretching out his legs in the passenger seat. "I have multiple calendar reminders set up. Every year, I agonize what to get you. I finally decide on something extremely sentimental but chicken out before I give it to you, so I have a decade's worth of gifts carefully tucked away in my closet for when I get the courage to tell you how I really feel."

"So hilarious," I say in my best Irish accent. "Really though. How do you know?"

"We just spent nearly three hours in the DMV together," he says. "Ample opportunity to see your date of birth."

"Oh. Right." I glance over. "Except I was in the DMV too and didn't memorize *your* birthday."

"I didn't *memorize* it, I just . . . remembered it."

"Fine, fine, but to even the playing field, when is yours?"

"March seventeenth."

I'm delighted. "St. Paddy's day! Really?"

"No."

"Oh. Damn. So when? Damn it, man, don't make me beg."

He sighs. "May. The second."

"May second," I repeat, trying to store it away in the spot of my brain that remembers details, which honestly, is not a big part of my brain. "You'll be . . . thirty-four."

"Thirty-five."

"Shoot. I was close though!"

"Congratulations. Are you going to tell me where exactly we're headed?"

"Hudson Valley. There are a bunch of cute little towns up there, but we're staying in one actually *called* Hudson. You been?"

"No car, remember?"

"Yeah, but the train drops off right there. You and Rebecca never take any getaways together?"

"We've been busy."

"With what, world domination? Surely even you can find time for a vacation."

"Not unless I'm kidnapped, apparently."

"You weren't *kidnapped*. Think of it as an extended driver's ed conference."

"That I didn't ask for, nor express any interest in."

"Don't act like I dragged you to the car. Obviously a *little* part of you wanted to get out of town."

"Or a big part of me didn't want to deal with your badgering if I resisted."

That too.

"Oooh. I *love* this song." I reach out and turn up the music and proceed to show him just how well I know my Madonna lyrics.

"God save me," he says. "It sings."

Yes, and passably well, thank you very much. "Open Your Heart" is my all-time favorite Madonna song, so I know every word.

I hold my right fist out in a microphone shape and extend it to Colin, who, shockingly, does not play along, so I bring my "microphone" back to myself and belt out the chorus.

He thumps his head back against the headrest.

"I should have gone with 'Danny Boy' after all," Colin says, raising his voice to be heard over the music.

But I'm pretty sure there's a slight smile playing around his lips. He can deny it all he wants, but he's having a good time.

Also, I make a mental note to learn all the words to "Danny Boy."

SATURDAY, SEPTEMBER 12

⌣

"*R*ight side, right side," I command gently, and Colin corrects the car immediately.

"Sorry," he mutters.

"Don't be, that's why we're here."

"And where exactly is *here*? These roads are barely paved."

"I'm not really sure." I look around at the trees surrounding us on either side. "I have a college friend who moved Upstate a couple of years ago, and she suggested we come out this way."

Jocelyn had assured me it'd be unlikely we'd see any other cars or people since it's mostly farmland, and so far she's right. There's nothing but Colin and me, trees, sunshine, and a car going about fourteen miles per hour.

"How's it feel? Just like riding a bike?" I ask, glancing across the car.

He frowns. "The mechanics came back relatively easily. Adjusting to the right side of the road is a bit harder than I expected."

"You'll start to get used to it," I say with confidence, adjusting my sunglasses. "We can take as long as we need. And let me know if you change your mind and want some music after all."

"Do you promise not to sing?"

"I do not."

"Silence sounds fine," he replies.

I let him have his silence for once, partially because I can see that his knuckles are white at their ten-and-two position, and partially because I'm genuinely enjoying myself. There's something surprisingly lovely about driving down a dirt road, the sun beating down through the windshield, and no one else around for miles, save for the person sitting beside you.

I wonder if this is why people used to go on Sunday drives back in the day. To achieve this perfect sense of contentment from driving for the sake of it rather than to get somewhere.

Colin makes a right hand turn down yet another deserted road then surprises me by being the one to break the silence.

"Can I ask you something without you getting mad?"

I snort. "Are you sure you're engaged? For having a wife *and* a fiancée, you know remarkably little about women."

"Can I ask the question or not?"

"You can ask. But if it's a jackass question, I make no promises about my resulting anger level."

"Your job," he says, glancing over at me briefly. "What is it?"

I look at him in surprise, both because he's never really expressed much interest in anything about me, and also because it's a pretty Google-able fact.

"I own a social media management company. Which is a fancy way of saying we implement Facebook, Twitter, and Instagram strategies for bigger companies."

"And that's profitable?"

"I'll rephrase," I say with a smile. "We implement Facebook, Twitter, and Instagram strategies for *really* big companies."

It's more than profitable. Some of our biggest clients, the behemoths of the retail world, see annual invoices from my company in the seven figures.

"And that's what you wanted to do?" he asks.

"What do you mean?"

"Well, as I remember it back when we got married, I needed a green card. You needed to get married in order to access your trust fund, which you told me was to start your own business, but you never mentioned any details. This is the business you envisioned?"

I think about it, trying to get back into the mental state of my twenty-one-year-old self. "You know, I don't really know," I admit. "I knew I wanted to start a company. I just loved the idea of it, all the more so because of the risk. The brainstorming, the planning, the securing of funds. Deciding when to bring on a team, how big the team should be. When to grow, how to grow, whether to invest in marketing or infrastructure first, and so on."

"Did it meet expectations?"

I ponder this. "It did. And by the way, Grandpa, if we're ever going to put you on the real road, you're going to have to go above twenty miles per hour."

We accelerate slightly. *Very* slightly. "You don't sound sure."

"That you're driving too slow? Trust me. I'm sure."

"No, about your company. About it meeting your expectations."

"I do genuinely love it," I say. "It was harder than I expected but more rewarding too."

"Okay, here's the line of questioning where you might get mad," he says slowly.

"Bring it on."

"When we were trying to figure out the logistics of this prenup arrangement, you didn't really fight me on my suggestion that you move here, rather than me move to San Francisco."

"Well, that's the benefit of it being a social media management. Most of what we do is online. I can work remotely, and you can't as easily."

"True. But . . ."

"Okay, fine, I promise not to get mad," I say. "Just spit out whatever you're dancing around."

"Fine," he says. "I guess what I'm trying to say is that you seem a bit bored."

I look at him in surprise. "I do?"

He nods. "Not unhappy. But I've seen you at your laptop, listened to some of your work calls. I've seen you when you head off to your makeshift office in the mornings, and I often see you when you get home. You seem a bit indifferent. Content," he adds. "But when it comes to your work, I don't get the energy I'd expect from someone with your—"

"Zeal for life?" I supply.

"Sure."

I turn my head and look out the window, thinking over his words, wondering if they're true. I haven't put all that much thought into my business lately, and *that* makes me realize Colin is right. I like my job, I'm proud of my company, but if I'm being really honest with myself, it doesn't feel like much of a challenge anymore.

Yes, the company is still growing, but at a slower rate. Plus, we already have some of the biggest clients, so we're already at the top of our industry. The options for innovation feel limited, the growth potential stunted.

Or maybe it's just that I can't *see* the innovation anymore.

Maybe it's time for me to move on.

The second the thought crosses my mind I realize it's been looming for months now. I've been trying to avoid it, but now that it's out there, it's not nearly as scary as I thought it would be. Or rather it is, but I *like* the fear. I *like* the little zip I feel in my stomach at the uncertainty of what might be next.

"You know for someone who's so emotionally stunted, you're quite introspective and wise," I tell Colin.

"Emotionally stunted," he repeats a little woodenly.

I look over quickly, wondering if I've hurt his feelings, but as usual, I can't read a damn thing on his granite jawline.

"I don't mean that in a bad way," I correct quickly, but he gives me a telling look. "You're just . . ." I blow out a breath, wondering how to backpedal. "Well, put it this way. You sensed that I'm a little bored with my job, and you were right. But gun to my head, I couldn't tell how *you* feel about *your* job. Or whether or not you like your apartment. Or if you like your wardrobe. I can't tell when you enjoy what you're eating, versus when you think it's bland. I can't tell if you like coffee as much as *I* like coffee. I can't tell if you're crazy in love with Rebecca or just sort of *meh* about her. I can't tell if you're as mad at my brother as I am. I can't even tell if I drive you as crazy as I think I drive you. I never know what you're thinking or feeling. Ever."

Colin doesn't respond. Not so much as a twitch—definitely not a verbal response—and I wonder if I've officially overstepped this time.

He finally responds, and true to form, it's with as few words as possible. "You do."

"I do what?"

He glances over. "Drive me crazy."

"Good to know," I say with a laugh, reaching across the car and tugging the steering wheel slightly to bring us back to the right side of the road. "What about the rest of the stuff?"

He exhales and taps his fingers against the steering wheel. "No complaints about my job. I like my wardrobe. And my apartment. Nobody enjoys coffee as much as you do. Yes, I'm angry with your brother too. Does that cover it?"

"What about Rebecca?" I ask, hating how much I want to know the answer to that question.

He hesitates. "What about her?"

"Are you crazy in love?"

"Maybe that's how you and I are different," he says slowly. "I don't believe there should be anything *crazy* about love."

"What should love be?" I ask.

"Calm. Comforting. Serene."

I wrinkle my nose. "Sounds boring."

But I feel a little pang. Because it sounds kind of nice too.

And very much out of reach.

SATURDAY, SEPTEMBER 12

*"Y*ou accused me of not expressing sentiment over food." Colin uses his fork to point at the plate of fried artichokes we're sharing. "These are surprisingly excellent."

"They really are," I agree, dragging an artichoke heart through the provided dipping sauce, something creamy and salty and delicious. "My friend mentioned the restaurants in this area were outstanding, and so far, she's right."

After a couple hours of driving, in which I'm proud to say, my husband worked his way all the way up to a respectable forty miles per hour while staying on the right side of the road, we realized we'd skipped lunch and opted for an early dinner before checking into the hotel for the night.

Joc had given me a handful of recommendations and I'd picked the one that was open, but it's been a good choice so far. The cocktails are strong, the appetizers flavorful, the company . . .

I look across the table at Colin, who looks more relaxed than I'm used to him being.

The company is growing on me. A little too much.

"Any questions about the menu?" our server asks, a relaxed twenty-something guy wearing jeans, flannel, suspenders, and a bright red goatee that suits him perfectly.

"Yes," I say, picking it up and gesturing at it. "How big are the plates over here on the Mains section?"

"Probably a little smaller than your typical entree size. Generous enough to work as a lighter entree, certainly, but we always recommend getting a couple of things for the table and sharing them. More things to try that way."

I glance at Colin in question, and he shrugs in what I'm pretty sure is acquiescence. As established, it's hard to tell with him.

"How are the scallops?" I ask the server.

"The mussels are better," he says without hesitation.

I look at Colin. "Mussels okay?"

"Sure. Order whatever you want."

"Okay, we'll do one order of the mussels, the sweet potato gnocchi, and . . . Brussels sprouts?"

Colin gives a quick shake of his head.

"Carrots," I correct. "We'll get an order of the carrots."

That gets me a slight nod of approval from Colin and assurances from the server that we chose well, as he picks up our menus and goes to place our order in the computer.

"Ah ha," I say, leaning forward, smiling gleefully. "I learned something about you. You, sir, do not like Brussels sprouts."

"I'll eat them. But I don't love them."

"Taste or texture?" I ask, sipping my drink, a light pink confection with something foamy and sweet on top.

"Shape," he says. "When I was a boy, I thought they looked like little alien heads."

I tilt my head back and forth, studying him. "Nope. I don't see it."

"What?" he asks, slowly chewing another artichoke heart. "Brussels sprouts looking like alien heads?"

"No, you as a boy."

"You thought I was born thirty?"

"No, I thought you were born eighty. Be honest, have you ever uttered the phrase *get off my lawn*?"

"I have not. Though, over the past few weeks, I sure have wanted to utter the phrase *get out of my house*."

I look quickly down, a little surprised at how much his comment stings. Not that it's been any big secret that he doesn't like me, but I hadn't realized it'd been *that* bad.

"Well, good news," I chirp, forcing the hurt somewhere else, to be dealt with at a later time. "Only two months to go, and then you're officially done with me."

"Charlotte. I didn't mean—"

"No, you did," I interrupt. "And it's okay. You've never pretended to like me. I'd be insulted if you started faking it now. So, I've been thinking, do you think we should have a divorce party?"

"A what?"

"A divorce party. I know it's not typical, but then we didn't exactly have a typical marriage, so why would we have a typical divorce?"

"Why in God's name would we want to have a party?"

"Oh, come on. You *know* you're going to want to celebrate being done with this."

"As will you."

Maybe. Maybe not.

"Well, to be honest," I admit, "I've been thinking lately that I was robbed of a proper wedding and a proper wedding reception, so maybe I'll just do it in reverse and have a divorce reception. We could have people come over for cocktails and canapés and dancing."

"A divorce reception," he says. "You are . . ." He rubs at his eyes. "I don't know what you are."

"I'm fabulous. And the party would be fun," I insist.

"It would *not* be fun. And I hardly think we need to spotlight the fact that we're parting ways for the immigration authorities. Why don't you save whatever plans you're cooking up in your head for your next wedding?"

"My *next* wedding," I repeat. "Do you know something I don't?"

"Don't you expect to get married again?"

I give it some thought as I chew on an artichoke heart. "I don't know. I hope so, but there's definitely nothing on the horizon."

"Hasn't there ever been someone—?"

"No," I interject. "I don't have a Rebecca. I mean, I've cared about people over the years, but I've never really been able to see myself growing old with any of them. I spent my twenties pretty focused on the company."

"What about your thirties? What will those bring?"

"I don't know yet," I say, dragging my pinky through the sauce on my plate and sucking it off. "Maybe starting something new? A new company?"

"Husband? Kids?"

I feel an unexpected tug at the thought of a family, and I real-ize that's part of what's been getting under my skin the past few weeks. It hasn't just been being back in New York, and it hasn't just been reuniting with my family, or even playing house with Colin. It's been the sense of wanting something *more*. My adult life to this point has been almost entirely about my professional development and having fun, and it's been great. Really great.

But lately it feels as though I'm ready for the next stage. One that involves diapers and dogs and someone to come home to. The *same* someone to come home to.

"I guess it's possible," I say, answering Colin's question. "A few years ago, I don't think it would have appealed to me, but the same ticking that's got Rebecca acting all crazy didn't pass me by altogether. I think I'd like being a mom. I think I'd be good at it."

"I think you would too."

"Wait." I wave my fork at him. "Did you just . . . compliment me?"

"It slipped out."

"Uh-huh. Anyway, if I do have kids, I hope I get boys. You going to eat that?" I point at the last artichoke heart.

"All yours. Why boys?"

"Girls are hard. I mean, you saw how I was ten years ago. If my daughter is like me, I'll go insane."

"We're all entitled to a few growing pain years," he says, his voice surprisingly kind.

"I bet you didn't have any. I bet you were the perfect son."

He shrugs. "I was easy. I tried to be easy."

"Tried. Why?"

"My parents wanted to have more children. They were devoutly Catholic, and I don't think it ever really occurred to them to have fewer than five kids. But it also didn't occur to them that they'd struggle to conceive. They were left with just me."

"Must have meant they doted on you."

"The normal amount," he says with a faint smile. "But they were fairly strict. Serious."

"*No*," I say in wide-eyed surprise. "But you're so fun-loving and free!"

He ignores the sarcasm. "I was always painfully aware that I was their one shot at being parents, so I tried to be what they wanted. Quiet. Respectful. Good grades, sat still in church."

"Was it easy or hard?"

"Easy," Colin says. "If you're hoping there's some wild child beneath the frown waiting to be freed, you'll be disappointed. Not that I was perfect. I put a frog in my babysitter's bed, broke a few windows with my friend—accidentally. But mostly I've always been, what was it—emotionally stunted?"

I wince. "I guess I could have just said you were quiet."

"You could have."

"Did I hurt your feelings?"

"Can someone who's emotionally stunted even have feelings?"

"That's not an answer," I challenge.

He looks down at his plate then slowly lifts his gaze back to mine, his eyes guarded. "Just because I don't show my every emotion, doesn't mean I don't have them."

"Fair enough," I answer carefully, knowing I need to tread lightly. "So, I'm curious . . . how did Rebecca coax you out of your turtle shell?"

He rolls his eyes. "What?"

"You know. If you're the turtle," I say, awkwardly miming a

little creature tucked into the safety of its shell. "How did she get you to show your soft side?"

"Why do you always have to make everything so weird?" he mutters, taking a sip of his drink.

"Emotions aren't weird," I say a little sharply. "If you don't want to be criticized for not showing every emotion, shouldn't the opposite also be true? Shouldn't I be allowed to wear my heart on my sleeve?"

He looks surprised by my outburst. "I guess it's never occurred to me that you ever wanted—or needed—to be *allowed* to do anything. You just . . . do it."

"And that drives you crazy. You said as much in the car."

"Well. Yes. You're a bit turbulent to be around."

"Turbulent," I say, my anger fading slightly. "I like that."

"You would." But he's smiling a little, and I can't help but wonder if he's starting to realize that a little turbulence might be exactly what he needs in his life.

SATURDAY, SEPTEMBER 12

"*H*i!" I say with a smile, setting my weekender back on the floor and greeting the woman at the front desk of our hotel. "I have a room reserved under Walsh?"

"Two beds," Colin says before the woman can say a single word. "We'll need two beds."

I step hard on Colin's foot, gratified when he winces.

"Yes, two beds would be great," I say smoothly. "My husband here has a pretty intense rash."

Now he tries to step on my foot, but I'm way ahead of him and shift out of the way.

The woman wisely ignores my overshare as she clicks away on her computer. "Ah. Yes. Here we are, one room for Mr. and Mrs. Walsh."

Colin gives me a sharp look, which I ignore. I've never pretended to take his name before now, and I'm not entirely sure what compelled me to do so when I made the hotel reservations. Nor do I completely understand why I like the idea of being a

Mrs. so much. Apparently, all it takes is a two-minute conversation about remarrying and having kids, and I turn into an aspiring June Cleaver.

"I see you're one of our Platinum members, which makes you eligible for an upgrade, but I'm afraid the only suite we have left has a king bed . . ."

"The regular room with two beds will be fine," Colin says, already handing over his credit card and ID.

"It's a really bad rash," I say in a loud whisper. "You remembered to pack your cream, right, darling?"

"Yes, my pet. I tucked it in right alongside your hemorrhoid cream so we could keep all the medicated ointments together."

I choke on a laugh. *Not bad, Mr. Walsh. Not bad at all.*

The woman completes the transaction and hands us our keys in record time, wisely wanting no part of our verbal sparring and medicated ointments.

"There's a complimentary breakfast from six thirty to eleven tomorrow, though I feel I should point out that tomorrow being Sunday, there are a couple of great brunches in town. We're also known for our antique stores, and a lot of people enjoy grabbing a bite on the main street before or after perusing the shops. Do you like antiques?"

I try to think of a polite way to say *not really*, but Colin answers first. "My mother loved them."

I look over in surprise, and I'm not the only one. Colin looks downright shocked at his own announcement. But the woman behind the counter isn't aware that my husband isn't exactly famous for sharing emotional anecdotes *ever*, and she merely smiles.

"Any era in particular?"

"No. She couldn't afford to buy much, but any time we passed one, she'd drag me inside. Said being surrounded by items with a story reminded her that we're all the same. That we're all just people, regardless of what decade we're born in. Anyway," he says quickly, looking embarrassed as he holds up the key cards. "Thanks for these."

She points us to the elevators, and the second the doors close, Colin speaks: "Be quiet. I don't want to discuss it further, so not a single word."

I stay quiet. I also do my turtle mime, which earns me a growl.

The elevator doors open again, and he hands me the keys then picks up both our bags, following me down the hall until I find our room.

Despite not being a suite, it's bigger than your average hotel room, and more modern than I expected, which is a welcome surprise, especially since we're still on the tail end of the heat wave; I was a little worried about the AC effectiveness in an older building like this one.

"Hmm," I say, gripping my chin, as I study the room. "Are these two beds far enough apart, or should I move one into the bathroom for your sake? Also, should we call the woman downstairs? Remind her one more time we're not sleeping in the same bed? I don't think she quite grasped it the first two times you made it clear."

He tosses my bag onto one of the beds and sets his own duffel on the other. "I'm already dreading enough telling Rebecca that we took this trip. I at least want to be able to assuré her that we didn't share a bed."

I hop onto my bed, kicking off my shoes and letting my feet swing. "Do you have to tell her at all? Not that I'm advocating keeping secrets, but based on what I saw last weekend, I don't know exactly how chill she'll be about this."

"Maybe you should have thought about that before you forced me on the trip," he said, unzipping his bag.

The brusque dismissal stings and because I'm not as adept as him at pulling back into *my* turtle shell, I let him know it.

"You just keep telling yourself that," I say, as I stand up. "Keep telling yourself that I'm some god-awful tornado that makes you do things you don't want to do. I'm sure it's easier than admitting that you're actually having a good time. And whatever you do, don't let yourself remember that the entire reason for me instigating this trip was to *help* you, and that I endured two *hours* going at turtle speeds while you remembered how to operate a moving vehicle."

"What is it with you and turtles?"

I stare at him for a moment. "*That's* your response? You claim to have emotions buried somewhere inside you, and I'm sure you're right. I'm just not sure you have any of the good ones."

I grab my toiletry bag and stomp to the bathroom, giving in to the urge to slam the door. Which does absolutely nothing to make me feel better.

I'm annoyed with myself for being upset in the first place. You'd think over the past few weeks I'd have gotten used to it—used to the fact that no matter what approach I take, he just plain doesn't like me.

But instead of becoming easier, the pain seems to get worse and worse every time he makes his disdain plain, every time he goes out of his way to keep his distance.

The Madonna song "Open Your Heart" has been going through my head ever since the car ride, and now I'm realizing that I hadn't made him listen to it on repeat simply because it was my favorite song.

Now I'm wondering if I wasn't subconsciously singing it to him.

"Stupid," I mutter, jerking open my toiletry bag and scrubbing off my makeup with more force than necessary. I brush my teeth and finish the rest of my night routine, taking my time to give my temper a chance to cool. Luckily, while my temper is fairly easily ignited, the flame dies down pretty quickly.

My good humor is mostly restored when I open the bathroom door a few minutes later.

"All yours!" I say, giving him a friendly smile.

He's sitting on the bed with clothes folded in his lap. I assume they're his, and he's planning to change in the bathroom, but he stands and hands them to me.

"What's this?" I ask, glancing down at the neatly folded white T-shirt and . . . blue boxers.

"To sleep in." His voice is gruff, and he doesn't quite meet my eyes.

"I packed my own pajamas," I say, as he walks past me toward the bathroom.

"Yes, I've seen your pajamas. I don't suppose you also brought the robe?"

"No. But—"

"Then you're wearing those," he orders, pointing at his clothes in my hand.

I wrinkle my nose. "But these are cotton. Mine are silk."

"Charlotte, for the love of—I'm engaged, but I'm not a saint, okay? Just . . . wear the ugly T-shirt."

Now he closes the door, and I stand still, a little stunned by the outburst and what he'd just admitted.

I bite my lip, thrilled at the prospect that maybe his insistence on the two beds hadn't been disgust at my proximity, or even appeasing Rebecca.

He hadn't wanted to be tempted.

Hmm.

I change into his shirt and boxers. Not because they're particularly comfortable or because he told me to, but because despite the weird feelings toward Colin, I'm not a home-wrecker. I may think Rebecca is all wrong for him, but the last thing I want to do is be *that* woman. The one who deliberately tempts a man who belongs to someone else.

I'm pulling back the covers on my bed when Colin comes out of the bathroom.

"Hey," I say, turning and glancing at him, seeing that he too is wearing an undershirt and boxers. "We're twins!"

I hold my hands to the side so he can see I've done as instructed.

Instead of looking pleased or relieved, he stops in his tracks and stares at me, his gaze drifting down to my bare feet then back up. He shakes his head.

I drop my arms to my side. "Now what?"

"Nothing," he says roughly. "Get into bed."

"Did you forget your rash cream or something?" I grumble as I climb into the plush, crisp hotel bed. "You're irritable."

"According to you, irritable is just my default state." He pulls back the covers on his own bed and climbs in.

I stare at the ceiling and take a deep breath, the sound unnaturally loud in the silent room.

"It's *really* quiet in here," I say.

"It is. I forget how accustomed I am to the subtle soundtrack of the city, even living in a high-rise."

"I could put on music on my phone. Or some sort of background noise," I say, pulling back the covers and starting to get out of bed to retrieve my phone where I left it charging on the desk.

"I've got it. My phone's right here."

I lie back down, and a moment later, soft music starts playing from Colin's phone.

I smile. He's playing "Danny Boy."

SUNDAY, SEPTEMBER 13

~

After another early morning driving session, during which I declare Colin fit for the open road, if not yet the crazy Manhattan roads, we take the hotel receptionist's suggestion and decide to stop for brunch before heading back to the city.

The French toast (mine) and omelet (his, I helped myself) are every bit as perfect as last night's meal, and I'm all but waddling as we leave the restaurant an hour later.

"Want to walk around for a while?" I ask, sliding my sunglasses onto my head. "I could stand to move before sitting in a car for two hours after eating all that."

"Sure."

Hudson's a cute little town and a refreshing respite from the rush of the city, both New York and San Francisco.

"You want to go in?" I ask, pointing at one of the half dozen antique shops we've passed.

He hesitates. "No, I'm okay."

"Come on. I'm still not ready to get into the car." I open the shop door and enter before he can come up with another pro-test. He follows me in, and a solid twenty minutes later, I realize my mistake. My stated apathy for antiques remains strong, but his enjoyment of them was understated last night.

I don't think I've ever heard him string so many words together at once, and he and the shop owner don't seem even close to wrap-ping up their conversation on mid-century something or other.

I don't mind, but I'm also bored, so I slip quietly out the front door of the shop to continue exploring.

It's clear that antiques are the thing in town, but I also find a bookstore, which I browse for a while, and then I find my way into a jewelry store, which I enjoy more than I expect to. Antique furniture and home goods might not do it for me, but antique jewelry is a whole other thing entirely, one that I like quite a lot, apparently.

I'm ogling a Georgian Pink Sapphire ring that the shop owner tells me is from 1820 when the bell at the door tinkles. I turn and smile at Colin. "Hey! You found me."

He holds up his phone. "I tracked your phone."

"That's creepy."

"You did it to me just last week to see if I was near a gelato shop."

"Which you were."

"I was eight blocks away."

"And yet, when you got home, there was coffee gelato in one hand. For me. And chocolate in the other. For you. So who's the real winner in this scenario?"

He rolls his eyes. "When the three months are up, getting off each other's family plan will be item number one."

"Fine by me."

In our effort to present the "living together, married couple" image, we went on a family plan. One of the side effects is that iPhones allow us to know the other person's location if we so choose. I'm not complaining. It got me ice cream.

"Buy anything?" I ask, extending my hand and admiring the ring one last time as he comes to stand beside me at the counter.

"A desk for my home office, but it won't get delivered for a few weeks."

"What home office? Where can you fit a desk?" I ask, reluctantly sliding off the ring and handing it back to the shop owner. I'm not above buying myself a little something, but a several thousand-dollar ring is pushing the limits of *treat yo'self*.

"Your room."

"I hope it's a small desk," I say, giving the shop owner a smile of thanks for his help and preceding Colin out onto the sidewalk. "The bed and dresser take up most of the room."

"I rented all that," he says, sliding on his sunglasses. "After you agreed to move to New York."

I look up at him. "My room wasn't always a guest room?"

"Nope. Office."

"Where's all the office stuff?"

"I sold it. I wasn't attached to it, figured I'd find something I liked better after you leave in November."

I nod but don't say anything as we head back to the car.

"Is something wrong?"

"No. Why?"

"You're quiet. Which feels akin to the calm before a storm."

Okay, fine. Something's a little wrong. I'm just more aware than ever how much he must be anxious for us to wrap this up so he can get his life back. His office. His quiet life. *His fiancée.*

"I'm fine," I say tiredly. "I guess I just didn't realize you had to rearrange your life so much when I came barging in."

"You didn't barge in. And despite my behavior that first day, I'm well aware that your life is the one that was upended. The least I can do is rent a damn bed for you."

"Yeah. Thanks," I say, as I sit behind the wheel, and we both close our respective car doors. "And I'm glad you found a desk you like."

"Yeah, thanks," he repeats.

Neither of us says much on the way back to the city.

THURSDAY, OCTOBER 8

꧁

*A*s has become my cooking ritual, Madonna is blaring, and as such, I don't realize Colin's come home until he's standing in the kitchen, wearing his usual *why is this happening to me?* expression.

"Oh! Hi!" I wave at him with the spatula, turning down the music on my phone with my free hand. "You're home early."

I try to keep my happiness out of my voice, but I'm pretty sure I fail. I'm already alarmed as it is with how much I enjoy being in the same home as this man, and how lost I feel when he leaves to go spend time with Rebecca. The last thing I need is for him to start realizing how I feel.

Colin lifts his eyebrows. "I'd say it's clear you weren't expecting me back so soon, but the kitchen usually looks like this even when you know I'm home," he says, pulling a beer out of the fridge.

He pops the cap with a bottle opener then, setting the bottle on the counter, and holds up both the opener and cap for me to see. "In case you want to take notes. This, in the garbage." He throws the cap in the trash. "This, back in the drawer." He puts the opener away.

"Are you *sure* that's where that goes?" I ask. "Because I can think of another place to put it. Here's a hint: the sun *nevvvvver* shines there."

Colin, as usual, is unimpressed with my wit. "I don't understand how someone cooking for one can make this much of a mess."

"But I always clean it up!"

"You do. But if you cleaned it up as you went along, it'd be easier."

"I trust the process," I say, using tongs to move the pasta from the boiling water into the pan where I've put together a lemony cream sauce. Three noodles slop onto the stove, and I wrinkle my nose, knowing it'll only fuel his argument of me being a messy cook.

"I see no process here," he says.

"That's because you lack imagination. Get me a plate, would you?" I lick sauce off my thumb.

"A bowl might be better."

"Oh my God, Walsh. Fine. Whatever makes you shut up."

He goes to the cabinet and comes back with a bowl. No, *two* bowls.

I look up in surprise. "I thought you ate with Rebecca."

"I did."

"And this is what, second dinner?"

"I ate light. I wasn't hungry before. Now I am."

Understandable. I wouldn't be hungry sitting across from that viper either.

And don't go accusing me of being bitchy, because let me tell you, I have *tried* to give that woman a chance over the past couple of weeks since we've been back from our Hudson weekend. I've even worn my frumpiest outfits to reassure her I'm not a threat. I've dropped everything to get out of the apartment so they can have *couple time* the handful of occasions she's come over.

I even asked if she wanted to grab a coffee or a glass of wine sometime, hoping that maybe if we got to know each other, she'd see that I'm not out to be a home-wrecker.

She told me, and I quote, "*I don't think that will be necessary.*"

I *do* not like her. Any more than she likes me, apparently. But I pretend to for Colin's sake, so I keep my mouth shut.

I've made plenty of pasta, so I dish up generous portions for each of us and carry them to the table, along with napkins and silverware.

"Anything to drink?" Colin asks.

"Yeah, sure." I turn around, intending to go to the fridge. "Whoa," I say, almost running into him because he's right there.

"What's this?" I ask.

He's holding out a fancy little gift bag, the tall skinny shape a dead giveaway of what's inside.

Sure enough, I pull out a bottle of Champagne.

I give him a puzzled smile. "Are we celebrating?"

"I thought we might. We made it past our halfway point."

"Of what?" I ask, studying the bottle. I don't know Champagne all that well, but I know this fancy-pants label wasn't cheap.

"Halfway," he repeats. "Of our prenup requirement. You moved in August twentieth. The prenup doesn't stipulate it has to be three calendar months, which means we're in the clear on

November twentieth." He taps the bottle and smiles. "That means we're more than halfway through this mess."

This mess.

"Wow," I say, struggling to keep my smile on my face. "You certainly have those dates at the ready. Do you have all the key milestones marked on your calendar?"

"Well, yes," he says, sounding puzzled. "Don't you?"

I nod, because marking my calendar with the end date of this situation was one of the first things I'd done upon learning of my brother's stupid trap. But honestly? I haven't looked at it in weeks.

Colin, on the other hand, apparently has the dates memorized.

He frowns. "You don't like the Champagne?"

"No, I do," I say, tracing a finger over the label. "It's just a bit jarring to realize that someone is counting down the days until they never have to see you again."

"That's not what I said. You're putting words in my mouth."

Someone has to—you're not exactly great about putting your own words in your mouth.

"Will you have a glass with me?" I say, starting to move around him to put it in an ice bucket.

He reaches out and grabs my hand. "Charlotte, wait."

For some reason, the touch makes the pain even more acute, and I look up to meet his gaze, trying mightily to keep the hurt out of my eyes, and not at all sure I'm succeeding.

"What?" I ask.

He says nothing.

His gaze drops to our joined hands, a line appearing between his eyebrows as he frowns, as though surprised to realize he's touching me. His grip tightens ever so slightly as though wanting to pull me closer and fighting the urge.

Don't fight it, I make a silent plea.

There's something *here*—something between us that goes beyond a green card, my trust fund requirements, and a prenup. Every day that's passed, every morning we share eggs and coffee, every time I manage to make him laugh, I'm more certain that Rebecca's not the one for him.

Every day, I'm more desperate for him to see it.

"Charlotte—"

Remember a few weeks ago when we had an almost-moment, and the doorbell rang? Well, there's a repeat. Except this time, it's a phone call that has him jumping back from me.

Moment. Over.

"Sorry," I mutter, reaching for my phone. I answer it, mainly as an opportunity to turn away from Colin.

"Hey, Kurt." I tuck the phone under my ear and place the Champagne in the fridge, fairly certain neither Colin nor I will feel like opening it anymore. "What's up?"

"Char, thank God you picked up," he says in relief.

"What's wrong?" I ask, because his tone is dramatic even for him, and my brain is already filtering through worst-case scenarios: We're losing a big client. One of the senior team members gave notice. Fire. Flood. Some sort of debacle nightmare.

"I just got *the* strangest call," Kurt says on a rush. "You remember how when you bought your apartment, you didn't want your name to be on the deed because of the tricky nature of your marriage, so Lewis and I are the official owners, and you paid us in cash?"

"Yes, Kurt, of course I remember," I say, panic making me impatient.

There are only a handful of reasons someone would be inquiring into my housing situation in San Francisco, and none of them are good.

I hear muffled voices and recognize Lewis's low timbre muffled against what is probably Kurt's hand over the receiver.

"Kurt!" I say loudly. "*Who called*?"

Colin is watching me now, looking up from the pile of mail I hadn't gotten around to sorting yet. He knows enough about my housing arrangement with Kurt to look as wary as I feel.

"Charlotte. Hi." It's Lewis who comes on the other end.

I close my eyes. "Let me guess. It's bad news, and Kurt didn't want to be the one to tell me."

"Bad news is not his forte," Lewis says in his usual calm voice, though he sounds grim. "He'll make it even worse than it already is.'

"It's that bad?"

"Immigration Services called us, Char. Some guy named Gordon Price wanted to know the nature of our relationship with you, most specifically, the living arrangements at your address."

"Oh God," I say, rubbing my forehead. "Oh *God*. What did you say?"

"We went with the script we all discussed for this type of situation. That it was our second home, and that you were a friend who had a key, and that we knew you stayed there sometimes, but that we couldn't speak to the nature of your personal life . . ."

"That's good, that's perfect," I tell Lewis. "I don't want you guys to have to lie for me."

Even though they sort of already had. They *do* know the nature of my personal life. They know that I didn't just stop into their "second home" occasionally, but I lived there twenty-four seven up until a couple of months ago. My friends had to lie for me, and it's my worst nightmare.

"What else did the Gordon Price guy say? Is he looking for me? Or Colin?"

Colin's attention is on whatever letter he just opened, but his head snaps up at that.

"I don't know," Lewis says regretfully. "He had sort of this fake nice vibe going on, acting like he was just a curious friend checking in on things."

"He was a passive-aggressive *bitch*," I hear Kurt announce in the background.

"He thanked us for our time and then hung up," Lewis said. "He didn't really indicate if he'd be calling back, or what they were after. I'm so sorry, Char. I can't believe after all this time they'd start sniffing around . . ."

"It's okay, thanks. I've got to run," I say, never taking my eyes away from Colin's. "Let me know if you hear from him again, okay?"

I hang up with Lewis and stare at Colin a moment later. "That was Kurt and Lewis. They got a call from some guy named Gordon Price, who somehow found them and was asking questions—"

"Gordon Price found us too," Colin says, holding up the letter in his hand. "We're under investigation for possible marriage fraud."

FRIDAY, OCTOBER 16

"*O*h God, what was your childhood cat's name again? Taffy? Taco?"

"Taz," Colin says patiently. "And he was just a mouser that lived in the barn, not a beloved pet or anything."

"You had a *barn*? Did we cover that? What color was it? Red? Please say red, it'll be easy to remember."

"It was brown, and don't stress about it. They're not going to care about the color of my parents' barn or a cat I haven't thought about in twenty-five years."

"But—"

"Remember, just keep your answers simple and honest whenever you can," Colin says, as he drapes a gray tie around his neck and begins tying it. "If they ask about the cat, or for whatever reason, the barn, tell them the truth. That I never talk about the cat, and you don't know any details about my childhood barn in Ireland."

"You're right," I say, taking a breath and sitting on the side of his bed. "You're right."

"Do you want to go over the San Francisco living situation again?"

"No, I think I've got it," I say, taking a deep breath. "It was a hard decision, but we made the choice for me to work primarily out of San Francisco because the proximity to Silicon Valley made the most sense for a social media company."

"And I couldn't join, because my specialty is financial law, and my primary clients are on Wall Street."

"Right. And we tried to see each other as often as we could . . ." I stand and begin to pace. "Damn it, we really should have bought plane tickets more than once-a-never. What if—"

"Hey," Colin says, reaching out and pulling both my hands between his much bigger ones. "Remember what we agreed. No *what ifs*. They lead to nowhere good."

I close my eyes and nod, trying to get my racing heart under control. It's been a week since we got the letter informing us of a required meeting with Immigration Services in an hour. It's given us a week to prepare, which I guess I should be grateful for, but I almost worry it has made everything worse. My head feels so full of facts about Colin, about our relationship, about my own life. Everything's so jumbled, half the time I find myself questioning the stuff that *is* real.

"What's going to happen?" I whisper.

"We're going to finish getting ready. We're going to go down to their offices, have a casual chat about how our marriage came about, and then I'll take you for a drink."

I open my eyes. "You make it sound so easy. How are you not freaking out? Also, why are you being so nice to me?"

"Just trying to soften the blow when I tell you that your dress is on backward."

"*What?*" I jerk backward, pulling my hands free of his to tug out the neckline of my dress. I look down and groan when I see the tag taunting me.

"I can't even *dress* myself," I wail. "How am I supposed to pull this off?"

"Charlotte, you are one of the most determined, successful people I know. Has there ever been anything you wanted that you haven't gotten?"

His question hits me right in the solar plexus, because up until a couple of months ago, I'd have cockily said no. That there *isn't* anything I've wanted that I haven't gotten. But looking at Colin now, I'm terrified that that's changing. That I want him more than I've let myself admit, and he's 100 percent, entirely unavailable.

I give him my sassiest smile and blow him a kiss. "Good point. BRB."

"Don't forget your wedding ring," he calls after me.

I stop and whirl around, my eyes wide. "Oh my God. I didn't even think—"

I slap my hand against the side of my head, panicking all over again. "I don't have one! I mean, I had that cheap, crappy one you put on my finger during the ceremony back then, and I wore it for a while, but—*damn*. I should have been wearing it this whole time, and . . . Colin, I don't even know where it is!"

I feel it should be noted that my voice went up about three octaves during that monologue, the last few words coming out as a mouse squeak.

Colin scratches his nose. "Yeah. I figured. To be fair, I didn't think of it either. Rookie move. I'm surprised nobody mentioned it during the party at your mom's."

"I'm not," I say with a sigh. "Everyone thinks we're edgy and modern and weird. They probably thought it was some sort of statement."

Colin goes to his nightstand and pulls out a small box. I assume it's his own wedding band—a boring gold one, if I remember correctly, which I don't, because he hasn't been wearing a wedding band either. At least he *has* one though. At least one of us is prepared.

But instead of putting on his own ring, he hands the blue velvet box to me.

"I picked up a new one for you in case you'd left yours in San Francisco. Or lost it altogether."

"Oh, thank God," I say gratefully, flipping the box open. "You saved my ass—"

I break off when I look down at the ring then glance up, knowing I must look as stunned as I feel.

"Don't be weird about it," he mutters.

"Where did you get this?" I whisper.

"You know exactly where I got it."

I *do* know. Hudson. It's the same ring I was trying on when he came and found me in that antique jewelry store. Not a look-alike. The *exact* same ring.

"When did you—"

"You insisted on getting a coffee before the drive back to the city, and the whole process took you damn near forty-five minutes. I ducked back into the shop and picked it up."

"It did not take forty-five minutes to get that coffee. And I told you, they were hand-grinding the beans—" I break off and hold up a hand. "You know what, it doesn't matter. What matters is . . ." I look down at the ring, still feeling a little dazed. "*Why?* You could have gotten one for thirty-five cents from that weird guy who sets up his table of random crap around the corner."

This ring is thirty-five cents times a thousand and then some.

He shrugs. "If you keep babbling about it, I'm going to take that one back, and the thirty-five cent one from around the corner is exactly what you'll have."

"Okay, okay, I'm quiet," I say, slipping the ring on and then clenching my fist in case he changes his mind and tries to take it back. "Can I at least say thank you?"

"You're welcome. Now, for the love of God, will you go fix your dress?"

I go back to my own room to do just that, but I take a moment to lean back against the closed door to study the ring, hating how much I love it, hating how much I wish he'd given me this ring for a reason other than us trying to convince the government our marriage is the real deal.

And yet, it has to mean *something*. He hadn't just picked out any ring—he'd picked *this* ring. One I hadn't even specifically mentioned I'd liked, he'd just seen me wearing it and known. Somehow he'd known how much I loved it.

And he'd bought it for me.

I fist my left hand and close my right hand over it, closing my eyes for a moment, wanting desperately to know what it means.

Colin knocks on the door. "Charlotte. We're going to be late."

"Coming!" I say, springing into action and peeling my dress over my head to fix it. A few minutes later, I've dressed myself—correctly this time—and Colin and I get into the back of a cab.

The immigration offices where the interview will take place

aren't nearly as far away from our apartment as I'd like. We arrive long before I'm ready, but then, I don't know that anyone's ever ready for this.

"Why am I so much more nervous now than I was back then?" I say out of the corner of my mouth as Colin holds open the door.

"Older. Wiser. More to lose," he says under his breath.

That's for sure.

But when I walk into the office, I deliberately banish my nervousness.

"Hi there," I say with a broad smile, approaching the woman behind the desk.

"Good afternoon." She's friendlier than you'd expect. "How can I help you?"

"I'm Charlotte Spencer, and this is Colin Walsh. Gordon Price requested a meeting with us?"

We'd toyed with the idea of introducing ourselves as Mr. and Mrs. Walsh to present a united front, but doing so at a hotel in a tiny town in Hudson Valley is one thing. Doing it in a government office is another thing entirely. A two-second glance at my ID would give me away as Charlotte Spencer.

Oh, and yes, our IDs with the new, shared address arrived in time. Granted, if they look too closely at the issue date, we're in for a whole slew of questions, but it's a hell of a lot better than me having to show a California driver's license.

"Okay, you're all checked in," the receptionist says, handing us back our IDs. "You're a few minutes early, so Mr. Price will be with you closer to your two o'clock appointment time."

The waiting room is empty except for us. "Ooh, new *Vogue*," I say, picking up the magazine.

Colin glances at it distractedly. "Don't we have that exact same magazine on our coffee table?"

"Yes, and I haven't had a chance to read it yet. It's been a busy week," I tell him pointedly, without looking his way.

He says nothing because he knows exactly how busy my week's been since his has been the same. Flash card trivia over coffee in the mornings as we memorized favorite foods and learned prominent childhood memories. Lunch breaks where we reviewed names of key colleagues and career-defining moments.

And over dinner, we'd defined our . . . um, love story. The moment we met. First impressions. How nervous we were on our wedding day.

Most of it true, but not all of it. A couple of things had to be fudged. The first kiss. The moment we realized we'd fallen for the other person.

The fake answer on that last one for me? Christmas dinner when I was twenty. In this version of our history, I'd watched as Colin patiently cut up my arthritic aunt's prime rib. And to be clear, that moment *actually* happened, and I *do* remember thinking it was sweet. But at twenty, those aren't exactly the things that make a girl's heart skip a beat. At least not the shallow twenty-year-old that I was.

They are the sorts of things that make a thirty-one-year-old woman's heart skip a beat in retrospect, but that's a whole other situation for me to deal with later.

As far as when Colin "fell for me," it was the first moment he saw me. I was wearing short jean shorts, an off-the-shoulder black T-shirt showing a pink bra strap, and he'd been a goner. Allegedly.

Now, as annoyed as I've been with my brother on the whole prenup mess, I will give him credit where it's due. Back when Colin and I went through the interview process the first time, Justin had insisted that we not only write down all of our interview questions and answers verbatim, but that we *keep* them in case we ever got asked the same questions again and needed to be able to ensure our answers lined up with what we said on the record back then.

His foresight saved our asses and might be enough for me to forgive him for the prenup sneakiness. Maybe.

Eventually.

Vogue is open in my lap, but for all my enthusiasm, I don't really see a single photo, much less read a single word. My gaze flits to my right, toward Colin as he reads something on his phone. Should I reach for his hand?

I should. It would be more convincing that we're in love if we're holding hands.

Or will that look like we're trying too hard?

But if we don't try at all, will they suspect? Maybe if I just casually rest my hand on his leg . . .

"Charlotte Spencer and Colin Walsh?" We both jerk to attention and jump to our feet. *Vogue* hits the table with a loud smack.

"Hi, there. I'm Gordon Price, come on back."

Gordon Price looks pretty much like you'd expect him to look. Medium height, medium build. His hair is medium brown; his blue checked shirt is tucked just a little too tight into navy slacks that are just a little too high.

The office is technically the same as when we came the first time ten years ago, but I don't recognize any of it. I'm not sure if that's because they've given it a facelift or because I was blinded by terror. Except I don't remember being blinded by terror. It's like I told Colin, back then I'd been a little jittery but not petrified like I am now.

Colin's right. Age and wisdom are a bitch. At twenty-one, it hadn't really occurred to me that anything in my life wouldn't work out the way I wanted it to. Now, I'm not even *close* to being confident of this going our way.

"Thanks for coming in," Gordon says, leading us into a small office that smells like old coffee. He gestures for us to sit.

Price waits until we're seated, his gaze flicking between the two of us before he gives us a bland smile. "You're wondering why you're here. Why you got that letter."

"Yes," Colin says, as I nod, remembering that for the purpose of this interview, we agreed to do things Colin-style. *Less is more; don't talk too much.*

"Well, I'll come right out with it," Price says. "We received a letter. An email, actually. Someone made the suggestion that perhaps your marriage came about due to Mr. Walsh's desire to become an American citizen."

"Who?" I demand. "Who wrote that letter?"

"Charlotte," Colin says in a low warning tone.

Price smiles, and it's not really nice, but it's not mean, either. To be fair, I don't think this guy wants to be here any more than we do, he's just doing his job.

"I'm afraid that's confidential information, but we do take these allegations seriously and do our due diligence to follow-up. Oftentimes, I get all the reassurance I need that everything is fine with a bit of my own research. But with you two, I have to admit a couple of things did look a little odd to me. Which is why you're here today." He reaches for a file on his desk. "Now, Ms. Spencer— it is Spencer, yes?"

"Yes. I kept my maiden name," I say, then bite the inside of my lip to keep myself from babbling on about how it's nothing to apologize for and *lots* of women do it these days.

"Ms. Spencer, am I understanding correctly that your primary residence has been in California?"

Oh dear. I swallow. "Yes."

"And Mr. Walsh. You live here, primarily. In New York."

"Yes."

Price closes the folder again and leans back in his chair, study-ing us. "Has that always been the case?"

"Mostly," Colin says casually. "Charlie moved back to the city a few weeks ago."

Charlie. Nice touch, although I've never heard him call me that *ever.*

"Why?" Price asks.

"I'm sorry?" Colin asks politely.

"Why did you move back?" Price addresses the question to me.

I give him the rueful smile I've been practicing in the mirror for days. "Maturity, I guess. I've always been pretty driven in my career, and if I'm being honest, I've let that take top priority the past few years. My job needed me in California, so I was in California."

"And that's changed?"

"Yes." On this at least, I'm quite clear and can answer honestly. "My parents live here, and it sort of hit me that they're not getting any younger. And Colin's here, and I realized I want a different sort of marriage than we've had this past decade."

Price's eyes narrow. "A different sort of marriage ... to be honest, what you two have had doesn't look like any marriage at all."

Ooof. The man has surprisingly sharp teeth.

He continues, reciting facts we already know, but that sound really bad said aloud. "You live on different coasts. Three hours' time difference. Ms. Walsh, you've founded a very successful social media company, you're quite active on social media your-self, and yet there's not a single mention or photo of your husband. Your relationship status isn't even mentioned."

"Social media is my job. I deliberately keep my private life private."

Gordon Price stares at me hard, and I try to keep my return gaze steady but non-confrontational. *Nothing to see here.*

His eyes shift back to Colin. "Mr. Walsh, how many times did you go to California to visit your wife?"

"Not as many as I'd like."

Good answer. He's good at this.

"I'm sure. But how many times? Estimate for me," Gordon says with a deceptively casual tone.

Shit. Shit.

Colin pauses for a long moment. "I didn't travel much to California."

"Hmm," Price says with a wan smile. "I'm not really a fan of the Golden State myself. So then, Ms. Spencer. You must have been the one to fly back to New York."

Less is more; don't babble.

I nod, even as my heart pounds. I knew this would come up, but I expected to have a few softball questions to warm up first.

What side of the bed he slept on. His boss's name. What he gave me for Christmas.

Damn it, I know the name of his childhood cat and that he had a brown barn! Ask me that!

Gordon Price does not ask me that.

"Ms. Spencer, how many times did you fly out to New York during the entirety of your marriage? Because I have access to flight records, and if the records are correct, I have you making three trips to JFK. Three. In ten years. And him not flying out to see you once?"

This is not going well. This is *really* not going well.

It's time for Plan B. A Plan B that I kind-of-sort-of didn't mention to Colin. He is *not* going to love it.

But it's necessary.

I let out a gasping sob then put my hand over my mouth, as though wishing I could pull it back. "I'm so sorry. I shouldn't—I promised—"

Gordon Price's gaze sharpens. "Ms. Spencer, if you have something to say, you'll help yourself most by saying it sooner rather than later."

I look nervously at Colin, whose eyes narrow, because we specifically agreed not to look at each other during the interview for answers, knowing it would look nervous.

But it's all part of Plan B.

My chin wobbles.

Forget San Francisco. I should have moved to Hollywood, because, baby . . . I'm about to deserve an Oscar.

I look back at the immigration officer. "I keep thinking it'll get easier—" I roll my lips inward and press my fingers to them, as though holding back another sob before I take a deep breath and press *oh-so-bravely* on. "They say that time heals the wounds, you know, and it has a little, but sometimes it's like I'm right back there again, and it hurts all over again—"

Price leans forward. "Ms. Spencer—"

"Are you married, Mr. Price?"

He's wearing a ring, so I'm pretty confident of my tactic here.

He nods once. "I am."

"So tell me. If you'd found the person you'd fallen in love with—the person you *married*—was cheating ... would you want to see them? Would you fly across the country, forced to be flooded by the memories, the mental images of their hands on someone else?"

Gordon Price blinks in surprise. "You're saying the reason—"

"What you're looking at isn't an illegal marriage, Mr. Price. Just a good old-fashioned relationship broken apart by an affair, and a couple's slow, painstaking attempt to put it back together again."

FRIDAY, OCTOBER 16

❧

"*I* don't know whether to kill you or applaud," Colin says, still looking dazed an hour after we've left our interview.

"Applaud *and* buy drinks. It's the least you can do after the havoc wreaked on my makeup from that performance," I say, gesturing at my still red eyes and general puffiness.

"Where'd you learn to fake cry like that?" Colin asks, lifting a hand to get the bartender's attention.

"I've actually never had to pull that move before. I just did the cliché thing. You know, thinking of the saddest thing I could."

"Delilah's death?" he asks, referring to my second-grade goldfish that lived about as long as goldfish usually live. Delilah had been in my flash cards.

I shake my head. "That wasn't the saddest thing. I remembered my brother ripping the head off my favorite stuffed dog, and the waterworks turned on immediately."

"What was his name?"

"My brother?"

He smiles. "The dog."

"Oh. *Her* name—Ariel. I was in a major *Little Mermaid* phase. But you don't have to gather Charlotte factoids anymore, remember?"

"That's not why I asked," Colin says lightly, turning his attention to the waiting bartender. "Two Vespers, please. Okay?" He glances at me for confirmation, and I nod, annoyed with myself at how much I like the fact that we have a signature drink together.

The downside being that I'll never be able to have that drink and not think of him. I wonder if he'll think of me. Five years down the road, will he and Rebecca sip Vespers together while they talk about where to send little Colin Junior to preschool?

I wrinkle my nose. *Yeeeeah*, I do not want to think about that.

"You could have warned me."

"Hmm?" I turn my attention back to Colin.

"About the interview. You could have mentioned your plan to blame our distance on my infidelity."

"I could have," I say with a grin. "But I wanted the surprise factor. Plus, I figured you'd have just told me not to do it, and then we would've fought about it. And then I'd have done it anyway, and been right, and you'd be in the very uncomfortable position right now of having to admit that you were wrong. So you're welcome."

A month ago, I'm pretty sure my babbling logic would have earned me a stern glare, but now he gives a slight shake of his head and an almost smile. "Your imagination is a spectacle."

"But you would have told me not to brand you a cheater. Right?"

"Probably," he concedes. "I can't say I loved being the villain.

Price was giving me nothing but dirty looks in between handing you tissues."

"Sorry about that," I say, not really that sorry. "I just figured that the entire point of these immigration interviews is to prove that people got married because of their heart, not citizenship status. So, I thought, why not show a *broken* heart? Reframe his image of you from an Irish immigrant to a cheater."

Colin winces. "I would love if we could not call me that."

"Right, sorry," I say, smiling in thanks as the bartender puts an icy-cold cocktail in front of me. "But we did say we'd tell the truth whenever possible. And you *are* in love with another woman, so it's not a lie."

"Except the part where you're completely heartbroken over that fact. That's a lie."

I hesitate for only a fraction of a second. "Right. So there was a little lie. But it worked, so . . . cheers?"

I lift my glass and smile, but Colin doesn't return the smile. Or the gesture.

"About Rebecca. I need to tell you something," he says.

Oooh boy. I take a big sip of my drink and set it back on the bar. "Okay."

"You know she's been struggling with this whole situation."

Understatement. "Yeah."

He scratches his temple, looking uncharacteristically nervous. "I did end up telling her about our trip Upstate a few weeks ago. It didn't feel right to keep it a secret."

"I'm assuming she wasn't thrilled."

"No. And not long after that conversation, she ran into a friend of hers. An ex."

My eyes go wide. "Oh my God. She hooked up with him? *She* cheated? Oh my God, they could make a movie about us. Or a soap opera."

"What? No, she didn't cheat." He frowns. "Why do you automatically go there? She just ran into her ex at a restaurant shortly after she and I got into a fight. They sat down to catch up, had too much wine—"

"Sorry, but how is this not leading up to a cheating story?"

He blows out an impatient breath. "*Anyway*. She told him about the circumstances of our marriage. The real circumstances. And I'm fairly certain the man still has feelings for Rebecca, and he's never liked me. Rebecca fears he's the one who sent the letter to Immigration Services, and I think she's probably right."

"Damn." I take another sip of my drink.

Colin stares at me. "That's all you're going to say?"

"What do you want me to say?"

"Aren't you mad?"

"At him? I don't even know the guy."

"At me. For confiding in Rebecca. At her, for telling her ex and probably resulting in this whole interview process?"

I shrug. "I mean, the situation sucks, but am I mad? No. Not really. Did you think I was going to pitch a fit?" I look at him. "Oh my God, you did!"

He looks at me for a long minute. "You are never what I think you're going to be."

I lift my glass. "Why, thank you!"

Colin rolls his eyes, and then catches me off guard by reaching out and putting a hand in my hair, pulling me toward him. He presses a quick kiss to the side of my head. It's a bit brotherly at first, but the way he lingers, holding me close, is not.

"Thanks," he whispers into my hair.

"For?" My voice is a whisper as well.

I feel him give a quick shake of his head. "I don't know. For being you, I guess."

I run my thumb over my wedding ring and squeeze my eyes shut. The depth to which I've come to care for this man over the past two months takes my breath away.

And the level to which I want him to care for me back nearly breaks me.

Instead, I think of Rebecca.

I pull back and give him a quick smile. "If you're done being weird, can we *cheers* to our victory? It was a victory, right? Price bought it?"

"He seemed to. And he didn't drag me off to be detained," Colin says, drumming his fingers against the bar. "But we still have two more meetings to get through. One of which is a home visit."

"Yeah, I've been thinking about that," I say, pursing my lips. "I have some ideas. What do you think the chances are of you getting that antique desk delivered early?"

SUNDAY, OCTOBER 25

I haven't been avoiding my parents, per se, but Colin and I have agreed to leave them out of the mess we've gotten ourselves into as much as possible, so we've missed the past couple of Sunday dinners.

This Sunday, my mom isn't having it.

Colin and I have been *summoned*. The mandatory, maternal kind of summons that's *way* scarier than any ominous letter from the government accusing you of marriage fraud.

We got to my parents' a few minutes ago, where Colin was immediately tasked with the unenviable job of showing my father how to update Microsoft Office on his Mac, which normally, would be my nightmare, but it beats my task, which is a staring contest with my mother.

I'm a little surprised when I win. She lets out a huffy sigh and takes a sip of her Chardonnay. "I swear, Charlotte, sometimes I just don't know what to do with you."

"I've been here all of ten minutes, and all I've done is compliment your new lipstick. How am I in trouble already?"

"Are you going to tell me what's going on?"

I take a sip of my sparkling water. "Nothing is going on."

She looks perturbed. "I thought we were making progress, and now you're clamming up. Is it The Rebecca Situation?" she asks, her tone implying she'd happily step in and *remove* the situation if I just asked.

I wish.

If I hadn't been watching her closely, I would have missed it— the ever so slight slump of her shoulders at what she perceives as my rejection, before she straightens them again, and pretends a fascination with her bracelet.

"Mom." I wait until she looks up at me. "I'm not shutting you out. I promise. It's just that Colin and I have gotten ourselves into a bit of a mess with Immigration Services . . ."

Her eyes widen in alarm, and I rush to reassure her. "It's fine. We're handling it. But we're trying to keep everyone as far away from the situation as possible. Should they choose to interview you and Dad, the more you can plead the Fifth the better."

She's silent for a long minute, considering this, and then she finally nods. "But if there's anything your father or I can do, you'll let us know?"

"Yes."

"Good. Now. What about the Rebecca situation?"

I let out an exasperated laugh, even as my gaze flits to the door, making sure Colin is still out of earshot in my dad's office. "I already told you—"

"That you weren't going to shut me out," she cuts in, trapping me in my own words. "What's going on there?"

"Nothing. No, it's the truth," I say before she can get on my case again. "Colin and Rebecca are still engaged."

"They're engaged?"

I wince. "Did I not mention that the last time we spoke?"

"No, Charlotte, you did not. I can't believe—how could he propose to her while he was still married to you?"

"I don't think it was a proposal so much as an agreement. But regardless, they're going to get married for real, just as soon as he and I can get un-married for fake."

"And how do you feel about the situation?"

"How do I feel about the situation?"

"Nobody enjoys an echo, dear."

I open my mouth, a saucy comeback on the tip of my tongue.

Then I shock her *and* me.

I burst into tears. Not the dramatic, chin-wobbling fake tears from that day in the immigration office, but real, *true* tears.

The kind that come from the deepest part of you, the kind that reveal your most forbidden secrets.

"Charlotte." My mom makes a *tsk*ing noise as she sits beside me and pulls me to her.

I let her. I let her hold me against her chest as I cling to her upper arm with one hand, my other clenched into a fist as I will the tears to stop, but they don't.

Instead of badgering me to explain my breakdown, she merely holds me, smoothing my hair back occasionally as she lets me cry it out.

"I don't even know why I'm crying," I say brokenly, when I can finally manage to get words out.

"Yes, you do, dear. Yes, you do." She pats my head as she says it, and she's right.

I know exactly what's wrong. I know exactly where these tears are coming from.

All this time I've been so focused on trying to get Colin to like me, that I haven't bothered to guard myself against a much more destructive reality: that I could come to *love* him.

"I feel like I can't stand it," I whisper. "When they're together, whenever he goes to see her, it feels unbearable."

"Have you told him?"

I make a clogged, snorting noise since my nose is plugged from the crying.

"So that's a no then," she says.

"That's a definite no."

"I think maybe you should," she says, easing me gently back into a seated position. "Colin deserves to have all the information. He deserves to know that you care."

I shake my head. "It wouldn't be fair. I can't just swoop into his life after ten years and turn it upside down. At least not more than I already have. He's already had one Spencer screw up the good thing he had with Rebecca when Justin wrote that stupid prenup. I won't make things even worse for him."

"And you think telling him how you feel would make his life worse?"

"I *know* it would," I say with miserable confidence. "He doesn't feel that way about me, Mom. I mean, he doesn't hate me anymore, so that's progress. I'd say, at best, he's hovering in the tolerance range."

"You're a fool to let a man like that get taken right out from under your nose."

I rub my temple. "I guess the doting, sympathetic portion of the evening is over."

"You're *good* together. For each other," Mom says, taking my hand and giving it a hard squeeze. "Why do you think I threw that party? Why do you think I was so determined to make him a part of this family? It's because I saw the very same thing your brother saw back then. *Potential.*"

"Respectfully, you guys are nuts. Back then, Colin and I barely even saw each other when we were in the same room."

"Ten years ago, perhaps. But now? I see you seeing each other," she says with a smug expression.

I rub my temple harder. "Yay. A riddle."

One that I'm thankfully saved from having to solve, as my father and Colin join us in the living room. Both men stop in their tracks when they see the two of us. Well, specifically me, and my not so pretty tear-stained face.

"What's wrong?" Dad asks in alarm.

"Hormones. I'm on my period," I say automatically, knowing from past experience there's no quicker way to get my dad to stop asking questions and back far, far away from the conversation.

As expected, his eyes go slightly wide, and he gives an awkward nod before making a beeline for the bar.

Colin, however, isn't so easily put off. His eyes narrow on me slightly. I try to hold his gaze and adopt a breezy expression, as though it really is just a rogue hormonal fluctuation at work, but the second our eyes lock, I realize my mistake and look away.

I don't have his protective turtle shell. I'm not at all sure that he won't be able to look into my eyes and know every single emotion running through me. Emotions that I'm positive he wants nothing to do with.

My mother's mundane small talk, once the object of my disdain, is my saving grace, and I start to breathe a little easier. The four of us sit in the parlor and conversation turns toward safer topics like the unseasonable snow expected for the week ahead, and whether or not they'll have more trick-or-treaters this year than last year.

At least, I think I'm safe. But when I finally manage to risk a glance at Colin, my breath goes haywire all over again, because he's watching me. Based on the intensity of his gaze, I'm not sure he's ever *stopped* watching me.

My mother's words from just minutes before drift back to me.

I see you seeing each other.

What do you know? I solved the riddle after all.

The question is . . . what do I do with the answer?

THURSDAY, OCTOBER 29

A few days later, I'm on all fours with my ass in the air when Colin comes home.

It's not what it sounds like.

"Charlotte?"

I jump at the unexpected voice, bumping my head on the bottom of the desk and slumping back down with a groan as I put a hand to my throbbing skull.

"Damn it." His voice is more urgent now as he crosses the room and crouches down. "*Charlotte.*"

I grunt and open one eye, still cradling my skull. "*What?*"

"What are you doing under there?" His tone is slightly chiding, but his eyes are concerned, his touch gentle as his fingers brush over my hair. "Are you okay?"

"Go away."

"You're so damn hardheaded, I'm surprised the desk didn't crack. How many fingers am I holding up?"

"I know how many I'm holding up," I say, pulling my hand away from my head to hold up my middle finger.

"Nice. Come on," he says, wrapping his hands around my upper arm and tugging me out from under the desk. "Dare I ask what you're doing on the floor?"

"I was plugging in your new desk lamp."

I let him haul me to my feet, but I bat his hands away when he begins messing up my hair looking for a lump on my head. "Stop. I'm fine. I spent forever getting my hair to look like this, and you're messing it up."

"It looks the same as it always does," he says, giving my hair a skeptical look.

"You're such a guy. I straightened it more than usual. The straight hair says that I'm a respectable professional with a side of doting wife."

"I see. What did your old hair say?"

"Sassy entrepreneur who wasn't about to be pinned down by a male."

He looks again at my hair then shakes his head. "Nope. I didn't get any of that."

"You look nice, Charlotte," I mutter. "Thanks for setting up my office, Charlotte. We're going to nail this interview, Charlotte."

Colin looks around the room, seeming to see it for the first time, a surprised look on his face. "How long have I been gone? It doesn't even look like the same room."

I bend my knees in a quick curtsy. "That's the *other* thing this hairdo says: home decorator extraordinaire."

Actually, I didn't do much of the real work. I had one set of movers come by at ten a.m. to haul away all the bedroom furniture that was in here. At eleven a.m., Colin's antique desk was delivered. After forty-five minutes of me freeing the damn thing from the miles and miles of bubble wrap it was wrapped in, the second set of movers arrived with the rest of the office furniture: an ergonomic desk chair, a couple of navy wingback chairs, an end table, copper bar cart, bookshelf, an antique globe, and even a Ficus.

I check my watch. We have an hour until Gordon Price gets here for the home interview, and the butterflies I've kept at bay all day by staying busy with changing my bedroom into a home office start to flutter.

I blow out a breath. "Okay. I just need to put some actual books on the bookshelf, and I think we're ready. Well, as ready as we'll ever be."

"You're sure your head's okay?" Colin asks, coming to crouch beside me at the bookcase, helping me move the pile of books from the floor to the bookshelves.

"Positive," I say, since the pain's receded almost entirely. "Just a bump."

He glances down at the book in his hand and turns it around so I can see the cover. *The Modern Woman's Guide to Leadership.* "Don't recall this one being in my collection."

"Some of the books have to be mine," I point out. "I'm supposed to live here too, and I can assure you, I wouldn't be touching your Edgar Allan Poe collection. It'll be weird if the room is entirely masculine, with only your stuff."

"Is that why there's a pink glittery stapler on my desk?"

"*Our* desk," I say, patting his knee and standing. "For the rest of the afternoon, it's our desk. Our office. Our home." I look him over. "You should change into something more comfortable."

He lifts his eyebrows.

"Relax. I'm not trying to get in your pants. You look like you just came from the office."

"I *did* just come from the office. Something Gordon will likely understand since he set up the meeting for three p.m. on a Thursday."

"Still, shouldn't we look a little more . . . domestic?"

"Which means what? Levis and slippers?"

"If I took the time to make my beastly hair pin straight," I say, pointing at my head, "the least you can do is ditch the jacket and tie."

"Fine."

He heads into the bedroom, and I take one last look at the office. Not bad—I can practically picture Colin behind the antique desk working, maybe the two of us reading side-by-side in the chairs, my legs draped casually over his knees . . .

I hope Gordon Price can picture it too.

The stack of mail looks a little too neat, so I pick it up and then drop it down again, letting envelopes and catalogs scatter a little, as though one of us tossed it there as an afterthought, the way a normal couple might.

I turn on the lamp and leave the room, going into the bedroom. *Our* bedroom. Because convincing Gordon Price that we sleep in the same bed is sort of a no-brainer if we want him to think we're trying to make this marriage work.

Hence the quick transformation of the second bedroom from guest room to office.

I've known all week what was coming, but I realize now that the *idea* of sharing a bedroom with Colin is different from actually seeing it in practice. Or maybe I just haven't let myself think about how intimate it would be. It's a little strange to see my water bottle and Kindle on one nightstand and his glasses case and book on the other.

Then there's my razor in his shower. Our toothbrushes side by side in his bathroom.

"Charlotte?" he calls from the closet.

"Hmm?"

I go to the walk-in closet where he's standing with his hand on his hips. "What's all this?"

"My clothes," I say, pointing out the obvious. "It'd be sort of a giveaway if I had all my clothes in the second bedroom closet."

"True. But why is it so—"

"Lived in?" I say.

"Messy."

"Well, believe it or not, some people have a wardrobe containing more than two colors."

"Don't you have a system?"

I blink. "A *system*? For a closet?"

He gestures at the haphazardly hung clothes. "To organize them in some way. Color? Season? Fabric."

"No, *dear*. I don't have a system."

"Sometimes I don't know how you get through the day," he grumbles.

"Ooh, that's good," I say. "Be sure and whine about that to Gordon. Classic marriage gripe right there. The uptight neat freak who tries to tame the free spirit."

"An interesting way to phrase the fact that you're a bit of a slob."

"Just because I don't alphabetize my stuff by brand doesn't make me a slob," I argue in exaggeration. "You act like my stuff's all over the floor. My clothes are hanging up!"

"The hangers don't even match."

My eyes go wide then narrow when I see his slight smile. "Oh, that's *really* fantastic. You tell jokes now."

"It's the only way I can think to cope with the pain of this," he says, gesturing at my side of the closet, which, I'll grant, compared to his side does look a little chaotic.

"I'll tell you what," I say. "If we pass this test, I'll let you rearrange my clothes however you want."

"If we pass this test, I can get your clothes out of my closet."

I'm glad his back is still to me, because I flinch at the reminder of just how eager he is to be rid of all things Charlotte. "Right."

I back out of the closet. "Okay, so you sleep on the left side of the bed, me on the right. Or do we sleep in the middle? Do we cuddle?"

He emerges from the closet. He's still wearing the tie, but it's deliberately loosened, and he's lost the suit jacket, his shirtsleeves rolled up to his elbows. "I hardly think Immigration Services is going to ask if we cuddle."

"Especially since you're a cheater," I say, turning toward him.

"Yeah, about that—what are you doing?" he asks in alarm as I reach out for his shirt.

I tug one side of it, pulling it upwards until the tail of his shirt is just *barely* tucked into his slacks.

"Trying to make you look relaxed," I say. "As though this is your haven, and when you walk in the doors, you let loose."

"I can't let loose with my shirt tucked in?"

I shake my head. "No wonder our marriage is crumbling."

I sit on the side of the bed and rub at the still slightly sore spot on my head from where it hit the desk.

He gives me a concerned look. "You're sure you're all right?"

I drop my hand. "My head's fine. But I have butterflies."

"About the interview?"

I nod. "I don't think my acting skills are up to snuff. I have no idea how to play the part of a woman who fell in love with her brother's best friend ten years ago, married him on a whim, got her heart broken when he cheated, ran away to California, stayed there out of pride, then came back to valiantly try to patch things up, all while trying to plant seeds that it's not working so there won't be a complete shock when you file for divorce in a month."

He slowly sits on the bed beside me. "Well. Thanks to your stellar performance last week, I think it'll probably be better if it's *you* that files for divorce."

"I just couldn't get past the betrayal," I say in a shaky voice, as though holding back tears.

He smiles a little grimly but doesn't respond.

I look down at my hands. "What does Rebecca think about all this?"

"She'll be as glad as the rest of us when it's all over."

More so, probably. "Does she know about . . ." I jerk my thumb behind us at the bed we're sitting on.

"That I'll be sleeping on the couch tonight?"

"I already told you I can sleep on the couch. It's your bed."

He shakes his head. "No. You've already done enough."

"Right. The office," I say. My voice sounds a little flat to my own ears.

"I was going to say your efforts with your hair. You're right. On second look, it does say everything you want it to say. It's practically screaming domestic bliss."

I smile because I know, in a rare role reversal, he's trying to cheer me up, even though I'm not exactly sure why I'm feeling so glum. Or rather, I do know. I just don't know what to do about it.

I don't realize I'm twisting my wedding ring until I see Colin watching the absent gesture, his expression darkening slightly, and I wonder if he's regretting giving me the ring.

"You can have it back when we're done," I say.

He frowns. "What?"

I hold up my left hand. "It's too much. I know what it costs, and it's way too much given our . . . situation."

"Keep it," he says gruffly.

"But—"

"*Keep it.*"

"Well, I guess you can't do anything with it," I say. "You probably don't want to drive all the way to Hudson to return it. Oh, I know! You could give it to Rebecca!"

He lets out a surprised laugh at my cheerful sarcasm. "That should go over well. Besides, it's not her style."

I scowl, slightly offended. "It's gorgeous. It's everyone's style."

"She's more . . . modern."

"Ah." I twist the ring. "I am too, usually, but this one . . . it's special."

There's another moment of silence.

"So you two have talked about rings?" I ask softly. "Have you shopped yet?"

This sense of not really wanting to know while also really needing to know is increasingly familiar and highly annoying.

Colin shakes his head and stands. "I'm not going to talk about ring shopping with one woman who's not even here, while I'm in the same room as a woman who's supposed to be my wife. You *are* my wife."

The words cause an ache deep inside of me, but I force a bright smile. "Good! That's good. That tone's exactly what you should use in front of Gordon Price."

"What tone?"

"You know." I flex my muscles and squeeze my own bicep. "All manly and possessive. It's good. Husbandly. Like I'm *yours*. Have you been practicing?"

Colin doesn't have a chance to answer because the doorbell rings.

My eyes go wide. "Is that him? I told the guys at the front desk to let him up whenever he got here, but he's super early!"

"It's a smart tactic," Colin says grimly. "Catching people off guard before they can put the final polish on."

"Well, he already knows our relationship's got a bit of tarnish," I say as we head down the hall to the front door. "All we have to do is convince him that everything was shiny and new back in the beginning."

He nods in agreement, glancing down at me before opening the door. I feel a moment of panic—a moment of *something*—and reach out and grab his hand. He squeezes my fingers briefly, his gaze holding mine before dropping my hand and opening the door.

THURSDAY, OCTOBER 29

"*W*e did it," I say, dropping into the new chair in the home office in a daze. "Holy crap, I think we actually *did* it."

"Well, I'm sure your descriptive accounts about our sexual proclivities helped," Colin says, handing me a glass of Champagne.

"It wasn't *that* pornographic. He just asked if you were a neat freak in all areas, and I said, no, not always. That in the more intimate areas of your life, you were actually quite—"

"Yeah," he interrupts. "I was there. I remember."

"This is good," I say, looking at the glass of Champagne in surprise. "What is it?"

"Expensive," he says, dropping into the chair beside me. "Think that bottle I bought for the halfway mark, and double it."

"Well, it was worth it. And we have plenty to celebrate," I say, lifting my glass. "Gordon Price all but told us that the third and final interview would just be a formality."

"Thanks to you," he says, watching me. "I'm fairly certain you saved the day yet again this afternoon by mentioning Rebecca's ex."

"I did, didn't I?" I say smugly, pulling my legs beneath me. "I figured if he knew *we* knew who'd tipped him off about our marriage and knew that the person had a personal vendetta, it might diffuse some of his interest."

"He didn't seem all that interested to begin with," Colin says, studying his Champagne.

"No, not really," I agree.

As nerve-racking as today had been, Gordon Price had seemed more like bored government employee than shark out to expose us for the frauds we were. His questions had been rote, his demeanor indifferent. Either he'd been trying to lull us into complacency so that we'd relax too much and slip up and spill the beans, or he'd been truly disinterested.

Mostly he'd wandered from room to room, checking boxes, asking the exact same questions I'd found on the Internet, with no follow-up. Who cooked? Me. Did I know how Colin took his coffee? Black. Who was the messy one? Me. What side of the bed did we sleep on? Left, him; right, me. Did my messiness bother Colin? "Most assuredly, yes."

On that, at least, he'd been able to answer quite honestly.

Just like I had quite honestly "let it slip" that Colin's lover had an ex with a vendetta who'd love nothing more than to see Colin deported. Gordon Price, God bless him, had eaten it up.

"Two down, one to go," I say, lifting my hand for a high five.

He stares at my hand. "Must we?"

"I saved our ass, remember?" I say. "You owe me."

He obliges me, slapping my palm. "Guess you were right about the hair."

I make a primping motion. "Don't get used to it. Tomorrow it goes back to tousled waves."

"The hairstyle has a name?"

I shake my head. "Of course it has a name. Jeez. You know—Rebecca owes me. I'm like your wife training wheels, teaching all the things you need to know about living with a woman, starting with the importance of our hair."

He gives a distracted nod and sips his bubbly. "I didn't realize the third and final interviews would take place with us separated."

"Me neither," I say. "But I guess it makes sense, separating the couples so we don't know what the other said. Come to think of it, you'd better bring your A-game." I point my drink at him. "I won't be there to save you that time, so don't screw it up."

He scrunches up his face in concentration. "Just so I'm clear, I should or should not mention that you and I had exchanged fewer than a hundred words prior to saying *I do*, and that I *really* wanted that green card . . ."

"Another joke!" I say, delighted. "I'm rubbing off on you."

"God save me." But he's smiling as he says it, and I can't help but think how far we've come in two short months, from two strangers literally counting down the days until this hell was over to . . .

Well, whatever we are now. I don't know that there's a name for it.

"Want to order in?" he asks.

I look up in surprise. "You're not having dinner with Rebecca?"

"She has a client meeting," he says, flipping through his phone. "Thai or pizza?"

I stifle disappointment that he's only doing dinner with me because she's not available, which I know is ridiculous. Rebecca is someone he chose. I'm someone he's stuck with. But selfishly, I'll take whatever time I can get with him, so I push the glum aside.

"How about Thai?" I say. "No, pizza. No! What about tacos? Ooh, or that Indian we ordered last week was super yummy. Or maybe—"

He holds his cell phone. "Thai. Ordered."

"You don't even know my order!"

"Coconut shrimp, chive dumpling, pad Thai, and you'll help yourself to my green curry without asking, eat half of it, and then tell me all the reasons you don't love it."

"Nice." I nod in approval. "Keep it coming with all this domestic discontent, especially during your solo meeting with Gordon Price. You'll sell not only our marriage but also our impending divorce."

"Only one month to go," he says, lifting his glass.

I manage to raise mine in an answering toast.

But I can't quite manage a smile to go with it.

THURSDAY, OCTOBER 29

⌒

"*D*id you find the spare sheets?" I call out, pulling Colin's pillow off his side of the bed. He's got a surprising amount of pillows on the bed for a guy who lives alone, and the Thai food churns a little in my stomach as I wonder if the mountain of extra pillows is Rebecca's touch. I wonder how many times she's slept over, I wonder . . .

No. *That's enough.* I'll *never* be able to get to sleep in this bed if I continue with that train of thought, and I'm not up for another fifteen-minute argument with Colin over who takes the couch.

If I had to guess, I'd imagine Colin a single pillow kind of guy, but on the off chance he likes a mountain of them, I grab three of them off the bed.

"Colin?" I call, tilting my head up so my voice can carry over the pile of pillows. "Did you hear what I said about the spare sheets? I put them in the—"

The rest of my sentence ends with an *oomph* as I step into the hallway and collide with something—some*one*. The pillows thump softly to the floor.

"What was the plan, building a fort?" Colin asks, as we both lean down to pick up the pillows.

"Nope. Smothering. I wanted to try out a couple different ones, see which felt the best as I held it over your face."

"Uh-huh. Also, I've already got a pillow," he says, a pillow under each arm, leaving me holding just one. "I grabbed the one in the linen closet with the guest sheets."

"Yeah, but these are *your* pillows. If you're going to have to sleep on the couch, your head should at least have a pillow that knows how to cradle your skull—"

"What are you—cradle my skull—you know what, never mind. Just never mind." He shakes his head and moves past me into the bedroom, tossing the pillows back on the bed.

"Well, I need the one that cradles *my* skull," I call over my shoulder, going to the living room couch and swapping the pillows.

I'm staring dubiously at the couch as he comes back into the living room. He's wearing flannel pants and a navy T-shirt; I'm wearing his boxers and undershirt, which has become my nightly uniform. As grumpy as I was about having to give up my expensive silk pajama set, I have to admit, the new PJs are growing on me. There's a certain comfort in oversized cotton.

Especially when, even after the wash, they still smell a tiny bit like Colin. At least that's what I tell myself. And yes. I am well aware that I'm acting like a crazy, obsessed weirdo. Don't worry. It'll fade when I move out, and he moves on. Probably.

"What's your issue?" he asks, coming to stand beside me as I stare at the makeshift bed. "Is that pillow not going to adequately *cradle my skull*?"

"I think you're going to have bigger problems than the pillow."
I point. "The couch is too short for you."

"I'll sleep on my side."

"You sleep on your back."

"How do you know?"

"It's what I told Gordon Price," I say.

"Who didn't ask, by the way."

"Well, I also shared a room with you in Hudson."

"And what, you watched me sleep?" he asks.

Maybe.

"And then there was the morning I brought you flowers in bed."

"Which I neither asked for, nor wanted."

"They were pretty!"

"They were, until they died and basically created their own
compost pile."

"File that one away too," I say, patting his arm. "Good marriage spat and divorce fuel stuff."

"You're really obsessed with this divorce material," he says,
looking down at me.

I turn to face him, hugging the pillow to my chest. "Well, that's
the whole reason I'm here in New York, isn't it? So we could live
together, in order to divorce?"

He studies me, his bright blue eyes even more piercing than
usual. "Do you regret it?"

I pluck at the tag of the pillow that's poking out from the pil-
lowcase. "We couldn't stay married forever. And while I'm still
pissed at Justin for this whole mess, I guess now is as good a time
as any to see it through and move on."

He nods. "You excited to get back to San Francisco?"

"Actually, I don't know that I'm going back."

He blinks. "What do you mean?"

"Well, I'll have to go back to California for a while, at least. My company's there, my apartment. But being back here in New York has felt really right. I want to mend things with my parents, continue reconnecting with past friends. I've been toying around the idea of starting something new, and New York's just as good a place to do that as San Francisco. *Better*, in some ways."

I haven't really realized that was the plan until I say it out loud. But saying it makes me realize how right it feels. There will be a lot of details to work out, obviously. Friends to say goodbye to, colleagues who will be more than a little shocked, but even knowing there will be some pain, I feel excited.

Colin had been right when he told me I seemed bored whenever I talked about my job, but diving a bit deeper, I've realized I'm bored when I think about San Francisco too. Not because the city itself is boring. I love that city.

But I'm also realizing that it's served its purpose. California was a place, first, for me to escape. And after that, a place to grow up. But it's time for the next chapter, and my gut tells me that chapter's here in Manhattan.

Colin is still staring at me in disbelief. "You're staying here."

"Well, not *here*," I say, gesturing around our apartment. "That might be a little cozy once Rebecca moves in. Unless you're moving to her place—or getting a new place, or—"

"We haven't talked about it yet."

I swallow. "Well, anyway. I don't really know the details, and I haven't decided for sure, but if I do stick around, maybe we could like, you know . . . be friends."

"Friends."

"Yeah, like ... maybe we could even double date!" I say brightly.

"With whom?"

"With you and Rebecca!" I say, exasperated.

"And? You and—?"

"Well, I'm not seeing anyone yet, but eventually I will. But look, if it's too weird, I'll get it. Even though we won't be exes in the traditional sense of the word, I can totally see how Rebecca wouldn't exactly love spending time with your ex-wife."

And how I wouldn't exactly love spending time with your current wife.

"Yeah. Sure. We'll figure it out," Colin says.

It's a classic blow-off, and I know chances of my double date scenario ever happening are slim to none, and that's probably a good thing.

"I'll miss you though," I blurt. "I mean I'll miss this. I'll miss ..." *Hmm.* "This whole situation hasn't been as bad as I thought it would be."

"Such lofty compliments." His eyes warm as he gives me a slow smile that's *extremely* appealing.

"Yeah, well. Don't let it go to your head."

He looks amused at the cliché, slightly lame comeback. His smile turns a bit cocky, as though he knows I'm off my game. Worse, as though he knows *why* I'm off my game.

"Right. Well, if you're sure about sleeping out here ... good-night." Still hugging the pillow, I step to the side to move toward the bedroom.

Colin moves at the same time, trying to move out of my way,

but moving in the same direction as me, blocking my path. I move to the other side just as he does the same, so we're doing that awkward "you go, no, *you* go" dance.

I let out a laugh, but it's more of an exhale because I suddenly realize how close we're standing. I freeze, my eyes lifting to his.

There's no hint of a smile on his face now, and his eyes seem to burn both bleak and hot as they lock onto mine.

His head dips lower, and I feel his breath on my cheek. "Charlotte."

"Colin," I whisper back.

He swallows and eases even closer, his gaze leaving mine to drop to my lips.

His eyes close, but other than that he doesn't move, his expression as tortured as I feel. "Damn it, Charlotte," he says on a breath, his voice rough.

My eyes drift closed as I feel his minty breath against my mouth, and even though I know it's so, so wrong, I *will* him to kiss me. I send a silent prayer to the heavens to do everything else right in my life to make up for this one wrong moment that I want more than I've ever wanted *anything*.

It feels as though we're locked in time, not touching, but not moving away from each other either, a million things passing between us that we don't dare say.

"I can't," he whispers, still close enough that I can *feel* the rejection.

Then he steps back and the air goes colder, my heart growing a little colder with it.

"Goodnight," he says, his voice rough as he stands a safe, respectable distance away from me.

"Night." My eyes water as I say it, and I move quickly past him before he can see the tears.

I go to the bedroom. I lie down on the bed.

I do not sleep.

MONDAY, NOVEMBER 2

❧

"*Y*our support means a lot to me, truly," I say into the phone as I pace around my temporary office space. "Yeah, it'll be a big change, for sure, but I know I'm leaving the company in good hands. And I'll still be around, just not in the day-to-day—"

I pause in my conversation with my CFO, giving a jolt of surprise when I see Colin standing in the open doorway. "Hey, Brian, I'm so sorry, but something just came up. Can I call you back in a bit?"

"You didn't have to hang up," Colin says, stepping all the way into the office as I end my call.

"Really?" I ask dubiously. "The expression on your face says otherwise."

"What expression?"

"The one that says you're making a rare emergence from your turtle shell. Not to mention the fact that you're here in the first place, when I didn't even know you knew where I worked."

"It was on the flash cards we exchanged about each other."

"Oh, right." He still hasn't moved, and I tap my phone against my palm as I watch him, trying to figure out what's wrong. "Sorry, I don't have a place to sit."

The office space I'm renting is really just more of a glorified cubicle, though with closed-in walls. It's got a desk, a chair, an ugly lamp, and really good Wi-Fi. Mostly, it's a place to get me out of the house when I'm feeling restless and all the tables are full at Starbucks, which in New York, is basically always.

"No, it's fine," Colin says, looking embarrassed. "I should have texted. Or maybe I shouldn't have come at all." He runs a hand over the back of his neck then drops his arm. "I didn't know who else to talk to."

My heart does something stupid and flippy that I am the one he's turning to. "You can always come to me."

"It's about Rebecca."

Or maybe not always *me*. Because my heart does something else now, decidedly less happy, at the knowledge that he's here to talk about another woman. A woman he plans to marry.

Still, I care about this man. A lot. And that means being here for him in the way he needs me to be, not how I want it to be in my daydreams.

"Ah." I step around him and shut the door. I usually leave it open because it can get stuffy, but I know him well enough by now to know that if he doesn't have complete privacy, there's every chance of him retreating to his shell.

"What happened?" I ask.

He sets his bag on my chair and goes to the window, staring through the glass, I imagine without really taking much in since the "view" is really just of the rooftop of the neighboring building. It doesn't offer much to look at besides pigeon poo.

He shoves his hands into his pockets. "I told her about the in-home interview with immigration. About how things went well and that we only had one more to go before we were in the clear."

"That must have made her happy."

"You'd have thought," he says in a low tone. "But then she asked about worst-case scenario—what would happen if Gordon Price *did* find us guilty of marriage fraud."

I tap my fingers on my cheek. "Well. Maybe she should have thought about that before telling her ex-boyfriend about us."

He gives me a sardonic look over my shoulder "I thought you weren't mad about that."

I grin. "I may have decided that I'm a little peeved after all."

He gives me a faint smile, though I'm pretty sure he knows I'm just trying to distract him by lightening the mood.

Colin turns back to the window. "So, I told Rebecca the truth. That we felt good about everything going our way, but if it didn't . . . we could be in a bit of trouble."

"*You'd* be in a bit of trouble," I say jokingly, leaning back onto the desktop. "I'd be in *a lot* of trouble."

"We've talked about this," he says, turning to face me. "You'd likely be looking at a fine. Jail time would be . . ."

"Unlikely, I know," I say.

And it's true. From what I understand, while technically people can be jailed for marriage fraud, it's generally only the people that facilitate fraudulent marriages on a large scale. When it comes to private citizens, it's a slap on the wrists, and writing a really big check, which I'm prepared for.

And hey, if I end up in prison . . . adventure, right?

Just kidding. I *really* don't want to go to prison. And to be honest, I do my damnedest not to think about it. Though, since we've brought it up . . .

"You know, you'd think she'd be thrilled with the possible repercussions," I say. "Let's not pretend that Rebecca doesn't hate my guts. Me having to write a six-figure check or get put behind bars must just tickle her."

"Probably," he surprises me by agreeing. "But we didn't really get that far in the conversation."

"I see," I say, understanding. "She wanted to know what would happen to *you*."

"That's the thing, she already knows," he says. "I've told her from the very start that worst-case, I get deported back to Dublin and can't ever come back to the States."

"She probably didn't love that."

"No. But in the past, we've always talked about it in a speculative way. It was never a real possibility."

"But it's real now."

"Yes." He clears his throat. "It's a little more real. A part of me has been mentally preparing for it, and I wanted to prepare her for it too."

He's been mentally preparing to be deported?

I have a million questions, but I stay silent, letting him gather his thoughts and say what he needs to say at his own pace. He turns all the way toward me, shoving his hands even deeper into his pockets, looking heartbreakingly vulnerable.

"I asked if she'd come with me if it came to that," Colin says quietly. "I asked if, hypothetically, she'd move to Dublin and start a life with me there."

My chest feels like it cracks a little in pain for him, because I already know Rebecca's answer from the fact that he's here and from the look on his face, but he says it aloud anyway.

"She *laughed*," he says. "She said she had no intention of throwing away everything she worked for to move to a place like Ireland."

His eyes are wounded. "What does that mean?" he asks. "A place like Ireland? She's never even *been* to Ireland."

We've established that I've never been particularly fond of the future Mrs. Walsh. And right now, I'm feeling something *much* stronger than dislike. But my feelings aren't what matters right now.

"That sucks," I say with a slow nod. "It *really* sucks. But keep in mind that you've been asking a lot of Rebecca lately. Her fiancé is living with another woman. Her fiancé is looking at being deported. Her ex-boyfriend is partially to blame for that. If I had to guess, I'd say Rebecca's probably not thinking too clearly. None of us say the right thing when we're mad and scared."

"You do," he says, surprising me.

"Hardly," I say, meaning it. "I just haven't been mad or scared in a while."

"Are you sure?" he asks softly.

My breath catches, because I have a sense that he can see all the way inside me to my biggest fear these days: losing him.

I force a lighthearted shrug. "Life is short. I just don't really see the point in wasting any more time than necessary being angry or fearful."

His expression turns thoughtful. "I've noticed that about you. It's . . ."

"Weird?" I supply.

"Refreshing," he counters slowly. "I was going to say it's refreshing."

"You're getting much better at the compliment game," I tell him. "But seriously, give this thing with Rebecca a day or two. I think she'll come around."

I pick up my purse, and he frowns. "You're leaving?"

"We're leaving," I say, lifting his briefcase off the floor and handing it over.

"Where are we going?"

"I'm taking you to lunch."

"Why?"

"Don't ask stupid questions," I say, leading him towards the elevators.

"Where?"

I sigh. "There's an Irish pub around the corner, and I'll tell you right now, we are ordering Guinness from the bar, and I don't want to hear a single peep from you about how it's 11:32 a.m."

The elevator beeps, and I move to step into it, but Colin grabs my hand and gives it a deliberate squeeze.

He lingers just for a second, then drops my hand before I can register the unexpected show of affection, much less analyze what it means. He steps into the elevator, holding the doors for me as I follow him.

"What was that?" I ask, feeling fluttery.

"Don't ask stupid questions."

WEDNESDAY, NOVEMBER 4

⌒

"*H*old on, coming," I mutter, wiping my damp hands on my blouse since the dish towel had an unfortunate incident involving a carton of chicken stock, and I haven't gotten around to getting a fresh one yet.

I tend to go *all in* when I cook, so I answer the knock at the door on autopilot, my brain still distracted wondering how much the dish will suffer because I forgot to get ginger from the store.

But all thoughts of my stir-fry scatter to the wind when I open the front door. "Oh. Hello."

Up until this point, I'd thought Rebecca's icy scowl was the scariest thing I'd ever seen. But nope. This facsimile of a smile she's pointing my way is much, much worse.

"Hi, Charlotte," she says in a sugary sweet tone. She presses her hands together in a pleading motion. "I'm so sorry to stop by unexpectedly like this. Do you mind if I come in?"

"Sure," I say, stepping aside and gesturing her to enter. "But Colin's not here. He's—"

"Attending a networking event in Midtown, I know."

She says it casually, but I've little doubt that there's nothing offhand about the comment. She's staking her claim, letting me know that *she* gets to announce Colin's whereabouts, not me.

"So." I gesture outward with my hands. "What can I do for you?"

Rebecca glances over at the kitchen, which is, as usual while I'm in the middle of a cooking adventure, a complete mess.

"You cook?" she asks.

"Not well, but I enjoy the process of it."

Her eyes narrow just the tiniest bit. "How adorably . . . domestic."

She doesn't even bother to hide the snideness in her voice, and I don't bother to get riled up. Clearly, she thinks my comment also came with an agenda, as though my stir-fry ambitions have to do with impressing Colin into thinking I'm a perfect little woman, as opposed to my real motivation: hunger.

I don't know why, since by my estimation, she doesn't deserve it, but I try to put my mind at ease. I think a part of me hopes the woman is wretched because she's threatened, and if I can just convince her that yes, Colin and I really are getting divorced in a few weeks, regardless of my cooking abilities, she'll finally be nice.

"I took a couple of cooking classes after I'd been in San Francisco a few years," I say with a friendly smile. "Cooking for one takes some getting used to, but I started to get tired of takeout."

See? Not trying to steal your man with my domesticated ways.

Don't get me wrong—I want her man. But he's made his choice, and I'm doing my best to respect it.

Rebecca gives me a plastic smile then looks pointedly at the living room. "Can we sit?"

"Of course," I say, even as warning bells sound a little louder in my head at the sense that while I may not have an agenda at the moment, she *definitely* does.

She precedes me into the living room, gesturing at the couch across from the chair she takes, as though welcoming me to her kingdom. As though I don't live here. As though I hadn't picked the throw pillow she's arranging behind her back. As though I'm not sitting on the same couch where Colin sleeps. As though I'm not the one that folded his blankets and sheets this morning after he got called into an unexpected early meeting.

I see her gaze lock onto the folded bedding and pillow I haven't yet bothered to put away, and I see the slightest flicker of relief cross her face. *Yes, Rebecca. He sleeps on the couch.*

Her eyes are slightly friendlier when they come back to me. Slightly.

"Look, Charlotte, I just wanted . . . well, to be honest, I wanted to apologize."

"Oh. Wow, okay!" I say, doing a terrible job of hiding my surprise. "What for?"

There are so many things . . .

"I've been *such* a bitch to you," she says with a smile that makes me realize how pretty she is. Makes me realize, maybe, what Colin sees in Rebecca. Her teeth are *perfect*. Maybe he's a tooth-man. And I bet her hair never frizzes. I bet she never has to tame it into submission for various looks—I bet her hair only has one look: thick and shiny.

"It's a difficult situation," I say, defaulting to my favorite go-to line for anything having to do with this woman.

"*Thank you* for saying that," she gushes. "It really is. I wish

Colin understood that better. I mean, I've known since the beginning that you had this *arrangement*, but I guess it was just . . . it was much harder to see you in person. To know that he was living with you. And well, you're not exactly a dog."

She gives a tinkling laugh, and I force a smile. "It's not a problem. I can't imagine how weird this must be."

Apology accepted. Are we done now?

"Very weird," she says in agreement. "And I haven't been handling it well. In fact, just the other day I made . . ." She sighs. "I've just been so *frustrated*, so freaked out, and I let Colin think . . ."

"That you wouldn't move to Ireland with him?"

Her eyes turn to ice.

Oops. I've just let it slip that he confided in me about their relationship, and I'll be really honest with you: I can't say for certain I didn't let it slip on purpose.

"He told you about that?" No sign of her perfect teeth now.

"Well, it's just . . ." I wave my hand around the apartment, grasping for a way out of this conversation. "We share a space, and we tend to step on each other's business a lot. It wasn't a big deal. But things are better with you two now?" I ask, hoping to distract her.

She smiles again, but the gaze remains cold and hard. "Much better, thank you. In fact, you may as well be the first to know . . . it's official!"

She thrusts out her left hand with a flourish, and . . . wow. *Wow.*

I'm really glad I'm sitting down, because I feel a little light-headed all of a sudden.

The ring on her fourth finger is massive. I don't know how I missed it before, but there's no avoiding its sparkle now, nor the way it seems to have sliced through my heart from three feet away.

"You finally went ring shopping," I manage.

"Yes, finally," she says, pulling her left hand back in to admire it. "I can't wear it in public yet, obviously. We have to wait another month until . . ." She waggles her fingers over me. "You know. The divorce. And then we'll probably wait a bit longer so as not to raise eyebrows. But at least when it's just the two of us, I can wear this and know that he's mine."

I barely manage to hold back my laugh at the lack of subtlety. There it is. Her real motive for stopping by. *To apologize, my ass.* She's here to remind me in no uncertain terms that Colin is hers, and she has the big-ass rock to prove it.

Well, sorry to steal your thunder, lady, but I've known he wasn't mine long before he put that behemoth on your finger.

"Have you set a date yet?" I ask, not because I want to know, but because if I have any shot at remaining in Colin's life after this is over, I'm going to have to at least try to make nice with this woman.

"No, we just want to enjoy being engaged," she says in a dreamy voice, still ogling her own ring.

"Well, I'm really happy for you guys."

A total lie, but I don't feel bad about it, because I'm *trying* to be happy, and I'd like to think that counts for something.

"Thank you," Rebecca says, standing. "I just wanted you to be the first to know, since . . . well, as you said—this whole thing is a difficult situation, and transparency will make it as painless for all of us as possible."

"Yes, definitely," I say, as we walk to the door. "I'm glad the end is in sight."

"Me too. And between us girls," she leans forward, conspiratorially, her left hand lifted to reveal her big ring *and* her crossed fingers, "fingers crossed that you two *sail* through that immigration interview tomorrow. I'll do what I have to do for that man, but the idea of moving to Ireland." She gives a drastic little shudder.

I'm all out of fake smiles now, so I open the front door with an icy coolness that would make my mother extremely proud. "I'll let him know you stopped by."

"Oh, don't tell him," she says breezily. "We swore we wouldn't tell a single soul about the engagement being official. He's just terrified about anyone catching wind of it and anything messing up the divorce process. I think he lives in constant fear you'll change your mind and refuse to sign the papers or something."

"Trust me. I'll have no problem signing those," I say with a cheerful smile. Oh look. I *do* have one more fake smile left. I paste it on as I calmly close the door in Rebecca's face.

I turn around, intending to return to my stir-fry, but my legs don't move. Instead, I lean back against the door, my breath coming in huge gulps as my eyes water. I lift my own left hand, looking at the antique flower ring. Older than hers. Less expensive.

Infinitely more perfect.

But given for a different reason than Rebecca's. And it's a crucial difference.

Rebecca's words cycle on repeat in my head. *I think he lives in constant fear you'll change your mind and refuse to sign the papers.*

I lose my battle with my tears, and I realize I can't do this anymore. I don't *want* to do this anymore. But more than what I want for me is what I want for *him*.

It doesn't occur to me until this very moment that this is what real love is about—wanting what's best for the other person. Wanting their happiness above your own because you love them.

Like I love Colin.

I wipe my tears on the back of my hand and go to the kitchen, picking my cell phone up off the counter.

I call my brother.

He doesn't pick up, but I don't expect him to since it's six hours ahead and I'm sure he's in bed.

Normally I'd just text, but there are some things better said aloud. I wait patiently through his nonsense voicemail recording, wait for the beep. And leave a message.

"Hey Justin, it's your favorite sister. Call me back as soon as you get this. I need some legal advice. It's about that stupid prenup agreement . . ."

WEDNESDAY, NOVEMBER 4

I'm wiping down the kitchen counters when Colin gets home a couple of hours later.

"Hey," he says, coming into the kitchen. "The scene of the crime must have been worse than usual tonight. It's nearly ten o'clock and you're still cleaning."

"Stir-fry. Lots of chopping."

"Did you eat any of it?" He glances down at two generous Tupperware containers I have yet to lid and put in the fridge.

"It made more than I expected." *And no, I didn't eat any of it. Your fiancée and her big ass ring stole my appetite.* "Help yourself."

"Already ate, but I'll take some for lunch tomorrow if it's up for grabs."

I make an *all yours* gesture at the Tupperware and swipe the rest of the crumbs into the sink.

I feel him watching me. "You all right?"

"Yeah. A little tired, and a headache that came out of nowhere."

"Stressed about the interview tomorrow?"

"Oh, you mean where one wrong word can get you banished to Ireland and me put in jail? Nah. Cakewalk."

I'm actually *not* that stressed about the final interview with Gordon Price tomorrow. I mean, I am. Of course I am. But not as much as you'd think. I've been a people person my entire life. I know how to read them, and I'm nearly always right. It's why I'm so sure that Gordon Price doesn't particularly care about Colin and me, beyond thinking Colin's a bit of a sleaze for cheating on his new wife, and I'm a bit of an idiot for sticking around so long.

He thinks we're guilty. Of being pathetic. Not of breaking the law.

But my excellent people-reading skills are also what have me feeling slightly queasy right now. Because just as I know Gordon Price is more or less harmless to Colin and me, I know that Rebecca is not so harmless.

And I know that no amount of me loving Colin gives me any right to stand in the way of him and Rebecca.

"All done!" I say brightly, putting the counter spray away and placing the Tupperware into the refrigerator. "Have a good night!"

I'm heading back toward my bedroom, but Colin steps in front of me, blocking my way.

I stop and look up at him. "What's up?"

His gaze takes its time, seeming to study my every feature before he frowns. "I'm missing something."

You're missing a lot of somethings.

"I told you. A little tired, a little headache, a little stress. I just need a bubble bath and a good night's sleep."

"All right," he murmurs. "All right." And then he steps

forward, his hands slipping around my waist and pulling me a little roughly against him.

A hug, I realize, after the jolt of awareness passes. Just kidding, it doesn't pass. But other things mingle with awareness as he pulls me into an embrace that's not quite sexual, but not quite platonic either. Want. Longing. Love.

Colin's arms wrap all the way around my waist, and my arms lift of their own accord to fold behind his head. He lowers his head slowly until his face is tucked into my neck, his breath warm against my skin.

I don't know what this is. It's less than a kiss, but it's also more than a hug, and for a moment something like anger splinters through me that he could be putting a ring on her finger one day, and holding me like this the next.

And though I know I should step back, the selfish part of me who knows my time with him is coming to a rapid end closes my eyes and pulls him closer.

I don't know how long we stay locked together. Minutes. Hours. Days.

He pulls back slightly and I force my arms to release him, to let him go. But instead of backing away from me, Colin pauses with his mouth just inches from mine, his gaze reflecting my own longing back to me as his gaze drops to my lips.

"Charlotte." It's a whisper, a plea.

I can feel his breath on my lips, feel frustrated tension in his body. Our gazes collide and the unspoken yearning in his eyes echoes everything I'm feeling so intensely that I ache from the inside out.

And then I remember Rebecca. And her ring.

I step back, watching the yearning in his eyes flicker and fade away, replaced by his usual impassive expression. And I wonder if I've imagined the entire moment out of a pathetic need to pretend, just for a second, that this *thing* is mutual.

But regardless, it doesn't matter. He's made his choice.

"Night," I whisper, sliding around him, careful not to make physical contact.

I stop before exiting the kitchen, realizing there's something that I need to say. I know it's selfish, but I say it anyway. "Colin."

"Yes." His voice is gravelly.

I don't turn around as I talk—I'm not *that* brave. "I'd have gone with you. To Ireland. If things tomorrow went badly."

I'd go anywhere with you.

He says nothing, and I flash him a quick smile over my shoulder to try and lighten the mood. "You know. Hypothetically."

He doesn't smile back, but I feel his thoughtful gaze on my back as I turn and head to the bedroom.

THURSDAY, NOVEMBER 5

*C*olin's gone the next morning before I wake up. I don't see him until he comes home around two so we can share a cab to the Immigration Services office, but we don't exchange a single word on the way there.

I don't know if it's because of the awkwardness of last night, because of the stress of the meeting to come, or if we're simply too lost in our own thoughts. A little bit of everything, probably.

A different woman checks us in this time. She's a lot less smiley than the last one, which I find oddly comforting. Her somber vibe suits my mood, and it suits this day.

"Who do you think will be first?" I ask Colin. I feel too jittery to read *Vogue* or any of the other glossy magazines this time.

"If it goes anything like last time, I'm hoping me," he says.

"Why's that?"

"I'm imagining you've got a hell of a grand finale up your sleeve."

Oh, soon-to-be-ex-husband. You have no idea.

"Well, regardless of who goes first," I say, "do you mind if I jet right after? I've got a couple of work things to take care of."

Colin looks down, confused and maybe a little hurt. "Yeah. Sure."

I know he wants to know why I'm not my usual upbeat self, but I don't have an answer for him. Not one I want to share, anyway.

"Ms. Spencer. Mr. Walsh. It's good to see you again," Gordon Price says, opening the door. He's holding a manila folder, and I don't consider myself a fashionista or anything, but the fact that the folder matches his tan suit almost exactly is . . . unfortunate.

"Ms. Spencer, we'll start with you. Come on back. Mr. Walsh, this should only take about twenty minutes or so."

"Sure."

I give Colin what I hope is a reassuring smile and follow Price down the fluorescent-lit hallway that I'm really hoping I'll never have to see again after today.

He shows me into the same office. I sit in the same chair.

"Ms. Spencer, thanks for coming in. How are things?"

"Actually, not great."

"That's good—" He breaks off and looks up from the open folder, realizing his mistake.

I smile to put him at ease. "Let me guess. Most people say fine?"

He laughs. "Actually, yeah."

"They're probably terrified to let you think anything in their marriage is less than perfect."

He closes the folder and tosses it aside, giving me a thoughtful look. "You do not share that fear."

"Obviously not," I say with a rueful smile. "I told you the first time we met that my husband had been seeing another woman."

"Yes. And that you two were trying to work through it."

"We were. But Mr. Price, can I be blunt?"

"Of course."

I take a deep breath. "Half of all marriages end in divorce. People drift apart. Cheat. Want different things. Couples in which one person is born in another country aren't exempt from any of that."

He nods slowly. "Go on."

"Colin and I *have* gotten closer since I've moved back from California. We've made significant progress. We've been kind to each other, respected each other, but Mr. Price, this is the part where I need to be frank . . . no amount of trying is going to make my husband love me again."

The addition of "again" is a *tiny* white lie, but I press forward.

"Our current situation has nothing to do with the fact that Colin's from Ireland. This is about emotion, not citizenship. And the brutal truth is that my husband loves someone else. And I can't change that, no matter how much I might want to."

Mr. Price blows out a long breath. "Ms. Spencer, your candor is noted, but I'm not entirely sure what it is you think I can do with that information."

"Nothing," I clarify quickly. "Nothing at all. But I wouldn't feel good leaving here today without telling you the truth: my husband and I plan to get divorced. Soon."

Price picks up his folder again and flips through it absently without really reading it. "This is . . . unusual."

"I know, but I've been thinking through this whole process.

Back when we got married, we went through these same types of interviews. The aim then, and I think now, is to prove that it was a marriage based on love, not the acquisition of a green card? Correct?"

He nods. "Yes. We want to ensure that a couple is married for the right reason."

I take a deep breath, ready to deliver my grand finale, as Colin had put it.

I lean forward. "I know I said that Colin doesn't love me, and I meant that. I can't change that fact, and trust me, I have tried. But Mr. Price, if you want to know if this is a love match, I can tell you at least that I love my husband. I love Colin." I reach down and take a document out of my bag. "And I can prove it."

FRIDAY, NOVEMBER 13

San Francisco

～

"*I* still can't believe you're not coming back," Kurt says. "It's not right. Nothing about this is right."

Lewis squeezes his husband's shoulder as he comes to top off our Sauvignon blanc. "We talked about this, Kurt. It *is* right. You're just sulking."

Kurt pouts as he looks at me. "Okay, fine. I confess, this whole situation does have a certain appealing symmetry to it. But I don't like it."

"Not even my corner office, which you now get to keep?" I say, nudging his calf with the tip of my Tory Burch flat. "Hmmm?"

He gives a sassy little wiggle in his chair. "Well, okay, that part's okay."

"Thought so," I say, smiling into my wine. I'm a bit surprised that my last night in San Francisco doesn't feel sadder. Don't get me wrong—it's bittersweet to think that this will no longer be my home. I'll miss the weather. I'll miss my job. My colleagues. My girl squad. I'll miss Kurt and Lewis most of all.

But as of today, I'm officially retired as the CEO of Coco. The reins have been handed over to Kurt as acting CEO, and the board of directors will have to vote on whether that's a permanent position. But I'm on the board, and I feel pretty certain that the corner office will be Kurt's to keep for as long as he wants it. He quit being an assistant a long time ago—he is Coco.

As for me?

I've got a flight from SFO back to JFK later in the week.

Toward what?

No.

Idea.

Yep. You're reading that right. I don't know what's next. I no longer have a job. Or a home. In a few days, I'll no longer have a husband.

Oh, yeah, and I'm a lot poorer than I was a week ago.

Why?

Because that's what happens when you file for divorce before the conditions of your prenup are met—everything I earned in the duration of our marriage is now half Colin's.

Oddly, the strangest part about all of this isn't that I walked away from a rather large sum of money in order to break my prenup early. It's that neither Colin nor I seemed to consider that possibility in the first place. We'd been so hung up on the single paragraph indicating that we must live under the same roof for three months in order to get divorced, we hadn't bothered to explore the consequences if we filed divorce papers before that. Or at least I hadn't. Not until last week.

That's what I called my brother about. And when Justin called me back—quicker this time, thank God—I'd learned that it wasn't that one of us *couldn't* file for divorce before living together for three months. It was just a *really* irresponsible financial decision, assuming either of us had amassed any amount of assets, which, we both had.

And honestly, even if I had known about the sort-of-loophole, I think I'd still have moved to New York. At the start of all this, the prospect of giving what was essentially a complete stranger half of everything I worked so hard to earn would have been unthinkable. Three months of living in New York City would seem a small price to pay for keeping what is *mine*.

Now though . . . well, as you know, everything has changed.

I truly don't feel I could have survived another day, much less weeks, of living side by side with Colin, knowing he was counting down the days until he could be with Rebecca. And more pressing than that, I'd realized how brutal it must have been to live with one woman while loving another.

It came down to this: I don't *need* that money.

I do, however, need Colin to be happy. I *need* it from the very center of my heart.

And he's not going to get there living under the same roof as me. Plus, my brilliant plan, if I do say so myself, did exactly what I wanted it to. It convinced Gordon Price that, yes, Colin and I were getting divorced, but there was nothing easy or planned about it.

Gordon Price correctly assumed that one does not willingly give up a very fat sum of money to one's husband if love isn't involved. I've told quite a few lies regarding my marriage. That wasn't one of them. I *do* love Colin.

"Oh, Char," Kurt says sympathetically as he sees my eyes watering. "No, no. Not that again."

"I'm not crying," I say, sniffling into the napkin he gives me.

"You are too. Is it for the guy or because you'll miss me?"

I honk out a laugh. "You. It's definitely because I'll miss you."

"I know you're lying, and I'll take it. Lewy! Bring the cheese puffs!" Kurt calls into the kitchen.

"I thought you went gluten-free. And vegan," I say.

"Lewis said the diet gave me the grumpies, so I gave it up," he says, getting a fresh tissue and dabbing at my eyes.

"Here we are," Kurt murmurs soothingly as Lewis brings a bowl of Cheetos into the room. Kurt picks one up and feeds it to me, and I eat it with a laugh. Salty, processed cheese snacks will solve none of my problems, but Kurt feeding them to me like some sort of mama animal at least distracts me for a while.

"I, for one, can't wait to see what's next for you, but I know you're going to crush it," Lewis says, sitting beside Kurt, who's feeding me another chip.

"Thanks, Lew," I say around the Cheetos.

Kurt tries to navigate my wine to my mouth, and I take the glass before it can spill. "I've got this part. Thanks."

"You'll come back to visit, right?" Kurt says.

"Of course. And seriously, you'll let me know everything I can do to help get the condo sold? Realtor fees, cleaning fees, all of that . . . I want to pay it all."

"Can you?" Kurt says teasingly.

"I'm not poor, just half as rich," I point out.

"Do you think he'll actually keep the money?" Kurt said. "That'd be pretty shitty."

"For that matter, why didn't you guys just agree to break the prenup from the beginning, do whatever had to be done to exchange funds, and then . . . hand them back after?" Lewis asks.

"Wonderful idea, Lewis," I say a little tartly. "Would have been a little more wonderful had you come up with it *two months ago*."

"You know what I think," Kurt says, giving me a little finger waggle indicating that I should listen up. "*I* think you didn't think of it because you secretly wanted to go back to New York. And *he* didn't think of it because he saw you again and realized his wife is super-hot."

"Fantastic theory." I point my wine glass at Kurt. "One you should *totally* tell his new wife."

Kurt and Lewis both wince. "Do you think you'll get invited to the wedding?"

"Probably," I mutter. "Colin out of guilt, Rebecca to rub it in."

"Would you go?"

"At the moment? It feels unfathomable. But I don't even know when it is. If I find a Thor-like date before then . . . sure."

And then, because I'm human and heterosexually female, I give myself a little moment of fantasy, imagining Colin's face if I really did show up with Thor. And because Lewis and Kurt are homosexually male, they let themselves fantasize too. I know, because they both sigh, "*Thor*," at the exact same time.

"And you really haven't talked to him?" Kurt asks with a wistful smile.

"Nope." I toss back the rest of my wine and hold my glass out for more.

Lewis nods approvingly. "You blocked him?"

"Nope," I say again.

"Wait." Kurt holds up a protesting hand. "So he hasn't even tried to get in touch? No email? No text? *Nothing*?"

"Well, to be fair, I *did* leave without saying goodbye," I point out.

"If you left divorce papers and your wedding ring on his kitchen counter, that was *definitely* a goodbye, babe."

"Exactly," I say, waving my hand, trying to ignore how bare it feels without my beloved ring. "I could not have been more clear about where we stand, so why would he get in touch? There's nothing to talk about."

"But you'll have to talk to him *eventually*," Lewis says, as he pours me more wine. "I mean, you said the guy's practically a surrogate son of your parents. Surely your paths will cross again. Oops! Hold that thought . . ."

Lewis sets the wine bottle on the table and goes to answer the front door.

"You expecting someone?" I ask Kurt around another Cheeto.

He shakes his head, making a *no idea* face.

Lewis returns a moment later, eyes wide, and his voice slightly terrified. "Char? It's for you."

"What?" I ask in confusion, turning to see who'd have shown up at Lewis and Kurt's house to see me. A moment later, I realize why Lewis is uncharacteristically terrified.

Eileen Spencer is standing in his living room.

My mouth drops open. "*Mom?* What are you doing here?"

"What I should have done ten years ago, Charlotte Elizabeth Spencer. Following you to California to tell you that running away from your problems is no way to live your life."

FRIDAY, NOVEMBER 13

~

"*She is so scary,*" Kurt mouths over my mom's shoulder as Lewis drags him away toward the bedroom.

He's not wrong. On a good day, my mom is a little scary. Right now, she looks battle-ready and downright terrifying.

I wait until I hear Kurt and Lewis's bedroom door close, making a mental note to thank them for retreating to their bedroom in their own house to give us some privacy. Though, if I know Kurt, and I do, his ear will be pressed to the door, and I love him for it. I'd be doing the same thing.

"Mom—"

She holds up a hand. "Me first. There's something I'm overdue in saying to you."

Oh dear.

"Will you at least sit?" I say, gesturing at the small dining table.

She does, looking adorably out of place in her pearls and pumps in Kurt and Lewis's trendy Nob Hill home.

She crosses her legs and sets her folded hands on one knee,

looking directly at me. "I want to apologize. I want to apologize for not respecting that you were your own person, with different dreams for yourself than I had for you. I was so fixated on the type of daughter I'd planned on having, that I didn't properly appreciate the daughter I had. *Have*."

To say that the apology catches me by surprise is an understatement. I don't realize how desperately I've needed to hear that, to know that I'm worthy of love and respect as I am, rather than if I'd been a little less headstrong, a little less ambitious.

"Thank you," I manage, my voice a little clogged. I sure am doing a lot of crying these days.

"When you told me you were going to California all those years ago to start your own business with your grandmother's money, I should have hugged you tight, told you to tell me when your plane landed, and that I couldn't wait to see you at Thanksgiving."

I brush impatiently at the tears on my cheek, and her face softens for a second before she seems to remember that she still has to deliver part two. "*But*," she says, lifting a finger. "First, I'd have asked if you were moving across the country for the right reasons. If it was truly a place you needed to be, or if you left simply because *staying* was hard given our acrimonious relationship at the time."

The rebellious Charlotte stirs immediately, and the million reasons why I had to be in San Francisco, about how it wasn't me running scared, it was me being smart.

But the adult Charlotte, the one who's learned there's more to life than proving her point and getting her own way, lets herself consider the possibility that my mom could be right. That my reasons for moving to San Francisco, while valid, were not *vital*.

At the very least, I could have done it better. I could have done a lot of things better.

"You're right," I tell her in a calm voice. "It was easier to leave than to try and fix things. But I should have tried. I don't regret coming to San Francisco. I'm proud of everything I've built here, and being near Silicon Valley did turn out to be essential. But I could have, *should have*, found a way to do both. To be an East Coast daughter, *and* a West Coast entrepreneur." I give a tremulous smile. "I should have come home for that first Thanksgiving. Whether or not I was invited."

Mom gives a shaky nod, her own eyes watering a little, before she lifts her chin. "And yet, here you are, doing the same thing. Moving back to California the moment a relationship gets hard."

"I'm not moving, Mom. Or rather I am, but not to California. I just came back to pack my things and tie up some loose ends. Ten years ago, my flight to San Francisco was one-way. This time, it's round-trip."

She sucks in a breath. "You're coming back to New York for good?"

I nod and smile. "Guess you'll have to make room for me at Thanksgiving *and* Christmas."

She smiles then promptly frowns. "Well, I'm glad, but you still ran away, young lady."

"*Young lady?*"

"Tell me, did you even stand still when you set the divorce papers on the kitchen counter for Colin to find, or were you still walking as you simultaneously rolled your suitcase out the door?"

I flinch, both at the mention of his name, as well as the fact that her accusation rings uncomfortably true. "You've talked to him?"

"Unlike you, he came to dinner last Sunday," she says stiffly. "Why I have to learn of your divorce from my son-in-law rather than my daughter directly—"

"You've known this was coming, Mom," I say gently. "I've never pretended we weren't getting a divorce. It's a little ahead of schedule but not much."

"But *why*? I thought you cared about him?"

This time I let the old rebellious Charlotte out just a little bit because I can handle *deserved* accusations, but not that one.

"It's *because* I care about him," I retort. "I want him to be happy more than anything. That meant letting him be with Rebecca sooner rather than later, so I made that happen."

"Yes, but I want *you* to be happy," she says stubbornly.

I laugh at the unexpected sweetness of that statement. "I know you do, Mom. I want that too, and I'll get there. It just won't be with Colin and me riding off into the sunset."

She doesn't relent. "I still think it should have been a conversation between you two, not just you leaving those papers for him to find."

"You're right," I admit. "But I'm not a saint. It was hard enough signing those papers as it was. I think having to hand them to him in person to watch him sign them might have torn me in two. And let's not forget," I continue quickly when she opens her mouth to argue. "It was Colin who initiated the divorce in the first place. I simply gave him what he wanted."

"Are you sure that's what he wanted? If you didn't bother to talk to him . . ."

"He gave Rebecca an engagement ring, Mom."

"But that was before you moved back, and you two—"

"No," I cut in, keeping my voice gentle since I know how much she loves Colin and had hopes of him being her son for real. "He gave it to her just a few days ago. I saw it myself. He chose her."

She lets out a long breath and slumps back in her chair. "Well, shit."

"Mom!" I don't think I've ever heard her curse.

She glances at the table and points at the bottle of wine. "Think I can get a glass of that?"

"Absolutely," I say with a smile.

I spend the rest of the evening laughing and drinking with my mom and two of my best friends. It's almost enough to make me forget about Colin.

Almost.

THURSDAY, NOVEMBER 19

⤻

*N*ow, look, I'm not going to call it rock bottom.

But I'm also not going to say that my pride isn't stinging a little about the fact that I'm thirty-one years old and *living with my parents.*

Granted, it's temporary, just until I find a place of my own and figure out what the heck comes next. I tried to tell my mom I could stay in a hotel, but you can guess how that went over. So, here I am. In my old bedroom.

Now, as I've said, it looks nothing like the room I grew up in, which is actually sort of a good thing. This way I'm able to tell my pride that I'm merely staying in my parents' guest room, not "moving back home."

I've been here for a couple of days now, but the unsettling sense of déjà vu hasn't faded yet. I'm uncomfortably aware that this is the second time in three months that I've gotten off a plane from San Francisco to New York armed with only one suitcase and one carry-on, my other belongings to follow. It's the second time in three months I'm living in someone else's home, feeling a little in limbo.

This time is even more complicated since I only have some of my belongings with me; the rest is en route from California, and I left behind a handful of items at Colin's place. I took the essentials when I ditched that whole messy situation a couple of weeks ago, but I wasn't able to fit everything in the suitcase.

I know eventually I'll have to coordinate with him to get my stuff back. *Or*, I could just resign myself to never seeing that portion of my wardrobe so I don't have to face him. Option number two is sounding *very* appealing.

It's seven o'clock on a rainy Thursday night, and the house is eerily quiet. My parents are at a dinner party, something I'd insisted they go to, despite my mother's offer to stay home. It's embarrassing enough to be living with them. I draw the line at letting them feel like they have to babysit me.

Still, I'm regretting their absence a *little*. I don't want to be alone. I start to text Meghan then delete it before hitting send. I start to text another friend then delete that too. I even start to text Drew, my high school boyfriend, thinking that might be just the distraction I need.

I can't make myself hit send on that message either.

I realize that I don't want to be alone, but I don't want to be with anyone other than . . .

Him.

I knew I'd miss Colin, but I didn't realize I'd *crave* him. I didn't realize how much I'd miss talking with him, even if it was to listen to him grumble about my cooking messes. I didn't realize how much his rare smiles could make my entire day brighter, or how much just being in the same room as him seemed to center me.

But, of course, that's a non-option. He's probably picking out freaking China patterns with freaking Rebecca.

Still, even though the pain is still alive and well, I don't regret signing those divorce papers. I really don't. Going on like Colin and I did wasn't good for either of us. It even occurs to me that maybe it was *supposed* to go down that way. Haven't I been sensing for weeks now that it's time for a fresh start? We all know when I want a fresh start, I go big, and well, breaking my prenup in dramatic fashion so that the love of my life can marry the love of *his* life feels like a suitably dramatic way to start the next phase of my life.

Resigned to the fact that I'd rather be alone than with friends tonight, I change into pajamas. As I lie back on my bed and stare up at the ceiling, I notice that my mom has replaced the light that used to look like a tit with a classier one, and I feel oddly disappointed. I used to love that boob light.

I hear a creak on the stairs and jump in surprise. I must have been zoning out for a hell of a lot longer than I realized if my parents are back from their party already.

I roll off the bed and open the door to greet them. "Hey, how was—" My question dies on my lips.

The creak on the stairs was not my parents.

"*Hi*." The word comes out breathy and lame, and I try again. "Hi."

Hmm, nope. The second attempt *still* sounds breathy and lame.

"Hello." Colin's voice, on the other hand, sounds low and confident.

Yep, that's right, I said *Colin*.

As in, my husband—ex-husband?—is currently standing in the doorway of my childhood bedroom and he looks . . . well, he looks so good I could cry.

Though, surprisingly, he's not in his usual suit.

Instead, he's wearing jeans—did *not* know that he owned those—and a gray crew neck sweater that makes his eyes look a little bit silver. There's a blue file folder in his hand, and my throat constricts because I can think of only one reason Colin would have brought a folder over to my parents' house.

"Can I come in?"

Faking indifference, I shrug and move to the side to let him in.

He steps into my bedroom, which I'd always imagined as being fairly roomy by Manhattan standards, but it seems to shrink to downright *tiny* with him in it. Or maybe it's that the room isn't big enough for him and my feelings for him.

"How'd you know I was here?" I ask.

He doesn't answer my question. Instead, he's staring at me. Hard. *All of me.*

Finally, he frowns. "Are those my boxers? And my shirt?"

"Um." I pluck nervously at the tee. "I guess I grabbed them accidentally when I was packing my bags."

"Uh-huh. And you were planning to keep them?"

"I was thinking maybe we could call them souvenirs," I say with a little smile. "Something to remember our time together?"

"Oh, so you *do* want to remember our time together," he says, stepping closer. "I figured from the way you left without so much as a goodbye, that you were anxious to forget it."

I flinch and want to close my eyes, but I force myself to meet his gaze. His eyes are accusatory, which I expected, but also a little bit wounded. Which I didn't expect.

"I'm sorry," I tell him plainly. "I really am. I *know* it was a kind of crappy way to go about things—"

"Kind of?" he breaks in. "*Kind of?* Charlotte, how do you think it felt that on the same day I find out I'm not getting deported, I come home to celebrate with my wife and get greeted by an empty house, and *these*?"

He holds up the folder in his hand, which I now know for sure contains our divorce papers. *Fine.* That's just *fine.* Colin's mad, and I get that, but now I'm mad too. Yes, I left without saying goodbye, and that wasn't well done of me, but I'm not exactly loving the way he seems to think that I should have just been waiting at home for him. For the first time, it hits me that Colin's been a little selfish in all this—he doesn't get to have the wife *and* the fiancée.

I poke a finger to his chest. "You wanted to come home and celebrate with *your wife*? Don't say it like that. Don't say it like the love of your life walked out your front door with your heart in her back pocket. I'm happy you're not getting deported, truly, but you should have wanted to celebrate with the woman you were going to marry, not the one you were going to divorce. What was the plan, you were going to come have a pre-dinner glass of celebratory Champagne with me before going off to dinner and more bubbly with Rebecca? Did it ever occur to you that it got old, Colin?" *That it hurt?*

Instead of apologizing or backing down, he only looks angrier. "It got so *old* that you deliberately broke the prenup? You were so desperate to get away from me that you couldn't have survived two more weeks?"

"Not *you*!" I shout. "I wasn't trying to get away from you, I was trying to get away from you and *her*!"

His eyes take on a steely gleam as he steps even closer. "Why's that?"

Realizing what I've just admitted, I tear my gaze away from his and try to move around him to escape his nearness, but Colin isn't having it and moves with me, blocking my escape route.

"*Move*."

"Why, so you can run away again?"

"I wasn't running away." I still don't meet his eyes.

"Bullshit." His voice is quiet but commanding. "Why'd you run?"

I keep my head stubbornly turned and remain silent.

"What happened that day in Gordon Price's office?" he asks. "I deserve to know that much, at least."

"What did he tell you?" I ask, keeping my gaze fixed on the wall to my right.

"Not much. My meeting lasted about three minutes, most of which was spent with him glaring at me, and ended with him begrudgingly telling me that he was closing the investigation without formal charges."

"Well then, see? All good."

"No, damn it, Charlotte, *not* all good. Why did you do it? Why did you break the prenup? You actually think I'd want your money?"

"I never thought that," I say, realizing he won't relent until he gets his answers. "It wasn't about the money. But it *had* to end. You've got to see that. We couldn't keep doing what we were doing—married, but not really. I couldn't . . ."

Remembering my mom's reminder that running from my problems was no way to deal with them, I do the *strong* thing and lift my gaze to his.

"I filed for divorce because I want you to be happy, Colin. I wanted you to be free to marry someone you love, not be stuck in a technical marriage for one day longer than necessary. But I also did it for me. I couldn't keep living with you, pretending to be your wife, when I knew you were counting the days to marry someone else. I *thought* I could survive it, but seeing that engagement ring on Rebecca's finger, it all became too real, and—"

"I never bought her a ring."

I blink rapidly through my tears, trying to comprehend this. "What? But I saw it. She came over and showed me."

He lifts a shoulder. "She bought it for herself. Or borrowed it from a friend. I don't really know, but I didn't buy her that ring, and I certainly did not put it on her finger. I didn't even know what had happened until after you'd left for California."

I stare at him. "Why would she do that?"

He hesitates. "If I had to guess, I'd say she thought it would get you out of the way, and I'd change my mind. She was half right."

"Half right?" I ask.

"She *did* get you out of the way. You fled the state. I, however, did not change my mind."

"About what?"

"About not being able to marry Rebecca."

I gasp, but before I can comprehend this, Colin tosses the folder on the dresser and steps closer, his voice a low rasp. "Do you know, when you first moved in, I thought those little pajamas you wore would kill me?"

"You want to talk about my pajamas? *Now*?"

"Yes, actually I do," he says softly. "I've seen women's underwear with more material than your pajamas, and I thought nothing could be more torturous."

Slowly he reaches out and roughly grabs a fistful of my T-shirt, pulling me closer. "I was wrong," he says on a growl. "Seeing *my* clothes on you, seeing *my* wife prance around in *my* clothes, wanting—*needing*—to know what was under them. Hating that my clothes could touch her skin in a way I couldn't . . . *that* was the real torture."

The hand not gripping the shirt finds my waist, sliding around to my back.

Under the shirt.

His palm spreads low against my lower back, and we both exhale at the skin-to-skin contact. I close my eyes, terrified this is the world's most wonderful dream and that my heart will break into a million pieces if I find out it's not real.

"You're really not marrying Rebecca?"

His forehead is still pressed to mine, and I feel him shake his head no, feel his breath near my lips.

"I'm a little confused," I whisper.

"I get that," he whispers back, as he gently pulls me all the way against him. "Maybe I can help make it clearer for you."

Colin's mouth lowers to mine, pausing for a fraction of a second, as though savoring the moment. The first brush of his lips is heaven. The second is ecstasy. The third feels a lot like *forever*.

And it seems to last forever, and yet not long enough.

"Clear enough for you?" he asks huskily when he pulls back.

"I think I'm starting to understand," I say on a smile, going to my toes and leaning in for another kiss. He leans back, staying just out of reach, and I open my eyes, ready to protest his withholding of kisses.

My protest dies at the look on his face, one I've never seen before, both tender and sure, as though he's looking at everything he's ever wanted. *Me*.

He lifts a hand and brushes back the hair near my face. "I'm in love with you, Charlotte."

Tears fill my eyes. "You are?"

He nods.

I glance hopefully at the blue folder. "Does that mean you didn't sign our divorce papers after all?"

"No, I signed them. And filed them. That there is your official copy."

"Oh," I say, my heart deflating. "So we're officially divorced?"

"We are," he says, his hands finding either side of my waist.

"Well, I guess that's practical," I say, trying to hide my disappointment. "We should probably start at the beginning, date, figure out if we're suited for the long haul—what are you doing?" I ask, breaking off when I realize he's digging in his pocket instead of listening to me.

He holds up a familiar navy box. "You forgot this."

"I told you, it was too extravagant for the circumstances. I couldn't—what are you doing?"

He's holding my left hand, the ring poised at the tip of my fourth finger as his gaze searches mine. "Do you love me, Charlotte?"

His accent's thicker than usual, his expression both adoring and a little unsure.

I nod emphatically, desperate to reassure him. "I thought you knew. I fell in love with you weeks ago. It was *highly* inconvenient."

He gives me a cocky, crooked smile, full of relief and joy. "Yeah?"

"Yeah," I whisper, brushing my lips over his.

"Marry me?" he whispers back. "Properly, this time? You sort of have to, I have half your money."

I laugh against his lips and nod as he slides the ring onto my finger. "*Yes.*"

Finally, Colin kisses me again. And again, and then one more time, until I realize something and pull my mouth from his on a gasp. "Wait. We can't get married. What if it turns out we're completely incompatible in bed?"

His lips find the underside of my jaw as he nudges me backward toward the mattress. "Excellent point. We should probably find out sooner rather than later if we can tolerate each other, no?"

Much, *much* later, I rest my cheek on his bare shoulder, pressing an absent kiss there. "Well, then. I think we're going to be just fine."

Epilogue One

My brother offers to help with the prenup. We respectfully decline.

Epilogue Two

My mom finally got to plan her daughter's big white wedding, which is just fine by me, since I was plenty busy launching my new company, a boutique consulting firm helping female entre-preneurs make their dreams reality.

Because my mother would have it no other way, the wedding goes off without a single hitch. My father walks me down the aisle. Justin starts crying during his best man toast, like *a lot*, and it's so sweetly unmanly that we decide to forgive him.

Kurt (now the official CEO of Coco, by the way) manages to

hold off his waterworks until after his man-of-honor toast. I, on the other hand, cry through the whole thing.

Colin and I sneak off to make love during the reception. We miss the cake cutting, but we've been making up for lost time. And some things are better than cake.

Epilogue Three

We honeymoon in Hudson. There is Champagne. Candles. Madonna.

No separate beds. No rash cream.

Also, Colin drives.

Epilogue Four

We name our first son Danny. He's nearly two now, and I have yet to *not* cry when I hear Colin quietly singing "Danny Boy" over the baby monitor.

We name our second son Spencer, as a nod to my maiden name.

Because this time around, we're Mr. and Mrs. Colin Walsh *for real*.

Epilogue Five

We live very, *very* happily ever after.

AUTHOR NOTE

Writing a book is hard. Nobody tells you that when you're nine years old and dreaming of being an author. You imagine that inspiration will never wane and that you'll choose all the right words the first time around. *Writer's block?* Not me. *Editing?* What's that?

The reality is, well, different.

The reality is that no matter how many times I sit down to an in-progress manuscript, writing feels like the hardest thing I've ever done in my life. Don't get me wrong, it's the best career in the world, and I wouldn't trade it for anything, even when I think it might kill me. But putting words on a blank page in coherent form day after day is no easy task.

Except when it is.

Every now and then, the writing gods give you a little gift. In between all the hard books, which is most of them, you get an easy one. You get a story that feels—not so much that you're creating something from scratch, but that you're merely conveying something that has already happened.

Some books aren't about writing a story. They're about sharing a part of yourself. They're the books that you can't tear yourself away from, the ones you cry when you get to The End because you're not ready to say goodbye. They're the ones where reviews can't touch you, sales numbers don't even cross your mind, because *nothing* is strong enough to diminish your love for the book.

I've had only a couple of those stories in my thirty-something book career. *Blurred Lines* was one. *Walk of Shame* was one. *Runaway Groom* was one.

And *The Prenup* is one.

Perhaps *the* one. All of my books are obviously written by Lauren Layne. *The Prenup* feels like it *is* Lauren Layne.

I have loved sharing Charlotte and Colin's love story with you. Thank you for letting me.

ACKNOWLEDGEMENTS

⌒

As you probably guessed from the author note, I wrote this book more or less in a vacuum. The outside sources were fairly minimal, and much of my time was spent hunched over my MacBook Pro in bed, completely lost in this story.

Eventually, however, I finished the first draft, and when I lifted my head, I had an entire team of people ready and willing to help me.

A *huge* thank you to Angela at Saffron Avenue for her amazing lettering skills. I tried not to get my hopes up that I could hire her to write the actual letters of *The Prenup* for me that you see on the cover, but she agreed without hesitation, which made my entire month.

I toyed with the idea of designing my own cover, but I couldn't quite seem to make my reality. I took the problem to one of my best friends, Laura Ashbrook Compton Treleven, a creative genius and design whiz. She agreed to take a stab at the cover, and when she showed me the comps, I confess . . . my eyes watered at how perfect they were. In the vein of a true artist, and perhaps more crucially, a true friend, she somehow seemed to know exactly what I wanted. And then made it even better.

To Kay Springsteen, who had the unenviable task of doing developmental edits on a book that is, essentially, *my precious*. I'm so grateful that you provided nudges on *improving* the story without *changing* the story.

To Kristi Yanta, I'm so glad destiny stepped in to allow us to work together on this one after all. As always, you know exactly how the details of my writing from "pretty good" to "exactly right."

To my copyeditor, Lori Sabin, I know this is our first time working together, but hopefully not our last, because you are an utter joy to work with. And the same goes to my proofreader Christine Estevez, both for your amazing work and for being so darn kind.

To my friends and family, I love you guys, I hope you know that. Anth, as always . . . well, no words. You let me gush about this one endlessly and never once complained about the days when I gave Colin more attention than I gave you.

A shout out specifically to Jennifer Probst, Jessica Lemmon, and Rachel Van Dyken, my writing squad, and three of the very few people who get me.

To my agent, Nicole Resciniti and to my UK team (especially, Kate!) thank you for believing in this story. Lisa Filipe, I'd be lost without you. Literally, just a little wisp of a writer wandering around with a manuscript clutched in her hands, if not for you.

And to the readers, of *course*, my darling readers. Thank you for loving love stories as much as I do, and for giving me a chance to share this one with you.

If you enjoyed

The Prenup

then you'll love The Central Park Pact
series from Lauren Layne!

Read on for a preview of

*Passion
on Park
Avenue*

Chapter One

*N*aomi Powell figured there was no good way to discover that the man you'd been dating for three months was married to someone else. But of all the possibilities, learning about the existence of a *Mrs.* Brayden Hayes via the cheating bastard's obituary?

Definitely the worst.

The taxi pulled to a stop outside Central Presbyterian, and Naomi nearly lost her nerve, her instincts screaming for her to tell the cabbie to take her back to the Lower East Side.

Instead, she handed the driver a twenty, shoved open the door, and stepped onto ritzy Park Avenue as though she belonged there. She pulled her Gucci sunglasses out of her bag and slid them onto her nose—the overcast July day didn't quite warrant the shades, but she was walking into a funeral. People would hopefully think the purpose of the sunglasses was to hide red, puffy eyes rather than what it really was:

A disguise.

Screw that, Naomi thought furiously, pushing the sunglasses back up into her dark red hair and marching with purpose toward the stately Gothic-style church. She didn't need a disguise. At twenty-nine, Naomi had spent most of her lifetime dealing with people trying to make her feel inferior, and she'd be damned if she let a turd of a playboy succeed from beyond the grave.

She had just as much right to be here as anyone else. It's not like she'd known he was married. She hadn't even known he lived in Manhattan. Naomi wasn't sure she knew a single damn thing about the *real* Brayden Hayes, but even around all her anger, she still wanted the chance to say goodbye.

The man had made her life better, for a while at least. Even if he was making it a hell of a lot worse now.

She sighed and slid the sunglasses back onto her face. Not to protect herself, but to protect Brayden's wife. Naomi had no idea if Claire knew of her existence, but on the off chance she did, Naomi didn't want to make this any harder on the woman than it already was.

Naomi walked up the steps to the church as Brayden's obituary rattled around in her brain, the way it had for days. *The victim of a tragic yachting accident, Brayden Hayes is survived by wife, Claire Hayes* . . .

A yachting accident. Really? *Really?*

Wasn't death by luxury boat just a *little* too good for a womanizer with the morals of a lump of coal?

The only saving grace of the situation, and Naomi had had to look *really* hard to find one, was that Claire and Brayden hadn't had any children. Thank God for that. It was the only thing that had kept Naomi from breaking completely when she'd learned of Brayden's double life. She knew all too well the havoc a philandering asshole could wreak on a child's life.

Naomi stepped into the dark, quiet church and walked

toward one of the back pews. Several people turned and looked her way, and her footsteps faltered.

On a rational level, Naomi knew they were merely turning instinctively at the sharp click of her Louboutin stilettos against the church floor. Some maybe even recognized her as *the* Naomi Powell from the latest 30-under-30 list, or from her interview on the *Today* show.

But everywhere she looked, Naomi saw only disdain. As though they could see beyond the conservative Chloé dress to her Bronx roots. As though they knew she was the *other woman*. The very identity that had destroyed her mother and that Naomi had sworn to avoid.

She sucked in a breath, trying to gather the defiance that had turned her from a nobody into one of the city's wealthiest women. She tried to gather the confidence that had earned her a spot on every "women to watch" list in the nation. But today, she didn't feel like a bright up-and-comer in the business world. Today she felt small. Worse, she felt *dirty*.

Naomi watched as a woman pursed her lips and turned away, as though unable to look any longer upon Brayden Hayes's whore. That's what he'd made her. A lifetime of trying to avoid her mother's footsteps, and one Upper East Side scumbag had turned her into her own worst nightmare.

Naomi didn't even realize she'd turned around and left the church until she felt the warm summer breeze whip at her hair. Didn't register what direction she was walking until she hit the eastern edge of Central Park.

Only then did she let herself truly breathe, sucking in big lungfuls of air. But she didn't cry. Naomi had promised herself a long time ago she'd never cry because of a man.

She was hardly dressed for a stroll, but the trees and winding path calmed her as she entered the park. A welcome respite from the nearby neighborhood and all its snobbery. In Central Park, it didn't matter what street you lived on, what borough you came from. Central Park belonged to all New Yorkers, one glorious shared backyard.

The park was mostly quiet. Most tourists entered at the south side, so she saw only a couple of joggers, a few elderly couples out for a walk, two moms on a stroller date, and . . .

Naomi did a double take at the blonde sitting alone on a park bench, and her stomach dropped out. *Are you* kidding *me with this right now, God?*

The first thing Naomi had done after the shock of reading that Brayden Hayes was freaking *married* was to google the crap out of his wife, desperate for an indication that the *Times* had been wrong about his marital status. That it was a misprint or he was divorced. The paper hadn't been wrong. There really was a Mrs. Brayden Hayes.

And she, too, had chosen Central Park over Brayden's funeral.

Nearly even with Claire Hayes now, and with the sunglasses still providing Naomi anonymity, she dared to sneak a look at the other woman out of the corner of her eye.

Brayden's widow looked pretty much like the picture Naomi had rummaged up online: a thirty-something Upper East Side WASP. Like Naomi, she wore oversize sunglasses, the Chanel logo glinting in a stray ray of sunshine. Naomi's trained eye pegged the basic black sheath as St. John, and the basic black pumps Louboutins—identical to Naomi's.

But *unlike* Naomi, Claire had a genteel poise about her. Like she'd never said *darn*, much less dropped an f-bomb. Naomi would bet serious money that Claire Hayes didn't eat Kraft Macaroni & Cheese straight out of the pan when she was stressed and that Claire had never been so poor that she'd actually once considered taking home a neighbor's discarded mattress, bedbugs be damned, simply because it was free.

Claire's placid expression betrayed nothing as Naomi passed her, the glasses too large to reveal any emotion on her face. For that matter, Naomi wondered if women like her experienced emotion at all. It didn't seem it. The woman was the picture of calm, except for . . .

Her hands.

Brayden's widow's hands were clenched tightly in her lap, the fingers of her right hand white-knuckled around the fist of her left hand. But it wasn't the subdued pink manicure that captured Naomi's attention. It was the bright red crescent moons *beneath* the nails.

Naomi had a lifelong bad habit of acting before thinking, and she did so now, crossing to the other woman and sitting beside her on the park bench.

"That's enough now," Naomi said, using her CEO voice, calm and commanding.

Claire didn't move. Naomi wasn't even sure the other woman heard her.

Naomi hesitated only for a moment before slowly reaching over and prying the nails of Claire's right hand away from her left hand. Little streaks of blood were left in the wake.

Claire looked down in confusion, as though just now registering the pain.

"Does that Givenchy have any Kleenex?" Naomi asked, nodding toward Claire's clutch on the bench.

Claire didn't move for a long moment, then taking a deep breath, she calmly reached for her purse, pulling out a travel-size package of tissue.

"We're wearing the same shoes. Same dress, too," Claire said, dabbing at the blood on the back of her hand with a tissue, using the same casual indifference of one dabbing up a drop of spilled water.

Naomi nodded in agreement, though Claire's St. John was a knee-length mock turtleneck, and Naomi's Chloé was a boatneck that hit at midthigh.

For a long moment, neither said anything.

"I'm supposed to be at a funeral," Claire said, balling up the tissue and dropping her hands back into her lap.

"Why aren't you?"

Naomi was genuinely curious. She knew why *she* wasn't at that funeral. But the widow being a no-show . . . that was some serious *Page Six*–worthy gossip right there.

Claire opened her mouth to respond but shut it when a pretty young woman with dark brown hair walked past them. Naomi waited for the other woman to pass and, when she gave the brunette a closer look, realized the other woman was walking a bit too slowly, as though tempted to approach. She looked vaguely familiar. Naomi was fairly sure they'd crossed paths at a couple of events, though Naomi couldn't put a name with the face.

Brayden's widow, however, could. Claire went rigid beside Naomi, even as she called out to the other woman, "Audrey."

Unlike Claire and Naomi, the brunette wasn't wearing sunglasses, and Naomi saw her round eyes go even wider. "You know who I am?"

"You're Audrey Tate. I did a little digging after you called the house that night," Claire said quietly. "I know you were sleeping with my husband."

Naomi's head whipped around in surprise, and then surprise escalated to shock as she realized Claire wasn't talking to her.

Meet *The Wedding Belles.*
They can make any bride's dream come true.
And now it's their turn.

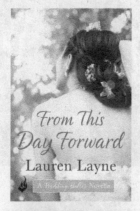

Available from

Meet the irresistible men of
Oxford magazine . . .

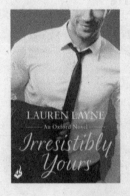

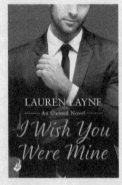

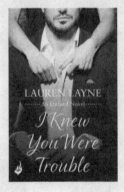

Available from

Discover five sexy, romantic standalone stories in the Love Unexpectedly series . . .

Available from

HEADLINE
ETERNAL

FIND YOUR HEART'S DESIRE...

VISIT OUR WEBSITE: www.headlineeternal.com
FIND US ON FACEBOOK: facebook.com/eternalromance
CONNECT WITH US ON TWITTER: @eternal_books
FOLLOW US ON INSTAGRAM: @headlineeternal
EMAIL US: eternalromance@headline.co.uk